SAM CRESCENT AND STACEY ESPINO

EVERNIGHT PUBLISHING ®

www.evernightpublishing.com

Copyright© 2018

Sam Crescent and Stacey Espino

Editor: Karyn White and Audrey Bobak

Cover Artist: Jay Aheer

ISBN: 978-1-77339-582-1

SAM CRESCENT AND STACEY ESPINO

BRED BY THE BILLIONAIRE

Breeding Season, 1

Sam Crescent and Stacey Espino

Copyright © 2017

Chapter One

"Where's my fucking coffee?" Tobias Bennett sifted through the files on his desk. He was getting too old for this shit—late nights at the office and staff who couldn't follow simple instructions. At this point in his life, he'd imagined living on a private island, a mojito in one hand and *The Wall Street Journal* in the other. But he was still running the family business with no sign of slowing down. He'd been termed a perfectionist, and probably a lot worse, but he strongly believed wealth was the measure of success.

A couple minutes later, one of the interns set a mug on the corner of his desk. She scurried out of his office, nearly breaking into a jog. Was he that much of an asshole?

Tobias scrubbed both hands over his face. He knew exactly what had been driving him crazy lately. His parents were riding him hard for an heir, another Bennett to carry on the family empire. The problem—he wasn't looking for a wife. His bachelor life suited him just fine, and even at forty-five, he wasn't ready to settle down. He would have told his aging parents to back off, but they had a point, one that kept crowding his thoughts.

Morgan peered in his office. "Why are you still here?"

"Work."

"Go home. It's Friday night, for God's sake." He'd gone to university with Morgan, and hired him to work on the Bennett Corporation legal team over a decade ago. Morgan was the only man who dared to speak freely with him.

"I've got that big bid on Monday. I need to be prepared," said Tobias.

"We've already got it covered. Everything's in order."

"It has to be perfect."

Morgan exhaled, then shook his head. "Well, I'm heading out." Then he added, "Don't push yourself so hard."

"See you Monday." Tobias leaned back in his leather chair and gave his friend a mock salute.

Once alone again, he pondered Morgan's words. Yes, he pushed himself. It was life as a Bennett. His parents expected perfection from day one, and he'd always delivered. The company was strong, profitable, and dominating the stock market because he didn't fuck around. He always put a hundred percent effort into everything he set out to do, and demanded the same from his staff. If one of his employees couldn't meet the mark, he didn't think twice about showing them the door. He had no room for weakness.

After another couple of hours, he packed up his paperwork and flicked off the lights to his corner penthouse office. As he stood in the darkness, the lights of the city sparkled with life beyond the floor to ceiling windows. He grabbed his briefcase and walked over to the window, looking down from one of the highest vantage points. It was one big party below, a city that never slept.

He'd put the Bennett Corporation on the map, made his father's business into something multi-national, but what happened next? What would happen when he died? The legacy he'd built would die along with him, all his hard work and sacrifices for nothing. The business might continue with the family name, but without the blood of a Bennett, it would be a soulless enterprise, nothing more than dollars and cents.

"Mr. Bennett?"

Tobias snapped out of his reverie, turning to see a silhouette in the doorway of his darkened office. "Yes?"

"Would you like some company tonight?"

He narrowed his eyes as he strode to the door. "Aren't you one of the new analysts we just hired?" Tobias had thousands of employees, so couldn't remember many names and faces. He only allowed minimal staff on the penthouse floor of his skyscraper. He remembered this woman from the new staff tour yesterday morning, and only because she'd worn a short skirt.

"Yes, sir."

"And why are you up here?"

"I wanted to offer my company." She ran her finger along the low collar of her blouse. Was she actually trying to seduce him? "I have many skillsets beyond analyzing, and I thought you'd like me to show you some."

He scoffed. "You thought wrong, sweetheart. If you'd actually done any digging, you'd know I never mix business with pleasure."

"But—"

"Stay on the fifth floor. I don't want to see you up here again."

She sulked off, clearly not expecting him to reject her. Tobias wasn't hard up. He had a long list of women he could call for a hook-up. None of them meant a thing to him. They were available for sex, and that's how he liked it—until now. If he wanted a kid, he had to find a decent woman to be the mother. Unfortunately, most of the women he fucked were gold-diggers, and he didn't want any baby drama. He just wanted the heir, nothing more.

He could already envision it, a life similar to his own childhood. His son would be raised by a nanny, go to boarding school, and be trained to be the best at everything. Tobias knew parenting wouldn't take much effort on his part—he'd rarely seen his own mother and father growing up.

Tobias took the elevator down to the parking garage, trying to push thoughts of babies and legacies out of his head. This responsibility shouldn't have fallen on his damn shoulders. He'd been the younger brother—until he turned sixteen. Maximus had been nineteen when he died of a heroin overdose. Of course, his parents made sure the real cause didn't hit the media, appearances being more important than the truth. Tobias had seen it coming. He'd done nothing. Unlike him, Maximus wanted more, wanted the love and warmth he'd seen in other homes. Their father said he was weak, he couldn't cut it, and that's why he killed himself. No one ever mentioned Maximus, like he never existed.

The elevator dinged, and Tobias stepped out into the secure garage. He dug the keys to his Mercedes out of his pocket, turning off the alarm system. Once behind the wheel, he tossed his briefcase onto the passenger seat and squeezed the steering wheel until his knuckles turned white. Reflecting on a past that couldn't be undone was pointless, and like his father taught him, emotions were for pussies. He needed to block that shit out, forget about the brother taken from him too soon. Trying to imagine an alternate reality would only break down his carefully maintained exterior.

He turned on the radio, hoping the music would drown out the noise in his head. Right now, he wished he could have fucked that blonde bitch over his desk to release the tension, but he refused to get involved with women in the office. Nothing was worth risking the reputation of the family business, certainly not a piece of ass.

Tobias hit the gas as he drove, the streetlights and bright signage disguising the fact the sun had set hours ago. At least leaving late thinned out the downtown traffic. His condo was only ten minutes from the office in one of the waterfront condos owned by the Bennett Corporation. There wasn't much they didn't have their hand in.

He nodded to the doorman as he walked to the elevator. Normally, he'd go out for a drink on Friday, maybe choose who he wanted to take home with him for the night. Today, he just wanted to crash. He'd pour himself a scotch on the rocks and drown out all the insecurities. Friday meant he could sleep in tomorrow, so he'd drink enough to keep all his nightmares at bay.

****

Adora Garcia had three major assignments due in the next two weeks, so her desk and laptop were going to be her best friends for a while. She'd been studying all morning, empty coffee cups and balls of scrunched up paper hiding her cellphone. When it began to ring, she remembered the promise to pick her mother up from work while her car was in the shop.

She drove out to the waterfront where her mother worked cleaning Tobias Bennett's condo three days a week and every Saturday. Adora hated driving in the downtown core, but it was the least she could do for the woman who raised her single-handedly, working her fingers to the bone to provide the basics.

"Can I help you?"

Adora had been wandering around the massive lobby of the condo, admiring the modern architecture, use of glass, and difficult angles. The security had apparently had enough of her presence. She was used to being questioned in stores when they assumed she was stealing something. Her absentee father had been a blue-eyed, white businessman who'd used and dumped her mother twenty years ago, leaving her alone and pregnant. Although Adora didn't have her mother's skin color, she had many of her Latin American features, including her long dark hair.

"I'm looking for Tobias Bennett," she said.

The security guard sauntered over, his thumbs hooked in his pockets. He looked her up and down. "Is he expecting you?"

She was going to give him the whole story, but decided to keep it simple. "Yes."

He tilted his head. "You're not his usual type, but who am I to judge? Top floor."

Adora bit her tongue and hit the elevator button. She'd grab her mother and get the hell out of this overpriced neighborhood. It was hard enough getting by without all the judgmental stares and stereotypes.

She wasn't one of Mr. Bennett's whores.

Her mother had told her all about the old bastard's weekly escapades. There wasn't enough money in all the world to pay Adora to sleep with him—not that he'd want her. She imagined a man in his position could have whoever he wanted. It made her sick thinking of all the beautiful young women who gave themselves to him in exchange for money or status. That would never be her. A degree in architecture would be her way out, a chance to make a real life for herself.

When she reached the penthouse suite, she softly knocked on the door. When no one answered, she turned the handle. She decided to slip inside and find her mother for herself. If she knocked too loudly, she could wake Mr. Bennett. Adora was used to finding her mother on the job. When she was younger, she'd helped her clean the condos and offices so they could get home sooner.

The condo was huge, and not what she expected. She knew he had money, but nothing like this. Adora whirled around in slow circles as she admired the vaulting ceilings, massive windows, and impressive collection of artwork. She couldn't even imagine living like this. It would be like stepping into a fairy tale. Mostly she craved the security that money could offer, not the luxuries. When she was a kid, she'd pretend to live in the homes her mother cleaned, role-playing and escaping into her imagination. Now she was an adult, and knew the only way she'd get ahead was working her ass off.

She studied the streets below from the massive floor to ceiling window, the people and cars scurrying about like tiny ants, when a throat cleared behind her. Adora paled, slowly turning to the sound. She swore her heart stopped when she saw a man standing there wearing an open robe. He wore navy pajama pants underneath and no shirt, an empty coffee mug dangling in his hand.

It couldn't be Tobias Bennett. She'd already envisioned exactly what her mother's boss would look like, and it was nothing like the man in front of her. This man wasn't haggard with sweaty palms and balding head. His chest was hard, with a light sprinkling of dark hair, and chiseled abs. A thin trail of hair led down into his low waistband … she averted her eyes. Adora swallowed hard, waiting for the shitstorm. She didn't want her mother to get fired because she was uninvited in Mr. Bennett's very expensive condo.

He didn't say a word, just stared at her, like a predator planning its attack. Should she say something? Apologize? Explain the situation? No words came out of her mouth, even when he started to walk closer.

"You're not Maria." His voice was deep, a hint of teasing, but no malice.

"I'm just picking her up. I'm sorry if I startled you."

He wet his bottom lip and moved to the side to get a better look at her. She felt as if she was on auction. This was exactly the reason she was enrolled in college, so she'd never be at the mercy of a man. She could only imagine the horrors her mother had to deal with over the course of her life, especially speaking minimal English.

"Do you work in the building?"

She'd kept her head down, but dared to look up into his eyes. "No. I'm her daughter."

He smirked, realization softening his features. His hair was still damp from a shower, and his dark, musky scent suited him perfectly. "You know, Maria's worked here for what? Ten years? I never knew she had a daughter."

"Did you ask?"

"My Spanish isn't the greatest." He held out his hand. "Tobias."

This was actually Tobias Bennett? One of the wealthiest men in the city? She wasn't sure how she felt about him now that she'd seen him in the flesh. Her mother had a job because of him, but Adora had always associated money with everything debased in society.

From her experience the wealthier the person, the higher they expected you to jump.

She shook his outstretched hand. "Adora Garcia." His grip was firm, and he didn't allow her to pull away. She looked down at his hand, and hers was tiny in his grip. Her body coiled tight, a wash of need taking her by surprise. When she glanced up to see his intention, her breath caught.

"Such a pretty name," he said. His words were slow and deliberate, mesmerizing her.

Then she thought better. He was a renowned playboy, and she had no intention of being his next victim. She pulled her hand back, which only served to amuse him.

"Have you seen my mother?"

"I don't know what I'd do without her. She knows exactly how I like things, and half the time I don't even know she's here." He ran the backs of his fingers along the length of her hair. She'd left in such a rush, she hadn't pulled it back into her usual ponytail. "I can see her in you."

She instinctively flinched away from his touch.

"Are you afraid of me?" he asked.

"I don't know you."

He moved toward his open concept kitchen, setting his mug on the counter. Tobias flicked on his coffee maker and then leaned over the counter, using one curled finger to beckon her closer. She took tentative steps, making sure to stay on the opposite side of the granite island. "How about we change that?"

"Change what?" she asked.

"I want to get to know you, Adora. Can I take you to dinner?"

She narrowed her eyes. "Really? Why would you want to take me to dinner?"

"Why wouldn't I?"

She scoffed. "Where would I start? You know nothing about me. What if I'm already dating someone?"

Tobias poured his coffee, then left it aside. He walked around the island to where she stood, bracing a hand on each side of the counter, caging her in. "Are you?" he asked.

Adora forgot how to breathe. He was so much taller than she was, his shoulders blocking out the rest of the room, making her feel small and feminine. He had such a commanding presence, and she imagined he got everything he wanted.

"Cat got your tongue?"

"Yes, I have a boyfriend," she lied. For all she knew he had another one-night stand still sleeping in his bed. Adora decided it was best to put up a wall to protect herself from this shark. If she rejected him flat out, her mother could lose her job. A boyfriend was a safe answer, an easy out.

He shook his head, his dark eyes stripping her layer by layer. "You're a terrible liar, little one." He ran the pad of his thumb along her lower lip, making her bolt back, hitting the counter. Tobias still wouldn't let her escape. "I'll bet all my shares in the Bennett Corporation that you're a virgin, too."

She gasped.

He chuckled, a deep, rumbling sound. "I didn't get this far by not being able to read people."

"Where's my mother?" she repeated, looking side to side for an escape. This stranger had unraveled her in just a few minutes. She felt so exposed, so deliciously violated. He had to be over twice her age, so why did he affect her like this? She wasn't used to watching all her control slip away.

"Relax, baby girl. I'm just playing." He stepped

back, running his hand through his dark hair, a bit of grey at the temples. Everything about him was composed and deliberate. "I'm just asking for one date."

"I don't think I'm your type," she said. "I'm not interested in a good time, and I can't be bought." She stood firm on her beliefs. No way would she be used and discarded. Not for all the money in the world, no matter how tempting he may be.

But a part of her, deep down to the marrow, wanted to be his. Wanted to be taken and claimed. Was she dealing with daddy issues? Was she sick for desiring a man exuding power and control? He was everything she tried to steer clear of, but she was inexplicably drawn to him. That one touch made her desperate for more, but she had to resist her twisted desires. Adora was convinced her DNA was against her, leading her to follow in her mother's footsteps. She wanted more from a man, demanded more from her life.

"Everyone has a price," he said.

She pushed away, finally able to breathe once she put space between them. His scent was addictive, pulling her under his spell. Adora turned around once at a safe distance. "Maybe in your world. Not mine."

"Then prove me wrong. One date."

It took all her willpower to refuse him. "Sorry, I'm not interested."

Chapter Two

In all of his forty-five years, Tobias couldn't recall a moment a woman ever denied him. The Bennett name got him what he wanted, when he wanted it. He knew women wanted him, craved him. Like last night. He didn't even remember the intern's name, but she'd been ready to give him anything he wanted, and then something more.

Adora was a beautiful young woman, and he knew for a fact he'd never seen her before. He wouldn't have been able to forget her. She was nothing like the women he usually brought home. There was an innocent air about her—youth and lush curves. She wore no make-up, and it was refreshing to see what a woman was supposed to look like. There's no way he'd ever let her go without at least knowing her name.

She licked her lips, and glanced over his shoulder.

The sudden smile transformed her face, a rare beauty, and he glanced to see Maria, her mother. They started talking, and he didn't understand a word of Spanish.

"Is it okay for me to take my mom home? She's finished for the day," Adora said.

"Of course."

Maria said something else before she went to put her supplies away. The stern look on Adora's face made him wonder exactly what her mother had told her. Maria had seen it all—the good, the bad, and the ugly.

Leaning against the counter, he reached for one of the grapes in the fruit bowl.

"What will it take?" he asked, popping it into his mouth.

She shook her head. "Nothing."

"Every single woman has their price. What's yours?"

It was clearly the wrong thing to say as she folded her arms, and began to glare at him. "You're used to clicking your fingers or signing a checkbook to get what you want. I'm not for sale."

"I didn't realize I was insulting you."

She rubbed at her temple, and he wanted nothing more than to pull her into his arms, to take the troubles away from her. Of course, if he took her troubles away, it meant she'd be giving him all of her attention.

Adora didn't dispute that he'd insulted her. He stared down the length of her body, wishing she wasn't wearing so many layers. Normally he dated women with fake tits, he'd even paid for some of them, but he knew Adora was all natural. Everything about her made his cock hard.

She was young.

"How old are you?" he asked.

"Why?"

"I'm curious."

She rolled her eyes, and with her arms folded, he saw how defensive she was. "I'm twenty."

He nodded. Picking up the fruit bowl, he held it out for her. "Want some?"

She shook her head.

"I'm not a bad man. I'm offering you some fruit."

"I'm sorry for invading your home. I just wanted to pick my mother up."

"Your English is impeccable," he said. He'd tried to have conversations with Maria, who he believed was a little younger than he was.

"I've known no different. My mom's tried to take lessons, but it didn't take." She shrugged. "I don't mind. I'm fluent in both."

She made conversation really difficult, and he found that she intrigued him. He usually didn't even care about a woman's name. She kept looking around his condo while waiting, and he saw the admiration of his décor, which he found interesting. She wasn't looking at his stuff, but the structure. Every now and again, she'd tuck her hair behind her ear, but it wouldn't stay there. She was nervous around him.

As he took another grape, any thought of the women he kept in his little black book slipped his mind. He'd intended to call a woman from the long list. Now, his focus was on Adora. He had to have her, at any cost. If Tobias was anything, it was persistent.

"Do you clean?" he asked.

She turned her attention back to him. "Sorry?"

"Your mother's a cleaner. I was wondering if you clean as well."

"No, not unless I'm helping her get home. Should I wait outside?"

He shook his head.

"You're a little … underdressed, and I really should wait outside before I say something I'll regret."

"Again, you don't have to." He took a step toward her. "Unless I make you uncomfortable."

She tensed up, and she shot him a glare. "I'm not uncomfortable. I don't like the way you jump to conclusions." She lifted up her sleeve, and he saw a simple black watch, the screen cracked, and he didn't like it on her wrist. Making a note to buy her another, he reached out, and tilted her head back to look at him.

"I meant no offense. Seeing as I don't know you, never seen you before, and you're in my place, it was a natural assumption. Tell me now, what will it take?" he asked.

"I'm not interested in going on a date with you, or

anyone. I'm busy with college and getting my life on track."

"You're in college?" He was surprised.

"What? You think a cleaner's daughter can't want an education?"

"Not at all. What are you studying?" he asked.

She shook her head, and he admired that fire. He wasn't used to reluctance in women. They were always ready and willing. It was somewhat refreshing having to do all of the leg work.

Just looking at her aroused him.

One day he'd own every single part of her.

I need an heir. The nagging thought wouldn't leave him the fuck alone.

This woman with fire in her eyes and a real chip on her shoulders would be an amazing conquest. He couldn't wait to get her underneath him, filling her tight, virgin pussy. He knew she was innocent to men the moment he touched her, and he liked the idea of being her only one. He couldn't resist putting his hands on her stomach, imagining his kid growing inside her.

Something dark and possessive ignited inside him.

She grabbed his wrist, and made to tug his hand away from her stomach.

"I'm not some whore that you can buy. This is my body and my life." She shoved him away, and before he could say or do anything more, Maria appeared.

He'd unnerved Adora. He saw the arousal in her gaze even though she wanted to fight him.

Maria said goodbye to him.

On the way out the door, he stood, watching them.

"Architecture," she said. "That's what I'm studying."

He should have known with the way she kept admiring his place. The elevator doors closed, and he walked back into his home, and went straight to his cell phone. Being the owner of the Bennett Corporation, he had a multitude of people and organizations at his fingertips.

Tobias gave one of his best investigators, a former FBI agent, Adora's name, age, and even what she was studying, and within the hour he had every detail of her life at his fingertips.

Flicking through the files that were emailed to him, he stared at several pictures that had also been attached.

He saw her birth certificate, which stated "father unknown".

Sitting back, he thought about Maria. She was a quiet woman, and stayed out of the way all the time, rarely making an appearance. Most of the time he imagined she was some kind of ghost.

Staring at Adora's finances though, he saw she was struggling, and she'd not been in college all that long either. The debt just kept rising, and even if she found a decent job, this would be hanging around her neck for a long time to come.

He needed a child, and she needed money.

Looking through some of the images, he saw she was a bright, intelligent woman. One of her graduation pictures had even made it onto the news. Her mother was there, and the two were hugging, a clear bond between them.

This was the kind of bond his brother tried to find and failed.

"There's no way you want this life, or what they offer. They're fucking liars, and they're cold as ice!" Maximus had been on another high, spouting shit off that

Tobias hadn't been interested in listening to. He'd wanted to keep his head down, and just focus on making his parents proud. He hadn't cared about anything else then. He wasn't blinded by their smoke and mirrors anymore.

When Maximus died, the guilt had nearly brought him down, but once again his parents had been there, telling him that he was the strong one, that it was now on his shoulders to carry the family name. Something had felt off to him, so he'd started to look into his family, and he knew things about his parents that were indeed quite shocking. Before he died, his brother had warned him to watch his back, so he did.

Tobias wasn't getting any younger. His parents had thrown prospective wife after wife at him, and he'd denied them at every single turn. He hated having this responsibility thrust on him.

Now his head was in the game. He wanted Adora in his bed, to fill her with his seed. Once she'd done her duty, she could do whatever the hell she wanted with her life. She'd be the perfect woman to be his child's mother.

It would piss his parents off that he hadn't picked their ideal woman. They'd never approve of his choice—her father unknown, her mother a mere cleaner.

His days of doing as he was told were starting to wear thin.

It was time to carve out his own life, and not one dominated by parents who didn't give a shit.

****

Sitting underneath a tree, Adora stared down at her course book, filled with descriptions of modern architecture, and all the while, her mind wasn't even on her studies. She rested her head against the hard bark, closing her eyes.

One of their neighbors had given birth to a new

baby, and all Adora had heard for the past six nights was the baby screaming. The mother was doing everything she could, but the walls were so thin.

She'd never been able to sleep with noise around her.

A couple of times growing up, her mother hadn't made rent in time, and they'd been tossed out onto the street. Shelters, buses, public toilets had been her bedroom for the night, and with it a whole set of nightmares she didn't even want to think about. As a child, she'd been scared, but like most kids, she'd dealt with it, holding her mother as she cried. She'd never understood why her mother cried, but then one day she'd found the diary that contained her secrets and her greatest pain.

Adora's father had been the love of Maria's life. At least, Maria had thought so. He'd been kind, gentle, building her trust. The affair had lasted a few months, and when she'd fallen pregnant, she'd been so excited. Of course, that excitement had turned to fear as he'd broken every one of her dreams, calling her a slut, a whore, and telling her if she even tried to pin the baby on him, he'd kill her.

Her mother had left, raised Adora all alone, and never once made her feel anything but love. It was part of the reason she wanted to really succeed in school. She had a plan. Get her degree, intern at one of the top five firms for young architecture designers, and build her career up. One day she hoped to have enough money that her mother wouldn't have to clean another house or office again.

There was one problem in her plan—the biggest firm was run by her real father. She wouldn't even think his name. She couldn't do it. The man meant nothing to her. He didn't want anything to do with her, and she never wanted to see his disgusting face in person.

"You're a hard woman to track down."

She opened her eyes, and saw Tobias Bennett in front of her. Glancing around the campus grounds, she saw that he'd gotten several curious looks. He was well recognized, and she didn't want this kind of attention. He took a seat, crossing his legs.

This was not the kind of thing she imagined from a wealthy businessman. He looked out of place in his impeccable designer suit as he sat on the grass in front of her.

"What are you doing here?"

"Well, I figured that dinner may be a little too soon, so I thought you'd be more comfortable with lunch or coffee. I'm inclined to have both, but it depends on you." She closed up her notebooks and began shoving them in her large bag, getting to her feet.

"I would really appreciate it if you didn't keep stalking me." She went to move past him, but he stopped her with a hand on her arm.

"I have a proposition for you. One I think you're going to really want to hear."

She pulled her arm out of his hold, and glanced around to see if anyone saw that.

"I don't think there's anything I want to hear you say. We don't know each other, not really."

He folded his arms, and, satisfied that she'd shut him up, she went to move away. "How would your mother feel if her job was given to someone else?"

She froze on the spot, and slowly turned to look at him. "No."

Tobias shrugged. "There are a lot of people who need a job. Probably more qualified."

"She's good at what she does."

"So are a lot of people."

"What do you want?" she asked.

"A coffee."

"You're blackmailing me for a coffee?"

"I tried to be nice, and you wouldn't buy it, so I'm stepping up my game."

She held her bag tightly on her shoulder, and took a deep breath before returning her gaze to his. "Fine."

"Excellent. My car is waiting."

"There's a perfectly good coffee shop there," she said, pointing toward the one near the campus.

"Not going to happen. I like good coffee. Come on, let's go."

He moved up behind her, and placed a hand on her back as he moved her toward his waiting limousine. She felt special in a twisted kind of way.

His touch affected her, and she tried to step away from his hand, but he wouldn't let her. His control, his ultimatum, his touch—it opened up that rift within her, that dark place she wished didn't exist. He opened the door for her, and she climbed inside. When he began to follow her in, she quickly moved over so she wasn't too close to him. She needed to be strong to resist him. He only wanted her in his bed.

Holding her bag in her lap, he told the driver where to go before putting up the private partition that separated them from his driver. They were completely alone, and she didn't have a clue what to say.

She couldn't believe that he'd just blackmailed her by using her mother.

"That wasn't so hard, was it?"

"I'd have preferred it if you'd not brought my mother into this. You know she's good at her job."

"I know she is. What do you have against spending some time with me?" he asked.

She took a deep breath. "We're in completely

different leagues."

"How are we so different?" he asked.

"You're a Bennett. You run a successful corporation, worth millions, if not billions, of dollars. My mom's a cleaner who earns less than the cost of most of your clothes." She'd never been afraid to speak her mind. Her mother didn't earn a lot from cleaning even though she worked for some of the wealthiest clients.

"And?"

Shaking her head, she gave up the fight and stared out of the window.

Tobias was friends with her father. She'd even seen pictures online, and in some of those glossy magazines that showed them laughing together. Until she'd seen Tobias in person, she hadn't realized it was him.

"What proposition do you have?" she asked.

"I'm in need of a certain type of person, and I have some … needs that have to be met. I think you'd be perfect for them."

"That's not vague at all," she said, not even trying to hide the sarcasm from her voice.

"Let's be clear, Adora. You've got debt. I've got money. I can help you out."

Just like that, she knew without a doubt what he wanted, and she just didn't want to know.

"No!" She turned toward him. "Sex. That's what you want, right?" She shook her head. "I want out of the car." She pulled on the door handle, and she started to get really angry. Her mother had been pulled in by a rich man and his false promises. This wasn't going to happen to her.

"Calm down."

"No. I won't calm down. Open the damn door now. I want out. I need out!"

She felt the anxiety attack begin to build. It had been years since she'd felt that clogging panic when she couldn't breathe.

Calm down.

He's not hurting you.

The limousine stopped, and the door finally opened when she pulled it. Bursting out of the limousine, she saw they'd stopped near an alleyway. Collapsing to the ground, she pressed her palms to the floor, not caring if it was dirty as her mind started to go fuzzy. Her stomach rolled, and she couldn't quite get her head together.

Tobias knelt beside her, and ran a hand down her back. "Are you okay?" he asked.

"Don't … touch … me."

She didn't expect him to listen to her, but he stopped touching her. He didn't leave her alone, staying close.

Minutes passed, and slowly, she got her breathing under control, and finally, she was able to stand up, and face him. Embarrassment overwhelmed her, and she quickly averted her gaze.

"Please, don't ruin my mother's job. She's really good and loves working for you." She didn't like how hard it was for her to not burst into tears.

"I'm not going to leave you here on the sidewalk, Adora. I won't hurt you, and your mother's safe. Just listen to me."

"I don't want to have sex with you, or to be with you in any way."

She held onto her bag like a lifeline. Tobias was a sexy, good-looking man, and even though he'd blackmailed her, she actually liked his cheeky smile.

From the moment she read her mother's diary, she'd promised herself she'd have a different life from her. It was why even at twenty years old, she was a virgin. Boys and men held no appeal.

Her studies mattered to her.

The plans she had in place were what she'd been focusing on all of her life.

"I don't want to just fuck you, Adora. I want you to be the mother of my child."

She stared at him, expecting for him to start laughing, but he didn't start laughing.

"You're joking?"

"No. I'm not. I want you to be the mother of my child, and for that honor I'll pay off all of your student loans, and set you up for life. You'll be at my beck and call whenever and however I want you."

For several minutes Adora stared at him, expecting him to say something else. There was no way she'd just heard that. Not after he'd threatened her mother, and attempted to blackmail her.

"What?"

Chapter Three

Tobias had expected this to go much smoother. Any woman would kill to be in Adora's position, but she acted like he'd forced her down the green mile. His initial plan only included using her to mother his child, but he'd spent the weekend unable to get her off his mind. He knew there was no chance of cutting her loose once he got what he wanted, so he'd set her up in an apartment to use at his leisure. She wouldn't have to worry for anything, so he didn't see an issue with it. Without his assistance, she'd end up scrubbing toilets like her mother.

"Don't look so shocked," he said. "I'm forty-five, and my parents are tired of waiting for an heir." He held the car door open for her and waited for her to take a seat, then joined her.

"You shouldn't have to pay someone to be with you. Why can't you fall in love like everybody else?"

"It's not so simple. I don't do love," he said. All his life, he'd been taught that love and empathy were weaknesses. The only way to move up the ladder of success was with a ruthless business drive and putting the almighty dollar above all else.

"Then why have a baby?"

"I need someone to pass my wealth to when I'm gone. It's important to keep the bloodline alive. Otherwise, it was all for nothing."

"Not everyone has children. Like me, for example, I'm only interested in my education."

He leaned back against the leather seat and massaged his temples, wondering why he tortured himself. Of all the women in the city, the one he wanted wasn't on board. He'd dealt with risk assessment and financial forecasting all his life. Taking his offer was in

Adora's best interest, she just didn't realize it yet. "Did you know I play golf with the president of your college every other Sunday?"

She twisted in her seat, her face blanched. "What is that supposed to mean?"

Tobias sat up straight, leaning into her personal space. "Use your imagination."

"You can't do this," she whispered. "You can't force me to be with you. Why would you want to?"

"Don't fight it. I promise you won't regret taking my offer." She looked so innocent, her lips full, her eyes wide with uncertainty. Part of him wanted to console her, but he knew he couldn't backpedal now.

"Why can't you just leave me alone?" Tears welled up in her eyes. "I'm nobody. And you're old enough to be my father."

"Is age that important to you?"

She paused. "No, but loyalty is. I don't want to be used and discarded. I deserve better than that."

He'd never had a deep-seated desire for any woman, young or old. Tobias always assumed he was a sociopath like his father, but fuck, he wanted Adora, regardless of her age. She tore down his resolve, making him weak, making him want things he'd never cared about. He held the side of her head, using his thumb to wipe away a tear. "It has to be you, Adora."

Until he'd first seen her on Saturday morning, the idea of an heir had been a burden on him. But the moment he saw her, it all became clear, and he had to move forward with his plan—to breed her, bind her to him for life.

Tobias used his free hand to drop her school bag to the floor of the car. She tried to reach for it, but he shook his head. He rested his hand on her thigh, making her flinch. This was new for him. He wasn't used to reluctance or purity in the women he dated.

"What are you doing?" She placed her hand over his, but he didn't move away.

"You want loyalty? Done. But I need to know everything. Tell me what experience you have."

"Experience?"

"With men, Adora. I want to know every detail."

After a brief silence, she answered. "There's nothing to tell. I have no experience."

His cock strained in his pants hearing the confirmation.

He knew she only obliged him by answering out of fear. She didn't want Maria to lose her job or for herself to get kicked out of the college. He was a bastard, always had been.

"What about kissing? Touching?"

She swallowed hard, wiggling in her seat. He decided he liked her shyness. It brought out his protective instincts, something he'd only associated with business. "I already told you I haven't done anything with men. I'm not a whore, so I don't know why you think I'll agree to any of this."

"Because you value your family and education, no?"

She frowned, but she looked more sad than angry now. "So you'll rape me?"

He chuckled. "Trust me, by the time I'm ready to deflower your pretty little pussy, you'll be begging me to fuck you."

Her mouth fell agape. "You're wrong."

"What do you have against me, Adora? Are you not attracted to me? What is it?"

She looked him in the eyes for a moment, but she kept quiet.

"Is it my age?" The thought of her wanting a man

her own age brought out an unexpected wave of insecurity.

She exhaled. "Do other women like being blackmailed by you?"

"I've never had to. I'm not used to women playing hard to get."

"This isn't hard to get," she said. "This is me refusing to jump to third base. You can't just buy people—well, not me, anyway."

Tobias knew she couldn't walk away because of her loyalty to her mother. But he loved her stubbornness. It brought out the hunter within him, made him feel ten years younger.

"I want a lot more than that." He moved his hand up higher on her thigh. She had thick legs, all curves he wanted naked and under him. Tobias looked forward to filling her with his cock, fucking her every day and night until she was ripe with his child. When he reached the apex of her thighs, she squealed and braced her hands on his shoulders.

They were so close, only a breath apart, so he leaned in and brushed his lips against hers. What surprised him most—she didn't pull away.

"Good girl," he said against her lips. She smelled like strawberry lip balm. He kissed her, softly, tentatively. This was going to happen, and he'd enjoy introducing her to every kind of wicked pleasure. The kiss deepened, still no hesitation. He slid his tongue along the seam of her lips until they were both tasting, melding into one. She whined when he slid his thumb between her legs, slowly rubbing up and down over her tights, so close to her virgin pussy.

She broke the kiss, gasping for air, her eyes hooded.

"It's just me and you," he whispered. Tobias slid

his hand under her sweater, taking her breast in his palm, caressing her pebbled nipple through her bra. She had big, juicy tits, and he couldn't wait to thoroughly enjoy them. Never in his life had a woman managed to unravel him like Adora. He could hardly keep himself in check, and he prided himself on his composure. "You feel so damn good."

"They're too big," she said. "Everything's too big."

"You're fucking perfect, sweetheart. Beautiful and perfect." His restraint was faltering. "Take your shirt off for me, Adora."

She hesitated.

"You don't have to be shy with me."

"But—"

He tilted her chin up, looking her eye to eye. "Please, baby."

She helped him pull the shirt up over her head. Underneath, she wore a black lace bra that barely contained her cleavage. Tobias peeled one of the cups down and licked her nipple before covering it with his mouth. He sucked hard, teasing with his tongue. She tossed her head back, her fingers combing into his hair. Her little mewling sounds drove him to the brink.

He lowered her to her back, rubbing his palm over the front of her pants, cupping her pussy as he suckled her breast.

"Tobias…" She moaned his name, her body becoming pliant. His girl was ripe and fertile, and he wanted to come deep inside her. No other man would have her, only him.

"You're mine, Adora. All of this is mine. Never forget that."

The limo came to a full stop. They were at the café, but the last thing he wanted right now was coffee.

****

Adora felt bereft when Tobias pulled off her body. The man didn't get his playboy reputation for nothing. With a few kisses and his very skilled touch, she'd fallen hard for him. How could a kiss like that mean nothing? It felt like the he was devouring her soul.

It felt like love, but she knew it was all part of his seduction.

His dark grey suit hugged all those hard muscles in just the right way. The scruff on his face and those evil eyes made her entire body take notice. He was masculinity and sophistication combined. Yes, he was much older, but his age and experience made her feel safe, special. That deep down need she wanted to ignore kept climbing to the surface, a craving for the security and attention she lacked in her life. She wanted to be his, to be cherished and owned by the billionaire, but her fantasies were just that. He only wanted to use her. Tobias himself said he didn't do love.

He winked at her. "Time for our coffee." Only then did she realize she had a death grip on his lapel, pulling him towards her. He took one of her hands, and kissed her knuckles. "Later."

How could he be so unfazed after what they just shared? No man had ever touched her the way he just had. She still felt lightheaded, her clit pounding and achy. She didn't dare trust her voice, so she nodded and followed him out of the limo after slipping her sweater back on.

He kept his hand at the small of her back as they walked into the swanky coffee shop. She could only afford the cheap stuff. His possessive touch made her feel good. Too good. Several eyes turned to them as they entered, making her feel self-conscious. Being a plus-sized girl from the poor side of the city, she stood out in upscale neighborhoods, and it didn't help that Tobias wore a full suit and walked in like he owned the place—maybe he did.

They sat at a small three-person table, the chatter of several conversations all around them. The rich scent of chocolate and coffee brought down her nerves slightly. "Do you come here often?"

"On occasion. Do you like it?" he asked.

She glanced around. Again, that feeling of not belonging weighed her down, and she just wanted to go home. Adora didn't want to be rude, and she didn't want to lie, so she shrugged.

"Hmm." He tucked some hair behind her ear. "I don't think you like it." That too-cute smirk tilted his lips.

"I'm just confused about everything."

This caught his attention. "That's why we're here—to talk."

Adora wasn't lying. She'd never been more confused and conflicted. All her life had been a struggle, and when she finally managed to get a student loan to attend college, Tobias showed up wanting to steal all her dreams. Yes, he tempted her with his promises and addictive kisses, but it was all false devotion. He'd probably get a kick out of fucking the maid's daughter, and then he'd move on without a backward glance. From her experience, that's what rich men did.

His offer included a baby, which meant she'd have to give up college, her dreams of making a mark in the architecture field, and her independence. She thought about running—her mother's job could always be replaced, but Tobias Bennett had a hand in everything, including her college and probably every company she'd ever want to work for.

"You know, there are surrogate mothers out there.

You could afford to hire one."

He shook his head. "It's not just about the baby."

She frowned. "I thought that's what this was all about, you and your precious *heir.* I can't even say the word with a straight face."

Tobias smiled, holding one of her hands on the table. He played with her fingers, then reached up her sleeve to hold her wrist. His warmth, his scent, his focus—it pulled her into his spell. "The kid's important, but it's *you* I want. I have more money than I can ever spend, but what I want to own is apparently not for sale."

"If you're talking about me, you can't own a person. This is the twenty-first century, Tobias."

He wet his lips. "I love the way you say my name."

She exhaled, trying to appear exasperated when all she felt was that same burning need she'd felt in the limo. "Can we focus, please?"

"Of course."

"You're a businessman, so I'm going to make a counter offer."

He nodded and sat straighter, trying to hide his smile. "Yes, ma'am. Let me hear this offer."

"I'm in college, and I'm not going to quit. My education is important to me."

"And?"

She struggled for words. What she wanted was his love, but she doubted that was on the negotiation table. "We take things slowly. If you want a relationship badly enough that you'd blackmail me, then we can start with dating. Like normal people."

The lines on his forehead creased. "Counter offer." He shrugged out of his jacket, carefully setting it on the free chair, then loosened his tie. She tried not to stare at his broad shoulders and toned biceps.

God, give me strength. "Okay."

"You'll get your education, I have no problem with that, and we can do the dating, but I want you in my bed tonight."

She pressed her legs together. "You're putting the cart before the horse," she said. "I'm not like the women you bring home Friday nights."

"So Maria's been chatty. Not smart."

The last thing she wanted was more trouble for her mother. "Okay, counter offer accepted," she blurted. "I'm just saying, I have no experience. Tonight seems too soon."

He appeared satisfied with her answer. "Okay, Friday night," he said. "Make sure those college boys keep their distance in the meantime. I don't want anyone touching you."

"What about you? Will you still be dating other women?" She held her breath. Adora knew the answer, but the truth would shatter her fantasy of being his special girl. She almost regretted asking.

The corners of his eyes crinkled. "Why would I date other women when I've found the one I've been looking for?"

"So you'll just keep sleeping around and not tell me about it? I don't want to be lied to. That should be in our agreement."

"You want the truth?" He shifted his chair next to hers, the legs scraping against the tiles. He put one arm around her, speaking in her ear, his voice deep and rough. "The only woman I'll be fucking is you, baby girl. All I can think about is burying my face into those gorgeous tits and filling you with my cock. I'm going to take my time with you, claim every inch of your body."

She focused on not stuttering. "I want more than sex," she whispered.

"Trust me, emotions are overrated." He raised one hand and a barista came right over. Tobias ordered their coffees. "I'll give you everything else: loyalty, money, education. That has to be enough."

She kept her mouth shut, wondering if he was even capable of love. They barely knew each other, so maybe things would change. Or maybe he'd break her heart and leave her alone and pregnant. She didn't want history to repeat itself.

Adora sipped on her coffee once it arrived. It tasted like heaven, and she could get used to drinking the good stuff.

"Good?" he asked.

She smiled. "I think it's the best coffee I've ever had. I think I'm in love."

He chuckled. "You're easily impressed. I like that."

"You know all this is crazy, right?" Even though she felt a thrill going along with this insane plan, she had to remind herself that he was forcing this on her. She had to keep up her guards.

"It's perfect," he said.

"I want you to know that I'm not as innocent as I look." Just because he was much older and experienced, didn't mean she was a foolish child he could toy with. She'd lived a hard life, and wasn't naïve to the darker side of humankind.

He used a crooked finger under her chin to get her attention. "But you *are* innocent."

Her face heated, and her fair skin probably looked bright red. "That's not what I meant. I'm talking about real life. Mine's been a struggle, and I won't be conned."

"That's a shame, but it all changes now," he said. "You're my woman. I take care of my own." He pulled out his cell phone and focused on the screen for a while.

When he finally tucked his phone away, he continued, "An offer of good faith."

She was confused.

"Check your accounts. Your student loan is paid off, and I've covered the tuition for the next three years. You're not being cheated."

Adora was speechless.

"I think you should do the same, so I know you're not a gold-digger."

"What?" She almost shouted. "This was your idea, not mine, Mr. Bennett."

He smirked, rubbing a hand over the salt and pepper stubble on his jawline. "Still, I need reassurance."

"How?"

He finished off his coffee, and stood up. Tobias grabbed his jacket and jutted his chin for her to follow him. Adora left her seat and weaved between the people in the line-up, following him to the back of the coffee shop and into the restroom.

"The bathroom?" She was going to complain, but when she glanced around, she realized it was nicer than her apartment, complete with sofas and artwork. "Wow, this is nice for a coffee shop."

"I only like the best," he said. "Now, for my guarantee."

"I have nothing to offer."

"Oh, but you do, Adora. You have no idea how valuable it is to me." He pressed her against the wall, his strong body trapping her in place.

He bent down and kissed her neck. She exhaled, a little moan escaping. When his hand slipped past the waistband of her pants, she tensed, grabbing his wrist. "What are you doing?"

"You're a virgin. I want to be sure."

His hand moved down her stomach, over the ugly

scar she kept hidden. When his fingertips reached her dark pubic curls, he growled. He suckled her pulse point. His warm hand touching her most intimate part made her knees weak. She held onto his arms to keep herself upright. When one of his fingers curled into her pussy, she let out a series of gasps.

"Fuck, you're wet, Adora." He pressed his finger in deeper, his thumb rubbing slow circles over her clit. "You're soaking my fingers."

"I'm sorry."

He smiled, stealing a kiss. Tobias continued to tease her cunt while she became lost in a kiss to end all kisses. His hard body was like an unmovable mountain, anchoring her from falling. When he slowly removed his fingers, she felt empty and achy, wanting so much more.

"Tobias," she said against his lips. "Don't stop."

He stepped back and checked the time on his Rolex. "I think it's time for my little girl to go back to school, no?"

What kind of monster was he?

Chapter Four

Tobias watched as Maria moved around his apartment. She'd been working late, and he'd come home early. He was taking her daughter out tomorrow night, and he'd not been in contact with Adora since his exploration of her body in the back of the coffee shop.

It had taken great effort on his part not to get in touch, to make this distance between them affect her. He wanted Adora to need him, to crave him, to want him so that by the time he took her out Friday night, she was desperate, and wouldn't argue with him. She wasn't like any other woman he'd ever known. All he ever had to do in the past was say his name, and women flocked toward him like a moth around a flame. Most of the time he didn't even need to say his name: in his circles, everyone knew who he was.

He was used to getting what he wanted, no questions asked, and yet Adora challenged him. She made him think, and just remembering her smart mouth made him hard.

When she began to make offers and counter offers, he'd known she'd be a damn good opponent in the boardroom. He intended to play golf with her professor this very weekend in the hope of finding out the other man's thoughts on Adora.

She already dominated a great deal of his thoughts. Not that he minded that at all. He loved thinking about beautiful things, and she certainly qualified. She wanted to date, fine. He had no problems dating, so long as she was in his bed. He also didn't mind her continuing college.

There would be no condoms involved. Just the thought of her being swollen, pregnant with his child, aroused him, had his dick aching in the most delightful of ways.

He'd already picked out the apartment he intended for her to stay in, along with the furnishings. She would want for nothing, and he'd even gotten a small place to set Maria up in. Adora loved her mother, he saw that, even though he didn't figure why. In a way he'd have dropped his own mother if their roles had been reversed.

Only love would have made someone take a deal they clearly didn't want.

Poor Adora.

She didn't want to be owned by him, and yet her body responded to him in ways that obviously confused her.

Tobias smiled, thinking of all the ways he wanted to pleasure her. He intended to get under her skin so there wasn't anyone else in the world she could think of. Staring at Maria, he saw a beautiful woman. She didn't appeal to him like her daughter did, but right now, he saw something … different.

Maria had to have been young when she had Adora, and with no father's name on the birth certificate, it piqued his curiosity.

Who had gotten Maria pregnant?

According to Maria's paperwork, when she had gotten pregnant she'd been working for a company who'd let her go a few months into that pregnancy.

He wasn't a fool.

Someone had gotten her pregnant, and seeing as the company she once worked for only dealt with wealthy customers, it made Tobias curious about who the guy was.

Did he know him?

Had he eaten lunch with a man who'd disowned his claim to his child?

He had no intention of keeping Adora his dirty little secret. She'd be the mother of his child, and once she was pregnant, he had every intention of doing things right.

She wouldn't fit with his parents' idea of a perfect wife, but he really didn't give a fuck about that one way or the other. She'd be perfect for him. It was like he woke up one morning and just wanted to have something for himself, to please himself, not his parents. He'd done that before, and they were never happy. He'd witnessed his brother's destruction at their hands. There was no way he'd go down the same way. They had a whole host of women lined up to fill the position of nursing a future Bennett. Women who came from wealth just like him.

None of them fired his blood the way Adora did.

When Maria finished her work, he noticed she went around his apartment another time, just fixing the odd thing that was out of place.

She was an impeccable worker.

The best really.

Within a few minutes she had her things, and was heading out the door.

"Thank you, Maria," he said.

She turned toward him, and nodded.

Her English wasn't great, which meant whoever had fathered Adora, spoke her language.

Tobias watched her leave, and he didn't like the twisting in his gut. Maria was a nice woman, kind and quiet.

Men with money, with power, with privilege, they'd have seen Maria, taken what they wanted, and spat her back out.

He didn't like that someone had shirked their responsibility in raising a child. In fact, it pissed him the

BREEDING SEASON: VOLUME ONE

fuck off. If he couldn't handle the consequences why not bag that shit up?

Sitting behind his desk, he logged onto Adora's banking accounts, and saw that she'd not touched a cent of the money he'd given to her.

Stubborn woman refused to take what he'd freely given her. The loans were all paid for, and her name was no longer marked by bad credit.

Flicking his pen between his fingers, he knew he was going to have to make her spend some money.

"Why are you so fucking stubborn?"

Bringing up Maria's documents, which he'd also requested, he glanced through her service history, seeing the company she'd worked for roughly around the time she'd gotten pregnant. He recognized the name, and attached to Maria's name was a list of houses she'd been dealing with.

He recognized every single name on the list. There was no way to narrow it down, which only served to piss him of even more.

His cell phone began to ring, drawing him out of his very pissed off mood at the fact he couldn't play detective, and when he saw Julia and Andrew Bennett's name on the screen, he groaned.

"Hello," he said.

"It's about time you answered, Tobias. I don't like to be kept waiting," Julia said.

That was his mother. A real piece of work.

He couldn't recall a time when she even asked him how he'd been.

"What is it?" He rubbed at his eyes, really not wanting to speak to his parents right now.

"It's Friday night, and we've invited the Clarkes. They're in finance, dear. You've probably heard of them."

And their three daughters.

"I'm busy."

"You're never too busy for your parents."

He nearly laughed. She rarely referred to herself as anything parental.

Glancing at the time, he realized Adora would be finishing up classes soon, and he wanted to be there to pick her up.

"I'm not going to make it. Enjoy the Clarkes' company. I've got plans." He hung up, turning his cell phone to vibrate as he left his condo.

His parents had a way of sucking all the energy out of a room without even trying. He didn't like them, not at all. In fact, he found their presence a pain in the ass.

Julia and Andrew liked to keep up appearances. They always brought up how torn he'd been over his brother's death, and of course how the family was dealing with it. There would be a few tears spilt for the sake of the cameras. Behind closed doors, however, was always a different story.

His father had been pissed off, angry that his brother had decided to be weak. Always begging to be loved, trying to find it in anyone who'd have him. The drugs had been a welcome reprieve from the emptiness.

Driving toward the campus, Tobias recalled one of the last days with his brother. How he'd found him in an abandoned building, naked, shaking from the shit he'd filled his body with.

"It's Tobias. Come to rescue me again, and take me back home."

"Why do you keep doing this?"

His brother had coughed and laughed at the same time. "I can't believe you're not *doing this. You spend so much time with your head in books, I'd think you'd*

*understand." Maximus looked up, and the sadness in his
eyes had really struck him. "But you don't get it. You're
as cold as them, aren't you, Tobias? You don't need love,
or to feel." Another cough, only this time it was a groan.*

"What you're trying to seek will get you killed."

*Maximus smiled. "Then I will die a happy man
rather than rotting in Father's library trying to please
him. He can't even disown me because he tries to keep
all of my secrets from the world. He's hoping I'll change,
that I'll become like him. A heartless, soulless bastard.
Let's not forget Mommy and her thirst for power. She'll
do anything for it. You go ahead, Tobias. Be like them,
and rot like them. Powerful they may be, but no one will
ever truly love them, and I feel sorry for them."*

Pulling out of his thoughts, Tobias realized he'd
parked at the campus already. He hadn't thought about
his brother for some time, and now he kept popping up in
his memories.

Love was an overrated emotion.

He had no intention of falling. Glancing around
the campus, he had an amazing vantage point, taking in
the students and the teachers. He spotted Adora speaking
to an older man around his own age, and Tobias didn't
like it as the two laughed.

There was a closeness there. He intended to put a
stop to it.

****

"I found your comparison interesting. Your own
apartment building to that of an upscale apartment—
fascinating. You've got an eye for differences, Adora.
It's very rare. Usually my students wish to talk about
modern architecture in buildings that have been erected
for special occasions, not general-purpose buildings."

Adora smiled. She enjoyed Professor Feswick's
class. Not only did he talk about historical architecture

and how it had evolved, he listened to everything. Out of all of her professors, she adored his class the most. He had a real passion for it, which hadn't died in the years of teaching.

"Thank you, I really do appreciate that."

"I'm not sure an examiner would agree. Even down to your notice of cheap materials between them. Also, you know you cannot compare the two as I also looked into it on my lunch break, and both buildings were constructed by different companies."

"I know. I looked into it as well. The company that built my apartment building is known for their cheap houses and apartments for the masses. The one where my mother works, they're known for only building for the wealthy, and tend to only be involved if the paycheck is high enough." Not only did she enjoy working on architecture, she loved going back to the nitty gritty basics, which again was why Feswick was her favorite professor.

"When you graduate, I hope I get a student with as much enthusiasm as you. You're a real treasure, Adora. Don't let any company that you decide to intern with take that out of you."

Before she could speak, someone pulled her into their arms. At first, she tried to pull away, but looking up into Tobias's angry glare, she found herself frozen.

It was Friday. She had no idea he intended to pick her up from campus. It wasn't late either, and in that moment, she couldn't remember if he'd given her a time when he'd pick her up.

Professor Feswick looked at her and then at Tobias.

"Tobias Bennett," he said.

She didn't like the way her stomach twisted.

"Professor Feswick."

They shook hands, and she noticed the way that Tobias gripped his hand.

Pulling out of Tobias's hold, she kept to her own space, not liking the way he'd claimed ownership of her in front of her professor. She wasn't an idiot. He clearly didn't like her talking to another male. She wasn't a slut.

Rumor had it that some professors were known for offering good grades for favors returned. She always made sure to avoid them, as she had no intention of ever being that kind of student.

"I was just telling Adora what a fine student she is, and when she graduates, I hope another is as fascinated as she is."

"I'll miss your classes, Mr. Feswick. You're an inspiration to me." She spoke up before Tobias had a chance.

"I was hoping we'd discuss where you wished to intern in the next few months."

Adora's stomach twisted once again. Her degree required a certain level of work experience as well as academic. Her father owned one of the best firms in the country, known around the world.

"What kind of work?" Tobias asked. "I've got Adora's best interests at heart."

"We believe our students need a level of hands-on experience to see the true potential. Adora's one of the top students in the class, and I was hoping I could put her forward toward the Hamilton program."

Hearing her father's last name filled her with anxiety. Pushing her panic away, she shook her head. "No, that's not where I'm hoping to go," she said.

Both men turned toward her.

She saw the confusion on their faces, and she didn't care.

"Adora, you're aware of the sheer volume and

respect Hamilton brings?" Feswick asked.

"I'm aware of them." And their lying, cheating, bastard of an owner. "They're such an obvious choice. I don't want to be obvious, so I was hoping to be part of the James and Co. program." They were Hamilton's biggest rivals, and she had no intention of ever, ever helping her father. That bastard had turned his back on her mother.

After reading her mother's diary, and knowing the pain she must have been through, she vowed to never give the man the time of day, and that included interning at his company. Adora was aware her father had a wife and children now. The family he acknowledged.

"That certainly does surprise me, Adora. I know you only wish for the best, but it's your future. Would you like me to put your name forward just in case? Hamilton is very … specific, so you may not even qualify."

"Put her name down. At least then she'll know," Tobias said.

She gritted her teeth, and stared at Feswick.

"I'll put your name forward for both." Feswick glanced at his watch. "I must dash. I've got to be home for tea. My wife has plans. Enjoy your weekend."

Feswick adored his children and his wife. He was always telling the class little stories, and she knew she wasn't the only one that adored her professor.

"He's an interesting man."

She turned toward the man that had her torn in many different directions. "Why did you insist on putting my name forward?"

"Why did you insist on *not* having it put forward?" he asked, staring at her.

The identity of her father was a secret. She intended to keep it that way.

"Did you forget we had a dinner date?" he asked.

She shook her head. "No. I didn't realize our date would be this early."

"I like to get dinner out of the way. We have more important things to get down to."

The wicked glint in his eye let her know exactly what he was talking about. Sex. He was going to be taking her virginity tonight.

"I've got to change," she said, glancing down at her jeans and shirt. She tried not to think about her nerves or her excitement about the coming night.

"You'll more than do."

"This won't be accepted in a restaurant."

"Then we'll stop over at one of the shops. We'll get you more suited." He placed a hand at her back, and guided her toward his car. Once at the door, she stopped, and turned toward him.

"You were jealous."

"Excuse me?"

"You saw me talking to my professor, and you were jealous."

"I don't believe in jealousy, never have. You're very much mistaken."

"You couldn't stand me talking to him." She smiled. Jealousy was a good thing. Well, not really a good thing, but it meant that he could at least feel something. "I'm not the kind of woman that screws her professors to get grades."

He stared at her. "You're aware that there are women who don't feel that way, right?"

"Of course I'm aware. I've heard of them, and I tend to steer clear of the professors who like to do such a thing." She stared at him. "You should know. Like you said, you go golfing with some of them."

She climbed into the car, allowing that piece of

news to simmer inside him. He closed the door, and she waited as he rounded the car.

Tobias climbed inside, and she didn't even have time to admire the décor. This wasn't like the limo he'd taken her inside the other day. Did he have a new car for each day of the week?

"Have any of your professors propositioned you?"

"No. Like I said, I avoid them. I've earned my grades with hard work, not because I've given away my body."

Tobias ran a hand down his face, and she wondered what he was thinking, what he was feeling. Had she finally gotten to him, or was it just an illusion? Was he putting a little show on for her to think that she was getting to him?

He confused her all the time.

From the first touch on her body, she couldn't seem to shake the feelings he inspired inside her, nor did she want to.

He turned over the ignition of the car, and they pulled away from the college campus, heading back into the city.

"If any professor ever tries anything, anything at all, you tell him no, and you call me immediately, do you understand?" he asked.

"I do."

Had she gotten to him? He didn't speak for several moments just driving his car.

"How was your day?" she asked.

"Long."

She smiled. He may not like it, but she hoped that she was getting underneath his skin just like he was hers. It would only be fair for the two of them.

He pulled up outside a very expensive designer

boutique, and her nerves hit her once more.
　　She didn't belong here.

Chapter Five

Tobias couldn't wait to spend his money on Adora. Most of the women he dated were only after his wallet, so it was refreshing to spend time with a sweet girl. *My girl.* He led her into the boutique, ready to spoil her before their date. Her clothes were cheap, and he wanted to see her wearing the very best. The mother of his child wouldn't want for anything.

"You don't have to buy me clothes, Tobias. I can go home quickly to change, or wear what I have on," she said, stalling at the entryway.

He shook his head. "Not happening."

Her reluctance was uncanny. He practically had to drag her into the shop. As soon as they entered, she dug her heels in and looked around with a childlike wonder.

"There're chandeliers," she said, barely above a whisper.

She was getting under his skin. How could she be so fucking adorable and sexy at once?

"I told you. I only like the best."

The white polished floors shone to a flawless finish. It reminded him of a dance floor, the clothing racks on the periphery. There were no other shoppers, but at this hour on a weekday, and with these prices, he didn't expect any different.

"Can I help you?" A tall, thin blonde walked toward them, her heels clicking on the stone tiles.

Adora held his arm, keeping close. He loved that she looked to him for comfort. She was his to protect and care for now. The new responsibility grounded him.

"We're looking for an evening gown, something she can wear to a nice dinner," said Tobias.

The blonde looked Adora up and down. She

looked like she'd just sucked on a lemon, and it pissed him off. "I don't know if we have her ... size."

"Then get a fucking tailor here," he said. "Have him at the ready."

Her mouth fell agape.

"Adora, take a look at some dresses you like, and then you can try them on together."

She looked up at him with pleading eyes. Didn't women like to shop? He prodded her to check out the racks of dresses, finally getting her to select half a dozen dresses and some heels.

They entered the fitting area at the back of the store, a massive circular room with countless mirrors and vaulted ceilings. He sat on one of the sofas, taking a quick look at his watch. They had plenty of time.

The saleslady approached him, bending over to whisper, "Our tailor is unable to come on short notice. Extensive alterations require at least a week turnaround."

"Do you know who I am?" he asked.

She shook her head.

He pulled out his wallet and handed her a card. "Tobias Bennett, Bennett Corporation. Call my assistant. She'll have a tailor here within fifteen minutes."

"Yes, sir. Of course, sir."

"Now, I want this changing room closed off until we're through, do you understand?"

"I'll be sure no one enters. If you need anything, please let me know."

Once the main door to the changing room clicked shut, Tobias smiled at Adora. She'd been standing nearby, looking at the dresses she'd selected.

"Take off your clothes," he said.

"What?"

"I want to see what I'm buying," he said.

"You heard her, Tobias. These are way too small

for me," said Adora.

"Don't worry about what she said. She doesn't know anything. We'll fix whichever one you like best."

She carefully took the first dress from the rack and started toward one of the smaller changing rooms.

"Ah-ah," he said. "Right there, baby doll. I want to see it all."

She looked like a deer in the headlights, but didn't argue. It surprised him. She hooked the dress back on the rack and pulled her sweater up over her head, her ponytail swinging down over her back once it was off. Then she slipped off her shoes and wiggled out of her pants. Once she was in just her bra and panties, his cock grew harder than the stone floors. He ran his palm over the front of his pants, trying to get comfortable.

"What if someone comes in?"

"They won't," he said. "Untie your hair."

She pulled out the elastic holding it back, her thick hair fanning out once released. It reached her ass, and she looked like a fucking angel. He'd chosen well. Adora had wide hips for child bearing and lush tits to nurse his baby. Just thinking about filling her with his seed made him feel like a horny teenager.

Adora wiggled into the first dress, a deep purple number. She couldn't do up the side zipper, but it hugged all her curves in just the right way.

"How fancy is this restaurant we're going to?" she asked, looking at herself in the mirror. When she glanced at the tag hanging from the dress, she gasped. "Tobias, do you realize how much this dress costs?"

"Let me worry about that."

"But—"

"You're worth it, Adora." It would take a while to get her used to being spoiled. And he didn't like her lack of confidence.

She tried on a few more, falling in love with the fourth one. It was black, form-fitting, with a deep plunging neckline. Her cleavage was killer, and he knew every man would be drooling over her tonight. The saleslady had been overdramatic, and the dress would only need some minor alterations.

"Are you sure you like it?" she asked.

"Come here." He patted his knee, and she tentatively sat down. Tobias cupped her cheek and kissed her once on the lips. "You're the most beautiful woman I've ever seen."

"Don't say that."

He growled in irritation. "I can have any woman I want, Adora, but the second I saw you, I knew it had to be you."

"I'm so confused," she said. "I should be happy. I mean, I feel like Cinderella right now. But I want more."

"What do you want?"

"I don't care about money. I want to fall in love with a man who loves me back, not one who blackmails me to have his baby."

He didn't know what to say. The one thing she wanted, he couldn't give her. How could he offer her love, something he'd never been exposed to growing up? He'd been taught to be strong, to be the best at everything. Love was a weakness. He'd been drilled to bottle that shit up. He wanted Adora, but couldn't offer something he was incapable of.

"You're right, this isn't a fairy tale. It's more complicated, it's real, but it doesn't mean I'm not giving you my all."

She fiddled with his tie. "It's just that my father never wanted me, and it hurt knowing that—more than you know. I had to watch my mother struggle, and had to live my life feeling unworthy. I'm an adult now. I want more."

"I'm not your father, Adora. He was an asshole to walk out on your mother. I'm nothing like him."

"You're more like him than you realize," she said. It sounded like Adora may know the identity of her real father, and it was something he was in the process of narrowing down.

He shook his head. "You don't even know me."

Tobias didn't even know himself. He'd been programmed to succeed, but at what cost? He couldn't help but remember why his brother took his own life. Most people needed more than dollars and cents—did he?

"But we're having sex tonight."

"Yes, we are," he said. "That's non-negotiable." He ran his hand up her thigh. "We'll have all the time in the world to get to know each other after tonight."

"What if I tell you I'm scared?"

He couldn't help but smile. "I promise I won't hurt you. We'll go nice and slow. I'll take good care of you." He gave her leg a little squeeze.

"I'm not worried about my body."

Tobias had a lot to prove, and it was all unfamiliar territory. But if he wanted to secure his legacy, he needed a woman. A wife. The longer he spent with Adora, the more his physical attraction morphed into genuine affection. It terrified him, this new vulnerability. His first reaction was to fight back and put up walls. He hoped he didn't fuck this up.

"One thing at a time," he said. Tobias slid his hand up her dress, holding her hip as he kissed her shoulder. "No more worrying."

"I haven't told my mother about us. About our date."

"You're doing it again. Tonight's about you and

me. I've been looking forward to it all week." He kissed her deep, holding her close. When her tongue slipped into his mouth, his eyes rolled back in his head. Never had a woman had such a profound effect on him.

****

Last week, Adora had been satisfied with her lot in life. Putting herself through college wasn't easy, but she was determined to make something out of her life. The studying, the working, the struggling—it would all be worth it one day.

Everything had changed.

In one week.

Adora was falling in love with a man twice her age, a man seemingly perfect in every way. She knew it was a mistake to go along with any of this, but she couldn't convince her heart otherwise. His words, his affection, and the way he stood up for her, everything kept pulling her in, and she was starting to change her hard-set views. Maybe things could work out. Maybe he'd grow to love her?

"If we don't stop now, I'll be taking you right here on the sofa. I don't think you'd want that." His voice always sounded rough and deep, having a direct effect on her libido.

She wanted to tell him that she didn't care one way or another. There was something about Tobias that demanded obedience, and she was helpless against it. She wanted him, wanted him to take control of her body in every way. Was she selling out? Putting her fears above her ideals? She didn't want to admit it, but even without the blackmail she wouldn't have been able to turn him down.

"I still say the dress costs way too much," she said.

He gave her that same evil smirk that made her

body fire hot. "You can thank me tonight."

Adora slipped off his lap, and changed back into her clothes. Tobias carried her dress to the front of the store. There was an older man in a suit waiting for them, a soft measuring tape around his neck.

"Carlos, thanks for coming by. Seems we have a bit of an emergency." Tobias winked and tossed the dress into his waiting arms, continuing on to the checkout counter. Adora followed behind him, but the tailor stopped her.

"A few measurements, please."

Adora obliged him as he quickly took all her measurements, then took the notepad to a wooden folding table with everything a tailor could need. She couldn't believe how much pull Tobias Bennett had. It made her feel special that he'd chosen her.

When she joined Tobias at the counter, he'd just swiped his credit card, tucking it back into his wallet. She couldn't even imagine how that would feel—buying anything he wanted, never feeling financially insecure.

"Give him a few minutes, then you can change. Are you hungry?"

She nodded.

"Where are we having dinner?" she asked.

"La Ballezza. Do you like Italian food?" He brushed some loose hair off her face, and she remembered it wasn't pulled back. The way he looked at her made her feel beautiful, like the only woman in the world.

"I love it," she said. He must have made reservations early in the week. La Ballezza was one of the most expensive restaurants on the downtown strip. All the celebrities and high rollers ate there. She never dreamed she'd see the inside firsthand.

"Excellent." He cupped her face and kissed her.

"I'm looking forward to tonight."

The lady from the store was only feet away behind the counter, but Tobias wasn't embarrassed or shy in any way about expressing himself. She liked that about him. He was confident and didn't care what anyone else thought. Adora wished she had a fraction of his self-assurance.

As soon as the tailor was done, Adora changed into her dress and shoes. The gown fit like a glove, hugging her curves like a second skin. She felt awkward being so formal, and walking in heels wasn't as easy as it looked. Before she had a chance to reflect and close in on herself, Tobias had his arm around her waist. He led her out to his car, opening the passenger door for her like a true gentleman. She wanted to hate him, but he made it so difficult.

The interior of Tobias's car was pure luxury. She sank into the lush leather seat, and watched the cityscape flash by the passenger window. The soft purr of the engine was the only sound in the car, and it unnerved her.

"Tell me something about yourself," she said.

"Like what?"

"I don't know. Your family, things you like to do … besides work."

His jaw twitched, his eyes focused on the road ahead. "There's not much to tell. I only see my parents on occasion, the less the better. Besides the odd game of golf, it's pretty much the office."

"You work too much."

"I built the business into what it is today. I like to have my finger on the pulse."

"There must be more than business. Didn't you have dreams when you were a boy?" she asked.

He scoffed. "To be the best. That's all that mattered. My parents demanded it, and I delivered."

There had to be more to Tobias. His life couldn't have been so cold.

"Siblings?"

"No." He cleared his throat. "Tell me about Adora. I want to know about the mother of my child."

She didn't like the sound of that. It seemed so clinical, so unloving. She didn't want to be his baby-maker, she wanted to be his everything. "I lived with my mother until last year when I moved to be close to college. I'm an only child, and you already know my mother raised me alone."

They pulled in front of the restaurant. The valets were already moving in, but it didn't appear to give Tobias any sense of urgency. He leaned over and tilted her chin up, looking her directly in the eyes. "It all changes now, baby girl. Today's the first day of better things."

She nodded just before her door was opened for her. Part of Adora wanted to argue, to tell him that setting her up in a condo while she baked his bun in her oven, was not an appealing prospect. She didn't care about money, not even security, if it meant a loveless life.

They walked up the steps to the massive glass doors, and two doormen opened them as they approached. Adora held onto Tobias's arm in fear of falling in her heels.

"Mr. Bennett, welcome to La Ballezza," said the hostess. "Would you like a table for two this evening?"

"Something private."

"Yes, sir."

They followed her into the restaurant, and Adora was fascinated by the mix of old world and modern architecture and décor. Her eyes adjusted to the dim lighting as they walked. The restaurant was as impressive as she'd imagined. The hostess led them to a small, private alcove at the back of the room with a circular bench. A candle flickered on the table.

"This is really beautiful," said Adora as she took as seat on the padded seat in the booth. She expected Tobias to take a seat opposite her, but he sat right beside her, their legs brushing.

"Not as beautiful as you."

Was her face as flushed as it felt? She swallowed hard, not used to this level of attention. "Did you have reservations?"

"I don't need reservations." He continued to stare at her as if amused by her discomfort.

"Do you always get what you want?"

"Always." He wet his lips, and she could envision the wicked things he was thinking. Her pussy tingled, the wave of need taking her by surprise.

"How old are you again?" She tensed after asking, wondering if she'd crossed a line, but he'd told her last time they'd seen each other. He was forty-five, and she was twenty.

"Is that important to you?"

She shrugged. "I guess not. I'm just wondering why you're not already married."

He smiled, his eyes crinkling at the corners. "I'm very picky."

"So you pick me?" She nearly choked on a laugh. Adora wasn't blind, and knew she was far from a ten.

"You're too hard on yourself. I'm not sure why, but it needs to stop," he said. "There's something about you, Adora. You bring out a part of me I thought was dead. Maybe your innocence, your beauty—all I know is I'm not letting you go."

"So, I'm your prisoner?" she teased.

It felt right to lighten the mood. Tobias was

scaring her with his intensity. Yes, she wanted him to be real, but her own emotions were a mess.

"Is it so bad?"

She couldn't answer. So far, he'd only spoiled her, making her feel like a princess. She wished he'd handled things differently, maybe dated her without demanding a baby. "I'm not sure yet."

"Fair enough. Tonight, I'll show you just how good things can be." He rested his palm on her thigh under the table, sparking every cell in her body to life.

She briefly closed her eyes, savoring the wave of need washing through her. Adora wanted to touch Tobias, to run her fingers over the stubble on his jaw, to unbutton his fancy shirt and feel those hard muscles firsthand. Maybe tonight she'd have the nerve to take what she wanted in return.

The waiter stopped by, introduced himself, and gave them menus. She was looking over the choices when she felt Tobias's body tense next to hers. He sat up straighter, staring at the other side of the restaurant. She couldn't see what he was looking at from her position in the booth, but she hoped it wasn't another woman. Maybe it was an ex-lover. Adora wanted to block out all the stories her mother had shared over the years. She wanted to be the only one for him, and the thought of him mentally comparing her to those beauties didn't sit well with her.

The new wave of jealousy surprised her, making her realize just how deep she'd invested herself in this venture. That's the only name she could give their relationship because it was completely unorthodox, but she knew she was all in at this point.

Chapter Six

Across the crowded restaurant Tobias caught sight of not only one of his ex's but also William Hamilton, the very owner of the company that ran the Hamilton program that Adora was determined not to be part of.

William was a known hound dog. He'd fuck anything with a pussy. Tobias's ex, Katerina, was well known for screwing anyone who'd pay her for the pleasure. He used to be one of those men like William, but not anymore. Looking at Adora, he saw the freshness, the innocence, the beauty within. He glanced at the other women, dressed up in their expensive dresses, the jewels, and wondered how many of them had a hard life. Did any of them worry about having a meal from one day to the next? Adora had helped open his eyes.

He'd read Adora's file and her mother's. They'd struggled most of their lives to make ends meet, and he was determined to make all that stop.

"Is everything okay?" she asked.

"It's fine." He reached across the table, taking her hand. She tensed up when he first touched her but slowly relaxed, and he gave her a smile, not wanting to think of William or anyone else. Tonight was about wooing his woman, and putting a baby inside her. If she'd not been hungry, he'd have already started the baby making.

"This is a really fancy place."

"So, how often do you speak to your professor alone?" he asked, abruptly changing the subject. Seeing Hamilton reminded him of the conversation he had with her professor, and it also made him curious to know exactly why she didn't want to go for the number one program.

"Really? You want to play the jealousy card again? I thought we went over that."

"Why don't you want to be part of the Hamilton program?" he asked.

He watched her tense up and pull her hand away from him. Being the astute businessman that he was, he knew something was going on there, something that he didn't like, not one bit.

"I don't like to do what everyone expects of me."

"There's something more going on there."

"Nope, nothing." She grabbed the menu, staring down at it. "Have you been here before? Do you know what's good?"

He signaled the waiter over, and ordered them both some steaks, potatoes, and vegetables. It sounded simple, but each item was made with the perfect amount of butter, garlic, and herbs, only the finest ingredients. He loved coming to this place.

Returning his attention back to his woman, he saw that she stared down at her lap. Once again, he was struck by how young she was. Not only her age, but also her insecurity came through. This world would take women like her, chew them up, and spit them back out, and he didn't want that.

"You remind me a little of a ... person I once knew," he said.

"I do?"

"He was determined to live life his own way. For a long time, he had these beliefs, searching for love, for something more." He hadn't told her about his brother, purposefully evading the question. Thinking about him now, Tobias was struck by a pain that twisted inside his chest.

"You make love sound like it's a disease or a curse."

"Love is overrated, and in his search for it, he killed himself."

Her lips fell open, and she glanced around the restaurant. "Why are you telling me this?"

"Love … can hurt a lot of people. You don't need to hunt for it. Ignore what you think the world expects of you. What I'm offering you is a future that no one else can. I'm a Bennett. I rule this world, and whatever you want, I can give it you."

Adora's eyes glazed over with a sheen of tears. "I want love, Tobias, and apparently that's one thing you can't give me."

"I thought it was you." They were both pulled out of their conversation by William's presence. Sitting back, Tobias didn't allow his annoyance to show. The Bennetts didn't need someone like Hamilton, but again, his parents would bitch and moan at him if he caused a scene. He always had to be perfect. There was never any wriggle room.

"Hamilton, Katerina, what a surprise to see you both," he said.

"Not that much of a surprise, I believe. This place is just lovely as you well know."

Out of the corner of his eye, he saw that Adora wanted to be anywhere but at the table. If it was possible, it appeared like she was trying to shrink away.

"We wondered if you and your date would care to join us?" Hamilton said.

Adora stared at him and gave a shake of her head. He saw the pleading in her eyes.

"I want her all to myself tonight, Hamilton. Thank you for the invite."

Hamilton finally looked at her. "Maria?"

Now this made Tobias tense up as Adora closed her eyes for a few seconds, and looked up at him. He didn't know what it was, but he suddenly saw a little of Hamilton in her features, and everything made sense. Maria had been cleaning for him roughly around the time that Adora was conceived.

Not only that, her determination not to join the Hamilton Program now made sense.

Staring at the man, then at the girl, then at the man again, Tobias knew that he was looking at her father. Not only that, her father was finally staring at the girl he clearly denied.

Adora turned toward him. "I need to use the bathroom. Is there one here?"

"I can show it to you," Katerina said.

Before he had a chance to dispute the two women leaving, they were gone. His anger started to build, especially knowing that she was about to be the mother of his child, and by right, she should inherit part of the Hamilton fortune. The man himself only had sons.

His parents would fucking kill to have a foot in the family, and right now, he was courting one of those chances, seeing as they didn't have a daughter to send off to marry.

Hamilton watched Adora leave.

The man looked positively pale, and everything seemed to become clear to Tobias. "You're a fucking asshole, you know that, right?" Tobias said, glaring at the man before him.

"Excuse me?"

"You know exactly what I mean. You fuck the cleaner, knock her up, and dump her on her ass." He snorted. "I always knew that you didn't own up to all of your shit, and Adora is one of them."

"You don't have a clue what you're talking about," Hamilton said.

"I know this is the first time you've ever seen

your daughter." Tobias laughed. "Wow, you know what? I want you to leave my table right now because when I look at that woman, and I think of all the shit she's been through, I don't like what I feel, or what I'm tempted to do." He stared at the man who he once respected. Sure, Hamilton was a bastard, but right now, it was glaringly obvious the guy fucked up, and instead of dealing with it, he just brushed it aside.

He thought about Maria and her lack of English, her innocence being taken advantage of, and struggling to raise a daughter alone.

Hamilton left the table, and seconds later Adora joined him. Her cheeks were red, and she stared at him. "You really know how to pick women," she said.

"Katerina is an ex. She's a whore who gives favors to men." He took a sip of his wine, her nerves palpable. "And William Hamilton is your father, which is why you don't want to work for him. On your birth certificate it states the father is unknown."

"How do you know that?"

"You're going to be the mother of my child. Don't you think I'd learn everything there is to know about you?"

She licked her lips, and the waiter came out with their food. Thanking him, he kept his attention on Adora.

"My mom kept a diary. She talked about him for a long time. Her time with him, and how she fell in love, how he made her think she was the most beautiful woman in the world. It was all lies." She glanced over at the table where her father sat. "Nothing was the truth. She fell in love with a liar. When she found out she was pregnant, he kicked her out. Told her to get rid of it. That she was nothing more than a cleaner and a two-bit whore." She paused, wiping beneath her eyes. "He broke her heart. I want nothing to do with him."

"You're entitled to your inheritance, and part of the Hamilton fortune."

She laughed. "I'd rather clean apartments and homes for the rest of my life than accept anything from him. I'm sorry that you don't understand that."

"I do understand. It doesn't have to be like that. Not for you, and certainly not for your mother."

"That's why I'm here though, right? You want me to give up my dreams for a baby. Tell me, Tobias, how are you any different from my dad?"

****

"You're nothing special. Men like Tobias use women and spit them back out. We're just a bit of amusement for him."

Adora rubbed at her chest feeling open, exposed, and cornered. The anxiety threatened to spill out, and she took a sip of her wine to try to blank everything out. Her father was here. He'd said her mom's name, and Tobias knew the dirty truth.

Katerina's words still echoed around her mind, and now she wondered how Tobias was any different from the man who donated sperm. She couldn't call William Hamilton her father. That bastard was anything but, and she wouldn't give him or anyone else the satisfaction of trying to get him to own up to his responsibility. She wanted nothing else to do with him. Simply being in the same breathing space was too much.

All she wanted to do was curl up with her mom, and forget about everything.

"I'm nothing like him," Tobias said.

She cut up the steak but didn't even bother putting it in her mouth. Katerina was Tobias's ex, and she looked like a super model. The few moments they shared in the bathroom had been a complete overshare. From the warning about how they were mere playthings, to talking about the length of Tobias's cock, it was all too much. "I need some air."

Without waiting for him to say anything, she left the table, stepping outside of the restaurant, and away from any prying eyes.

Grasping the wall several feet from the building, she took deep breaths. In a matter of days, she'd suffered with two anxiety attacks.

She had to get out of this deal with Tobias. She couldn't handle it. She'd never be cut out for that kind of life. He didn't do love, and all she wanted was someone to love her.

"Don't leave like that," Tobias said.

His hands stroked up and down her arms, and she kept her eyes closed, welcoming his comforting touch.

"Come on, the car's waiting."

"No, I can't. I can't do this." She spun to face him, tears spilling down her cheeks. "I'm sorry, but I need you to leave me alone."

Tobias stepped up close to her, invading her space. "Remember how good it feels to have my hands on you?"

She shook her head. "No! I don't want to remember. I don't want to continue this. Your ex was right there. My own father, who is married with kids, was right there. I don't want this life. When I have a child, it's going to be with a man I fall in love with. A man who will love me unconditionally and doesn't care about me being a cleaner's daughter."

Tobias grabbed her arm, and pulled her toward the waiting car. She began to fight him, and he yanked her so she fell against him. To anyone watching, they were embracing.

"If you don't get in this car, I'm going to cause a scene you're really going to regret," he said.

She hated scenes, not that she'd created many herself.

Adora much preferred to be out of the way of prying eyes. When Tobias opened the door, she didn't argue. Climbing inside the car, she buckled her seatbelt, resting her head in her hand. Her elbow rested on the frame of the door.

She didn't say anything to him as he got behind the wheel, and drove away from the restaurant. Their date and meal had been ruined.

He didn't take her home, nor did he take her to her mother's. She didn't argue as he pulled up into the private parking lot of the condo where he lived. Opening her door, she followed him to the waiting elevator. Neither of them spoke as they made their way to his apartment.

Tobias closed and locked the front door while she moved toward his large window, which overlooked the city. He held so much power that it was almost frightening to think about. She saw his reflection in the window as he held up two glasses with dark amber liquid.

"I'm nothing like your father."

She took the glass from him with a thank you. She stared down at the liquid, the scent of whiskey making her nose wrinkle.

"It's not a taste you'll like, but it'll put some fire back inside you."

Sipping at the dark liquid, she coughed as it hit her throat. "Thank you."

"William Hamilton is not a close friend of mine. My parents would love me to marry into that family."

She laughed. "Wow. He only has sons." Younger brothers she'd never met. She didn't know if they were like her father or not, nor did she care to find out.

"I wouldn't ever allow a woman to raise my child alone. Even if I had nothing to do with a kid, I'd make sure they were taken care of. Everything their hearts desired would be theirs."

Looking at Tobias was hard to do. His words were always so blunt that it was impossible to believe that she found herself falling for him. She wanted love. He refused to give it, told her constantly that she wouldn't ever get it from him.

"It was hard for you and your mom, wasn't it?" he asked.

For some reason she didn't think it was a question that needed answering. "Seeing him tonight was … hard." She finished off the whiskey, handing him back the glass, and finally looking at him. "It's the first time I've ever seen him up close. Mom doesn't even know that I know about him. I read her diary without her permission. I don't want to be in her position. She never found anyone else. Her love has always been for a man who'll never love her back. Tonight, he's married to someone else, and he was with another woman."

Tobias once again pulled her into his arms, and she didn't fight him.

"I'm not like him. I'd never leave you, and I will always care for you and our child."

She gripped the lapels of his jacket, and pressed her face against his chest. It wasn't enough.

Tobias rubbed her back, and as the time passed, she closed her eyes, basking in his touch. His hands were so large and smooth. There were no callouses that scratched her as he touched her skin. Slowly, the tension in the room changed.

She became aware of the beautiful dress she wore. How her nipples tightened at the rub of fabric against them.

Biting her lip, she stared up at him, trapped by his gaze.

"I know you're not like him," she said.

He stroked her cheek, his hand cupping her face as his thumb ran across her lip. She closed her eyes, gasping as he pressed his thumb inside her mouth. Instinctually, she sucked on him, loving his moan as she tasted him.

"I'll do anything for you, Adora. All I want is you, your body, and for you to be the mother of my child." His hands moved around her neck. He stroked over the pulse before going to the straps of her dress, pushing them down.

Her pussy pulsed as arousal hit her.

His gaze was always so intense, so focused that she struggled to break free from it, not that she wanted to. She loved his gaze on her, the fire directed on her alone. She'd seen the annoyance in his eyes when Katerina had been close. He'd not been happy to see his ex.

Pushing away thoughts of the other women in his life, she followed his direction, turning so that he could slide the zipper down.

There were no words as the dress fell down on the floor, and she stepped out of it.

"You can take off the heels." Kicking them off, she lost a couple of inches. "One day I'll stare at you completely naked with only heels, but tonight's not the time."

He picked her up, and she wrapped her arms around her neck with a gasp.

"You feel perfect in my arms. I won't have you any other way."

She didn't complain that she was too heavy as he carried her toward his bedroom. She held onto him tightly, afraid that he'd drop her. His strength was only another turn-on.

His bedroom door was already open, and he placed her on her feet. She watched as he removed his jacket, and became aware that she stood before him in only her underwear. He'd seen her before, touched her body, but right then she felt too exposed.

Tobias stepped in front of her after tossing his jacket on a chair. "Take off my shirt."

She rubbed her arms, and reached out, sliding the buttons open, mesmerized by his hard, muscular chest as she opened his shirt.

"Now take it off."

Her mouth went dry. Sliding her hands from his stomach up, she watched the crisp white shirt fall to the floor.

This is really happening.
I can't believe it.

Her heart pounded, threatening to explode from her ribcage.

Tobias circled her, one of his hands going to her waist, trailing a circle around her body. She didn't pull away from him, not that she wanted to. Away from the prying eyes of the people in his world, she lost any reason to deny him, deny this. He made her ache in ways that she couldn't begin to think about, or describe. There was no way she'd ever feel this way about anyone else.

Does it matter he'll never love me?
I can live without love.

She'd been doing it for years. His lips trailing across her collarbone, making her ache in all the delicious ways. He stepped behind her. His touch made her skin burn. She couldn't wait for more to come.

Chapter Seven

Tobias supposed this was like any other business transaction. He'd made Adora an offer she couldn't refuse. It all started because of his parents nagging him for an heir. Instead of allowing them to hook him up with some rich bitch, he'd decided to make a baby with no attachments. But all his well-laid plans had gone out the window the moment he set eyes on Adora.

She was sweetness and innocence personified.

Now the dark-haired beauty was becoming the center of his universe, and he wasn't sure how the fuck that could happen in the span of a week. Yes, he needed the heir, but he wanted Adora even more. She didn't care about money or fame, and it was refreshing. Tobias had never realized how shallow his life was, and now he wanted more. For the first time, he had a glimpse into his brother's torment. He wouldn't allow his parents to steal away his newfound happiness.

"Your skin is so soft," he whispered, leaving a kiss on her bare shoulder. Tobias had a lot of experience behind him, but he'd make sure to go slowly for Adora's first time. Now that he thought of it, he'd never had a virgin. In his fast-paced world, the women were anything but sugar and spice. Not his Adora. She was his prize, a woman just for him.

He hadn't thought of another woman since Adora walked into his condo. And now he'd claim her, breed her, bind them together for life.

She inhaled sharply when he ran his hand over her stomach from behind.

"You're shivering." He lifted her hair to one side, inhaling deeply at her neckline. She smelled like strawberries and sunshine, and he was already addicted.

"I'm just a bit nervous," she said. "Maybe a lot

nervous."

"You're in good hands, Adora."

She twisted around in his hold, resting her forearms on his chest. "That woman in the restaurant. She told me things about you. Private things."

He scowled, wishing he'd stayed away from that tramp all those years ago. Everyone he knew had taken a ride on her. Knowing their brief relationship made Adora insecure pissed him off. How could he explain that Katerina meant nothing to him?

"Like what?"

She bit her bottom lip, her cheeks changing to a pretty pink. "She thinks you'll use me, that after tonight I'll never hear from you again."

He had to tamp down the rush of venom that raced through his veins. Anyone who threatened his relationship with Adora was on his shit list. She brought out all his protective instincts.

"I hope you know that's not true. I'll admit I've always thought of women as playthings, but I've found the one woman who can tame me," he said. "But that's not what's bothering you, is it?"

"She told me personal things … about your body."

He smiled. "You've made me curious. I'd like to hear this."

Adora shook her head, her breathing picking up. "Just that it was big and had a beauty mark on it."

"*It*?" He took her wrist and pressed her hand against the front of his suit pants. "Do you mean this? My cock?"

Adora attempted to pull her hand away as if it burned, but he wouldn't allow it. She could remain shy, but not with him. He was about to open her up to a whole new world.

"Listen to me, little one. This is yours now. Only yours. I don't care what some old fling had to say because she meant nothing to me," he said. "You mean everything."

Her fingers twitched.

"Go on, Adora. Touch me."

She squeezed lightly, and he clenched his jaw down hard. The pleasure of her little fingers wrapping around his erection was too damn much.

"It's really hard."

"What's hard?" He tilted her chin up, looking deep into her dark eyes. "Tell me you like my cock."

He pulsed in her tender grip, his blood engorging him to the point of pain.

"I like it. I like your *cock*."

Tobias growled the second the word slipped from her lips. He reached behind her and unfastened her bra, her big tits spilling out of their binds. "Tell me these are mine." He held her waist and bent down, suckling her beaded nipple before gorging himself on her soft flesh. She was fucking heaven—all real, and all his.

"Yes," she cried out. "They're yours, Tobias."

He stood up, and knew his eyes were glazed over. "It drives me crazy when you say my name. I can't wait until you're screaming it." When he began to peel down her panties, she tensed.

"Can we turn the lights off?" she asked.

"Now why would I do that?"

"Please?"

There was no light on in his bedroom, just the soft glow from the living room. He wanted to get these granny panties off her. She needed to take a trip to the lingerie store to pick up some sexy little numbers. He'd be sure to get a credit card in her name. "You're not hiding from me, baby." He proceeded to remove her underwear, and her hands slapped over her lower stomach. "What are you hiding?"

"I don't want you to see."

He frowned, forcing her hands away. A large, thick scar covered the area below her navel, slightly darker than her fair skin. "What happened, Adora?"

She covered her face with her hands for a minute, then took a cleansing breath, looking defeated. "It's an old burn. I was helping my mom when she worked in a kitchen. I had to have some skin grafting done, but it will never look normal."

"And you think you have to hide this from me?"

"It's disgusting."

He shook his head. "It's a burn. If you think this changes anything, you're wrong." Tobias leaned back to get the full view of Adora's naked body. He loved her full, rounded hips, and all those explosive curves. The short, dark curls between her legs hid her pussy, and he needed to know every inch of his woman.

"But—"

"I like everything I see, Adora." He unbuckled his belt, the metal jangling as he unzipped his pants. "You drive me crazy."

He didn't want her to feel insecure around him. She was perfect. Tobias cupped her face and kissed her, slowly walking her backwards toward the bed. She invoked such passion in him. The women he used to fuck around with meant nothing. He'd almost become numb to sex, going through the motions but never giving a shit. Adora held him captive with a single kiss.

When the backs of her legs hit the mattress, he lowered her down until he dominated. She held onto his bare shoulders, kissing him with a hunger that matched his own. His dick ached, the lowered zipper only offering a bit of respite.

He trailed his kisses to her neck, teasing her erogenous zones with his tongue. She was so receptive, her little coos and sighs prodding him to take more. Tobias stood up, bracing one knee on the bed. He bent forward and pressed her tits together, creating a mountain of cleavage. He flicked her nipples, licking and sucking until her back arched up off the bed.

"Oh God." She whimpered as he kissed lower, focusing on her scars, not missing a spot. He'd prove to her exactly how he felt about her beautiful young body. Tobias had always been a superficial asshole, but Adora changed all that.

"Open your legs."

"Tobias, I can't."

"Be a good girl for me." He lifted her legs so her heels were on the bed, then spread her open at the knees. She fought him, trying to keep her thighs together, but he wouldn't be denied. Her pussy spread open looked so fucking pretty. He licked his finger, then slid it inside her, watching it slowly disappear. She gasped, closing her legs, trapping his arm. "Don't fucking close these legs, baby. Let me play."

She opened up for him, her chest rising and falling rapidly. Tobias had to remind himself he was dealing with a virgin. He kissed the soft, pale skin of her inner thighs, higher and higher until he painted a line along her slit with this tongue. She grabbed his head, squirming on the bed.

"This is mine, Adora." He dropped down to his knees on the floor, slipping his hands under her ass to pull her right to the edge of the bed, her legs over his shoulders. "When I want to eat this pussy, don't stop me." He firmly lapped his tongue up from her puckered little asshole to her clit, over and over, until she cried out.

Such a delicious virgin pussy—all his.

He fucked her with his tongue, savoring the fact he was the first man to enjoy her, before settling over the tight bundle of nerves. He sucked and rolled her little pearl with his tongue until she writhed on the bed, her screams echoing in his condo. His composure faded, a new feral need taking over. "Come for me, baby. Come all over my tongue."

Within seconds, she arched her back, her fists clenching the comforter. "Tobias!" Then she detonated, her pussy pulsing against his mouth as she moaned with each wave. He didn't release her until every quake had settled.

Her eyes were half-lidded, her mouth parted as he stood up and kicked off his pants and boxers. She leaned up on her elbows, staring at his dick. Adora was about to know it intimately.

****

She could blame the shot of whiskey for her lack of inhibitions, but knew otherwise. It was Tobias and his mad skills. Nothing about her seemed to repulse him, and he ate her pussy with enthusiasm, so there was no mistaking he enjoyed every second of it. Something about him made her crave to submit, to give in to his sexual domination. Her body still hummed, and the delicious high from her orgasm had given her an out-of-body experience. She was completely at Tobias's mercy, desperate for more of what he could give her.

When he began to undress out of his pants, her curiosity soared. Katerina had said Tobias was eight thick inches that would ruin her for other men. Adora had no plans on visiting another man's bed, and she hoped Tobias wasn't lying when he said she was one of a kind. She had dreams of forever, and hoped she wasn't being naïve in believing she could tame a playboy.

Tobias's cock was impressive and intimidating,

jutting up like a virile arrow, thick and beefy. Just imagining all those inches claiming her virginity made her wet all over again.

When she attempted to close her legs, he shook his head. "Keep them just like that. You're making my cock rock hard."

Tobias had the body of a god, all hard, chiseled muscle. She knew she was staring, but couldn't look away. The corded muscles in his shoulders tensed as he briefly stroked his erection. He stared at her like she was something to eat, something irresistible, and she loved his undivided attention. His dark eyes roamed over her body, heating her up from the inside out. She was ready to beg, so desperate to feel his warm skin against hers, to taste his lips, and feel his cock filling her.

"Tonight, I make you mine, Adora. I plan to fuck you every night until you're ripe with my child." He licked his lips. "I'm going to fill you with my seed, stretch your pussy with my dick."

She swallowed hard, her lips suddenly too dry. Her pussy tingled in anticipation, the slight breeze from his movements were beautiful torture to her oversensitive clit. Adora needed him, wanted him, and prayed she could keep him.

He crawled over her, hoisting her up to the center of the bed. She couldn't hold back, running her hands over his shoulders, down his biceps. He felt so good, all male power. Once over her, he parted her legs with his thigh. His cock pressed against her pussy, the friction unraveling her. After tucking his forearms under her shoulders, holding her close, he kissed her forehead.

"I wouldn't have fired your mother," he whispered. "I just wanted you to know that."

Part of her knew, but she wasn't ready to take any chances when he'd propositioned her. Now, it didn't even matter, because she'd devoted her heart to this affair.

"So I can leave?"

He chuckled, a deep rumbling sound, before he kissed her hard on the mouth. "That's not going to happen, little lamb. I've already made it clear there's no going back."

"What are you going to do to me?"

Tobias smiled, sex and sin. "Soon all you'll think about is the next time I fuck you." He rimmed the shell of her ear with his tongue. The world stopped, only the warmth and rasp of his breath keeping her grounded. "I'm going to enjoy taking your innocence, and then you'll be mine. Only mine."

She wanted to be his, wanted Tobias Bennett to be the one to take her virginity. After a lifetime of feeling rejected by her father, she thrived on Tobias's attention.

He kissed and gently sucked her pulse points in just the right way, as if he knew every secret pleasure center. She was lost, riding the wave of desire, and helpless against it. Her eyes were closed, her body floating away.

When he slid one hand down her side, slipping it between her legs, she blinked open her eyes. He stared at her as he slid two fingers into her pussy. Every movement sent a rush of erotic heat soaring through her body. She clamped down on his fingers, and he moved them with expert skill, hitting her hidden G-spot effortlessly.

Adora gasped, holding him tight.

"You have no idea what I have in store for you," he said. "I pride myself on being the best in *everything* I do." He began to fuck her with his fingers, his thumb teasing her clit. The sound of her wet folds was the only sound in the room besides their heavy breathing. When he slid one of his moist fingers into her asshole, she jerked, the explosion of sensation startling her.

"How long should I tease you?"

"Stop," she said. "I can't take any more."

"You're ready for me?"

"Yes," she practically shouted the word. The man was wicked, teasing her to the point of insanity. When he shifted his weight to one side, grabbing the root of his cock, some of her bravery slipped away. He was well hung, and she'd never had a man.

He ran the smooth head of his cock along her slick folds, over and over, hitting her sensitive clit with each pass. When she began to writhe, he pushed in an inch. Adora gasped, more from satisfaction than the shock of fullness. He kissed her closed eyes, her cheeks, then her lips. Then more inches pushed inside her.

"You're so tight, Adora." He grunted, showing exactly how much restraint he was using. "I love your pussy."

"More," she said.

Tobias growled. He was losing his precious control, and didn't stop until he was fully seated, his entire dick stretching her. The moment was surreal, bonding, perfect. She'd never felt so full in all her life, no cell left unstimulated.

"Am I hurting you?" he asked.

She shook her head, looking up at him as he brushed her hair back. Adora wanted to ask him how he could separate sex from love, because the two felt like one and the same.

"Good girl." He slowly pulled his hips back, his big cock rubbing along her inner walls before he pushed back in. He kept moving slowing, rhythmically, the pressure building towards another release. It was so much better with Tobias inside her, claiming her. His skin was hot, a sheen of sweat covering his back, and his hard muscles tensed. She wrapped her legs around him, prodding him with her heels, needing more. "Careful, baby. I'm trying to go easy."

"I want you," she barely managed to say. "*Please.*" Adora didn't care that she was begging. She was beyond any rational thought.

He pushed up on his arms, his cock still inside her. Tobias looked down at her. "If you want more, I'll give it to you. Just ask." He lowered his head for a moment to kiss her lips. "I love having you in my bed. In my life."

Why couldn't he love *her*?

Tobias lowered his push-up until they were skin to skin. He began to pump his hips faster, and the speed increased the pleasure tenfold. The longer he pistoned into her body, the more feral he became. He was a beast in bed, better than Katerina's depiction. His stamina was unreal, the entire bed rocking as he fucked her.

"Oh God," she cried out, the beautiful pressure nearly reaching the breaking point.

"I'm going to fill you with my cum, baby. Make you mine."

She clawed his back as her orgasm hurtled to the finishing line. He picked up the pace, and she exploded. The powerful waves rocked her body, her pussy squeezing Tobias's cock. She felt the moment his came, his hot cum filling her.

A few moments later his weight dropped over her briefly, before he rolled to the side. "You were worth the wait, Adora." He draped an arm over his forehead, his chest still heaving.

Her orgasmic bliss wouldn't allow her to worry about anything beyond the perfect moment they were in, but this was the time she'd been terrified of. Once he got what he wanted, would everything change?

She attempted to sit up, but he was quick to pin her down. "What are you doing?"

"You need to stay still for a while, let nature do its thing."

Right. The baby.

This wasn't what she expected getting pregnant would be like. It felt more like a business deal or science experiment than the happy family she'd dreamt of. "I doubt I'll get pregnant after one night." Then she tested him. "Maybe you won't get me pregnant at all." If she couldn't give him a baby, she had no purpose in his life.

"Is that a challenge?" He narrowed his eyes playfully. "Get ready for lots of practice."

Chapter Eight

Tobias stared down at his beautiful woman. Adora was passed out, and he couldn't blame her. He'd taken her enough times last night that she had to be sore. Her pussy was perfection, so tight, so wet. All he had to do was touch her, and she melted in his arms. She was responsive, eager, and refreshing.

There was no doubt in his mind. He'd picked the right woman. Pushing some of her hair off her face, he couldn't wait to see her pregnant, so full and ripe with his kid. His cock began to harden again, but instead of waking her, he ignored the urge. Her pussy wasn't used to taking a cock so often, so he wouldn't be fucking her today, even though he wanted to. Being inside Adora was like going to heaven. He didn't ever want to stop.

What he didn't want to do was hurt her, and she deserved some attention today.

He pulled the sheet from her body, and cupped her stomach. She was a fuller woman anyway, so it was already rounded. Soon it would be big, her tits larger, if that was even possible.

"What are you doing?" she asked, turning her head toward him. There was a smile on her lips, and she reached out to cup his cheek.

"I can't get enough of you. I think that's clear. You're like a witch. You've put spell on me."

She chuckled. "I'm not a very good witch. I tried to avoid you, remember?"

"I do." He took possession of her lips, and she moaned as he plunged his tongue into her mouth. When she moved, she drew back a little with a wince.

"I, erm, I don't think…"

He pressed a finger to her lips. "Already there,

baby. Don't worry. We're not going to be doing anything else today. We have plenty of time for that later."

"Oh, okay. I should go home then."

"Now I should be the one that's insulted," he said, laughing. "I don't want you to go home. You're using me for sex, I get it. You just want my body."

She rolled her eyes. "So, you don't want me to go home?"

"Not at all. I don't need to be in the office today. Besides, it's slow on Saturday. I figured we could spend some time together. Share breakfast, maybe some lunch, and you can tell me all about you."

Her hand lay on his chest, and he saw she was thinking. He wondered, not for the first time, what was going on in that head of hers.

"You're keeping me in suspense here," he said.

"Okay. I'll talk about myself, but you've got to talk about you," she said. "And I don't mean the stuff you give at interviews either. I'm talking real stuff. From the heart." She patted his chest. "The truth."

"You don't ask for much, do you?"

"You know a lot more about me than anyone else. You know who my father is, and how much I can't stand the thought of being near him. You've met my mother. She works for you." She shook her head. "There's so much, and thinking about it now, how can I be the mother to your baby, Tobias? My dad screwed the cleaning lady."

He silenced her doubts with his lips. Stroking his tongue across her bottom lip, he once again deepened the kiss, and relished her moans as he felt her turn toward him. Running a hand down to her ass, he squeezed the plump flesh.

"Don't ever doubt who you are or what you mean to me. I don't give a fuck who your dad is, or isn't."

He'd seen Hamilton in a whole new light last night, and it wasn't a good one. Of course, he knew Hamilton was an unfaithful bastard. Who didn't? The woman he'd married was just as money hungry as he was. They only wanted to get stronger, get wealthier, have more power. That was what he was used to, the power-hungry circle of people he mingled with, Hamilton being at the top just like him. "This changes nothing."

"I'm sorry. I just … it was the first time I ever saw him, and I know my mom still loves him, but seeing him with that other woman. It just … she'll never get her happy ever after. She's still hung up on that one guy who broke her heart."

"Katerina is nothing special. She's known for spreading her legs for the next big thing. If someone else catches her eye, Hamilton will be passed over."

She pulled away from him, sitting up. "You think that makes me feel any better? You've just told me that my mother is in a long line of women that mean nothing."

He really didn't have the first clue how to do all this emotion crap. He was used to people being cold, not giving a shit.

She got to her feet, and he watched as she placed a hand on her stomach, wincing. Getting to his feet, he picked her up in his arms, and carried her through to the bathroom. He already saw his sticky cum on her thighs, and he didn't mind. In fact, he hoped right now his cum was doing its job. The sooner he had a baby inside of Adora, the happier he would be. Especially as he kept putting his damn foot in his mouth, and ruining everything just by fucking talking.

The women he knew didn't need love or kind words. They wanted money, jewels, and were used to being told shit the way it was.

Adora's not like them.

He had to keep remembering that.

Running her a bath, he made sure to add some soothing bath salts, and when the water was right, he eased her into it, following her in, as he got her to lean against his chest. Wrapping his arms around her waist, he took both of her hands, and locked their fingers together.

"You're going to have to give me time to get used to all these changes," he said.

"What do you mean?"

"I'm not used to watching my tongue."

"It's like you live on a whole other planet where nothing affects you."

"It doesn't, baby. That's the point. I'm not used to having to watch what I say. Love really doesn't happen within my world."

"I can't believe that. Love is everything, Tobias. I probably sound fickle, but I've seen it. I've seen how it can bring people together, and I'm not just talking about sex either. What is life without love?"

Once again, he thought of his brother, and the memory was a sharp one. Since meeting Adora, he'd thought more about his brother in the past week, than in all the years since Maximus had died. Tobias had filed each memory away, as if it was just another contract that slipped his mind. "My brother would have adored you," he said.

She tensed up. "You didn't say you had any siblings."

"I don't have any that are living."

"Oh, I'm so sorry."

He held her hands tighter, and he closed his eyes for a second. "His name was Maximus, and he was my older brother." He laughed. "I was the spare heir."

"What?"

"You never heard of it? It's what I think is termed as the heir and the spare. Powerful families, even the royals, were always advised to have a son, and then another in case anything happened to the other."

"That's barbaric, and outdated."

"Not in my family. They're very much believers of it."

"I don't like this, Tobias."

"My parents believe in business, in order, in structure, and control. They don't believe in getting sticky with emotion. Everything is clean cut. More power, more influence, more wealth. When you have wealth and knowledge, you have power, and that keeps you on top. Maximus was … flawed, according to my parents." He heard her sharp intake of breath. "He didn't want the nannies or the money. He didn't believe in power, or wealth, or furthering the family line."

"What did he believe in?"

"Love. That's all he wanted, all he searched for. He believed it was the answer for everything wrong in the world. In his quest for love, it got him killed." It was on the tip of his tongue to give her the lie. The one his parents told the world, but wasn't the truth. "No one knows this, but Maximus died of a heroin overdose. He used drugs to numb the pain. Our parents wouldn't give him what he wanted, and he tried to find it himself. They considered him an embarrassment, and a waste of time."

She turned in the bath, cupping his cheek. "Did you love him?"

"Yes. I didn't have a clue what he was searching for though, and I couldn't help him. He kept telling me there was more to life than studying, than being the perfect son, and I ignored him." He laughed without humor. "I told him to grow up, and to stop believing in fairy tales."

"You blame yourself?"

"If only I'd listened, he could still be alive, no?"

"You can't blame yourself."

He cupped her cheek, running his thumb across her bottom lip. She was so incredibly beautiful, so warm, so right. He didn't deserve her. He'd blackmailed her to get her into his bed, and now he was set to impregnate her.

"What are you going to do when she sees through you, Tobias? When all of her hopes and dreams are crushed."

It was like his brother was speaking to him, but that wasn't possible. No one would ever be good enough for Adora. Only him.

Kissing her lips, he pushed his thoughts to one side. His parents had raised him to be strong, merciless, but he was starting to believe they'd created a monster. The longer he spent with Adora, the more he resented his upbringing. He just wanted away from their control, and any power they believed they had over him.

****

"Do you even watch any of the DVDs?" Adora asked. There had to be close to three hundred different kinds of movies on the shelves. They were all hidden behind a wall so no one saw them. Seeing as he didn't want her to go out because it was hurting to walk just a little bit, he wanted to spend some time together, watching a few movies, doing normal things. She didn't know what was normal or not.

Tucking her hair behind her ears, she walked toward the kitchen, and wrinkled her nose. The scent of burnt egg filled the kitchen. "Do you know how to cook?"

"You're all for the questions today," he said.

She watched as he scraped the pan, and shook her

head. "Lucky for you, I can cook, and I happen to be willing to answer any question."

"Fine, what was your favorite bit about last night?" he asked.

Adora saw the challenge in his eyes, and she rolled hers for good measure. "If you must know, I liked your mouth on me."

"Where?" he asked.

She sighed. "I liked your mouth on my pussy, and you know it."

"See, that wasn't so hard," he said. "Now, you know how to cook?"

"I do. My mom showed me at a young age. She always believed that a woman should know how to take care of herself. It was like her crash course in living alone in the big bad city." She moved him aside, and dumped the pan he was holding into the sink. "You do at least know how to scrub dishes clean, right?"

"I can certainly give it a go."

She took his hands, placing a kiss to them. "They're so smooth. They don't look like they've done a hard day's work in your life."

He pulled her to him, tilting her back, and slamming his lips onto hers. She didn't fight him, and melted against his warmth. Her pussy burned from all the sex it had taken last night, and he'd already told her he wouldn't be taking her again today even if she wanted him to. She didn't mind waiting at all.

"I will prove to you I know how hard to work."

While he got stuck into the dishes, she served them up a breakfast of bacon, eggs, and some tomatoes. This was something her mother had often cooked for her. It was cheap, and easy, and with some bread, filling. This, along with noodles and rice dishes, had made up most of her childhood diet.

By the time she finished dinner, the dishes were done, but Tobias had to change his shirt, as it was a mess. He came back shirtless, which was very distracting. The man didn't have any extra fat, only lean muscle.

They sat at his table, and she found that when he wasn't being all so bossy, she enjoyed being with him. He was witty, smart, charming, and funny.

Their date last night had been horrible. It would never win awards or anything, but afterward, that had been perfection. She couldn't have thought of a better way to lose her virginity. What did suck though, was she knew she was falling for him, even though it had only been a week.

She liked that he trusted her enough to talk about his brother. Listening to him, she actually believed that Tobias hadn't been given the time to grieve. He'd been forced to be stoic from a young age. It wasn't healthy.

"Well, I am lucky that you can cook."

She finished off her eggs as Tobias mopped up the last of his juice on his plate.

"Mom loves to cook. She really believes the kitchen is the heart of the home." She smiled.

"Your mother will want for nothing."

"She wouldn't want that. She likes earning a living."

"I can make all of her troubles go away," he said.

That's what Tobias Bennett was used to. Throwing money at a problem instead of dealing with it. "You don't need to keep spending money. My mom's not greedy."

"Did she ever ask your father for money?"

"No. Once he kicked her to the curb, she never went begging for help. My mom's a very proud woman, and whatever she couldn't afford, she did without. Your parents are going to hate me, aren't they?" Since he told her about his brother, she knew that his parents would despise her. She wasn't what they'd want for their son.

"It doesn't matter what they think."

"It doesn't? What about when they meet me? Do you really think it's going to be easy for them to accept their son being with the daughter of a cleaner?"

"I don't care. You're giving me an heir, Adora. They didn't tell me how to make one, and they're not going to control me regardless."

She nodded, and pushed some of her hair out of her eyes. "I don't even know them, and I'm scared to meet them."

"Don't be. When you meet my parents, I'll be there."

Taking a sip of her coffee, she tried not to let her nerves show. He'd also confirmed that soon she'd meet his parents. Tobias only seemed to work on one speed, and that was super-fast. She struggled to keep up.

"Has your mother seen your father recently?" he asked.

They were still asking questions of each other. Questions were good.

"No. Not that I know of." She really believed if her mother saw Hamilton again it would break her heart.

She wanted to delve deeper, to know the man under the skin. He may not admit it, but there was much more to Tobias Bennett.

"Do you love your work?" she asked.

"What do you mean?"

"I love everything about architecture. The different moods of each person who designed a building. How they all seem to have that one element that's like an artist's signature. It's a passion that I think I got as a child going from different apartment buildings, fancy homes, and of course the apartments that were made cheaply. Your work, does it fill you with excitement, with passion?"

"I work for the family company, Adora."

"What was your passion growing up? What did you love more than anything else?" she asked.

She saw that she'd stumped him.

He smiled. "I don't know if you'd call it a passion, but I loved music."

"Did you sing?"

"I liked listening to different kinds of music— soul, country, rock, pop, you name it, I wanted it. It was an escape from the pressure."

"Why didn't you pursue it? The music industry has more than just singers. It has people who manage, own companies, distribute."

"My life and what I'd do was set out before I was born, Adora. Music is just something I enjoyed."

She sat back and rubbed her arms, suddenly feeling a chill. They were going to have a baby. There was no doubt in her mind that they were. She couldn't resist him, and he wouldn't let her resist him. What she didn't like was the fear that he'd be exactly like his parents. That he'd expect their son or daughter to work for the family company. To learn all the ropes, and never follow their own passion. She couldn't speak. So much anger and fear swamped her, that she grabbed their plates, and headed into the kitchen.

"What have I said now?"

"Nothing."

"Clearly, I've said something to upset you, and doing that is not my intention."

She put the dishes in the sink, and turned toward him. "You really don't see it, do you?"

"See what?"

She laughed. "I haven't even met your parents

yet, and I know they've got one hell of a control lock on you. It's not even funny."

"You don't have a clue what you're talking about."

"You're good with numbers, great at it, I bet. You seem to know when to spot an amazing deal and one that's little shady. You have all the mechanics of a fantastic businessman. You've taken the Bennett name from strength to strength."

"You researched me."

"Why not? You pursued me. You threatened me. I had to find out what I was up against, and what I found out was exactly that. But your work is not exactly thrilling to you. You don't find a rush, do you, when you enter that boardroom? There's no real excitement over what you do. You're just going from one motion to another."

He didn't say a word.

"And that's what you want for our child." She placed a hand on his chest. "Think about that. Think about what you're going to want for our little kid. Will our child end up like Maximus?"

He stepped away.

Before she could say anything else, the ringing of the telephone stopped her. Biting her lip, she watched as he left to answer it.

Finishing the dishes, she was drying them up as Tobias rounded the corner, looking really pissed off.

She hadn't meant to cause a problem or to upset him. They weren't even pregnant yet, and already she was worried about the future of her child. She didn't want them to grow up hating their parents. Her mother had told her love and passion were the key to enjoying life. Tobias told her they were useless emotions.

"What is it?" she asked.

"My parents are here. They're on the way up."

Oh great!

Chapter Nine

The second his mother said she was entering the lobby with his father, Adora's words rang in his head. His parents *did* like to control him; they had since he was a kid. He wasn't a fucking pushover, and wouldn't let them drive him to the breaking point. They'd trained him well, too well—he'd surpassed his father's strength in their industry well over a decade ago. Tobias had protected himself and his investment in the Bennett Corporation, so his parents could never fuck him over like they did with Maximus. He'd been drilled to be the perfect son, but his parents had shown their true colors too many times over the years. His loyalty had begun to fracture long ago.

"Why are they here? Do they usually just pop in?" asked Adora. She was distraught, trying to arrange her hair and fix her shirt. Actually, it was his shirt, and she looked fucking adorable in it.

"Relax. I'm sure they're not staying. We're not exactly a close-knit family."

Tobias decided this was as good a time as any to break the news to his parents. Adora would be the mother of his child, and, he hoped, his wife. This all happened so quickly, he still wasn't sure how it would all work out. He knew he needed an heir, but didn't have a plan of action until he saw Adora standing by his window.

A loud knocking echoed in the room. He could only imagine why they were stopping by, but he didn't have a good feeling about it. Tobias had made sure there was plenty of distance between his condo and his parents' home when he'd bought the penthouse suite. It had been one of his major deciding factors.

He opened the door.

"Tobias, is that any way to answer the door?"

asked his mother. He glanced down at himself, not really giving a shit that he only had jogging pants on.

"What does social protocol tell us about showing up uninvited?"

She ignored his question and pushed past him into the condo, followed by his father and another woman. "Tobias, this is Gloria Ellen Palmer. You remember her, don't you?"

"Should I?"

"Don't be rude. She was at the country club golf tournament last year," said Julia, his match-making mother. He was forty-five, not twenty-five. Tobias did not need help finding a woman, certainly not from his family.

"Julia, it's early Saturday morning, and you've shown up without calling. I'm not in the mood."

"I've tried calling, but you never answer your phone."

His father, Andrew Bennett, stood there with the same miserable frown permanently creased into his features. He'd been a cold, demanding father growing up, never accepting an ounce of weakness from him. Tobias had to remind himself he was no longer a helpless child, and the old bastard no longer called the shots in his life.

"Your mother went through a lot of trouble to arrange Gloria's visit today. I'd think you'd at least be grateful," said Andrew.

"I never asked to be set up," he said. "But if this has anything to do with the heir you're so insistent on, I've got it covered."

His mother looked back and forth from him to his father, confusion on her face. "I don't understand."

Tobias closed the front door and walked through the great room to the kitchen. Adora was still standing behind the counter where he'd left her.

"I'd like you to meet Adora Garcia," he said, waving his hand in her direction. "Adora, my parents." He internally cringed. This was not the first face-to-face he'd planned. It was supposed to include a nice dinner and grand introduction, everyone on their best behavior.

"It's nice to meet you," said Adora, her sweet, shy voice making him smile.

His mother didn't even acknowledge her, rolling her eyes less than discreetly. "Now, what were you saying about an heir?"

He ground his teeth together. No one tested his patience more than his own family. "I'm trying to introduce you to the mother of my child."

Julia's jaw dropped. "The maid? What are you talking about, Tobias? Explain yourself."

This was turning out to be worse than dinner last night. He kept fucking up over and over, and how long until Adora had had enough?

"Why would you assume she's my fucking maid?"

"Language, Tobias."

"You know, I thought you'd be happy. I entered this whole 'keep the Bennett name alive challenge' because of you. Now, I'm telling you there'll be a baby here in nine months, and not even a congratulations?"

"You've impregnated this girl? I can't even count the number of eligible women I've introduced you to. Are you purposely being defiant?"

"If either of you think I'm going to let you pick my wife, you don't know me at all. I call the shots. I pick my own woman, and Adora's the one I choose."

Just then the sound of the front door opening and closing caught everyone's attention. Maria came around the corner with her cleaning supplies in her arms for her usual Saturday morning shift. Tobias scrubbed both hands over his face. *Fuck me.*

"And who is this now?" asked Julia. "Another maid?"

"That's my mother," said Adora.

His mother snorted.

"Can we talk in private?" asked Andrew. "You're going to give your mother a nervous breakdown."

His mother would need emotions in order to have a breakdown. She was just pissed off she didn't get her way. Appearances and the right people meant everything to her, so Adora would be a major letdown. He wasn't desperate for their approval like he was years ago, but a small part of him had hoped his parents would accept Adora with open arms.

He wouldn't hold his breath.

"Anything you have to say, you can say right here."

Andrew adjusted his jacket and shoulders. "I was too lenient with you. Gave you too much freedom. Why else would you shame the Bennett name like this?"

"What shame? Because I won't jump into bed with Rod Palmer's daughter? You wanted a baby, I delivered. If you can't accept my choice, then I suggest you refrain from popping in again."

His dad began to lead his mother to the door, turning back once. "We *will* talk about this later."

"Unless you're planning a baby shower, we have nothing to talk about."

When they got to the door, his father glared at him, only a couple feet away. Tobias waited for some smart-ass comment. "I can't believe we put all our hopes on you. Such a mistake."

Tobias held his arms out to his sides. "Well, I'm all you've got. Or have you forgotten what happened to your first son?"

They left without another word, and he locked the door, resting a hand against the wood as he collected himself. His parents' reaction didn't surprise him. What mattered was the fact Adora had witnessed the freak show. He didn't want their behavior to impact him, but their bullshit parenting was deep-seated. Maximus had been right. Tobias was chasing the wind trying to please them. Nothing would ever be enough, and they'd destroy him if he kept striving for their version of perfection.

He took a cleansing breath and returned to the kitchen. Adora was in the same place, no expression on her face. She'd been talking to Maria, but her mother quickly left the room as he entered. "I should go," she said.

"No."

Her eyes began to glisten. "I don't belong here. It'll never work between us and you know it."

"You can read my mind now?" he asked.

"That was Gloria Palmer, Tobias. She's a model, for God's sake. Her father is a billionaire hotel mogul. Even I know that."

"And?"

"She wanted you, probably wanted to have your baby. That's what you should want."

"Because my parents say so? That's not how any of this works, baby. I make the decisions for my own life, not them," he said.

"They'll never accept me."

"Fuck them."

Adora put her face in her palms. When she finally looked up again, he hated the insecurity in her eyes. "I told my mom about us. I didn't exactly have a choice standing in your kitchen in just a t-shirt."

"What did she say?"

She shook her head, coming around the kitchen

island. "What do you think she said? She doesn't approve. She expected to clean up after one of your one-nighters this morning, and didn't expect to find me here. My mother wants better for me."

His parents wouldn't understand that logic. To them, better meant wealthier, having more power and influence. In Adora's world, it meant happiness.

She tried to skirt around him to get to the bedroom. He grabbed her arm, yanking her against his chest. She struggled, tears filling her eyes. He refused to release her, letting her vent her emotions. Adora was such a sensitive little thing. It would be a full-time job to ensure the darkness in his world didn't destroy her. He had to shelter her, make sure she never felt the same desperation Maximus once suffered through.

"Stop," he whispered, kissing her atop the head.

"I'll never work," she repeated. "We're too different. I need to get out of here."

"If you think it's over, you're wrong," said Tobias. "When you took my cock last night, screaming my name, you signed up for the long haul, baby. I never plan on letting you go. I don't give a shit what my parents think, what your mother thinks, or what the whole goddamn world thinks. This is between you and me. You're *my* woman now. Nothing and no one is going to change that."

He released her.

After stepping back, she stared at him for a moment.

"Have a little faith in me, Adora."

She walked away.

****

What was I thinking? Adora hailed a taxi on the downtown strip. She could only imagine what she looked like with her black evening gown on and oversized t-shirt tossed over it. Her hair was in tangles, and her eyes felt sore and puffy from crying.

She hadn't bothered saying good-bye to her mother, not when she was an emotional basket case. Why was she a mess?

Because she was in love.

And it could never work.

He may say his family didn't matter, but given time, he'd start to resent her. She'd always be the black sheep, and her baby would probably never be loved by his family. Adora clutched her stomach as the taxi weaved through the morning traffic. Could she be pregnant? If she was, history was about to repeat itself.

Adora arrived at her apartment in the shitty part of the city, a sharp contrast to where she'd been picked up. She slammed her door behind her, threw her purse, and dove onto her threadbare sofa in tears. Adora was angry with herself for going along with Tobias's plan, for giving up her life for him. And now for not wanting anything more.

Why did she leave? She should have stayed and talked things out, allowing him to fend off her fears. But his family had made her feel so small, and that woman had been beyond beautiful. Adora had been standing in his kitchen in just an old t-shirt with morning hair, and her insecurities had gotten the better of her. It was hard to believe that Tobias could want her more than a fashion model.

She cried until there were no more tears. All she wanted was Tobias, and for their circumstances to have been different. Adora was in mourning, wanting something so badly but knowing it was forever out of reach. But she had to be strong, to try to pretend none of this whirlwind had ever happened. The midnight hour had passed, and her Cinderella fantasy was over.

Adora hung up her dress in the closet and jumped in the shower. She needed to wash Tobias's distinct scent off her body, to start anew, and focus on her homework. Her mother had managed to move on after heartbreak, so she could do the same.

When she finished changing, still towel drying her hair, her cellphone rang.

It was *him*.

She reached to answer it, but stopped herself. Her emotional state was too fragile right now, and she'd too easily fall for his sweet words and promises. For the rest of the weekend, she needed to focus on her priorities.

By the time Monday morning came around, Tobias had called well over a dozen times before she finally turned off her phone. He'd have to give up sooner or later. Maybe a little time would help him realize how stupid it was to hook up with the maid's daughter. Maybe his mother would help him see thing clearly.

She strolled through the campus grounds to her first morning class, her books cradled in her arms. The birds sang in the branches above her, the usual sights and sounds soothing her. *You can do this*, she assured herself. It was any other Monday.

Before she reached the building, she heard someone jogging close from behind. When she turned to look, the man stopped beside her, walking at her pace. He worse a suit and carried a briefcase. At first, she assumed he was a professor ... until he spoke.

"I'm Jeff Langley. I represent Mr. and Mrs. Bennett. I've been authorized to pay a generous amount in your name."

She stopped dead and faced him. "And what do I have to do?"

"It's free money. You just need to keep your distance from their son, and not to list him on your child's birth certificate. If you don't want to go through with the pregnancy, the payout could be even higher."

Adora seethed on the inside, a mix of shock and disgust twisting her gut. Just because she was poor didn't mean she'd sell out for money. Tobias's parents were too much, and she wondered if he knew what they were up to.

"Tell them to keep their money. I'm not interested in any of it." She wanted to say so much more, but wouldn't stoop to their level. Adora began to walk up the path at a faster speed.

"You're making a mistake if you don't take their offer. They're a very powerful family."

"Stay away from me!"

Adora rushed into the building and down the hallway toward her first class. Tears clouded her vision. If Tobias was able to blackmail her into having his baby, she could only imagine what his parents were capable of. She didn't want any more problems in her life, and certainly not in her mother's.

Before she got to the lecture hall, a strong hand grabbed her, bringing her to a stop.

"Adora."

She looked up into Tobias's face. His eyes were narrowed, his forehead creased, but her body still melted in relief. She'd been dreaming of him every night.

"Why are you crying?"

Adora shook her head and huffed. "You don't know?"

"No, I don't."

"Your parents want to pay for my abortion. I don't even want to imagine what they'll do when their lawyer tells them I refused."

If she thought he looked pissed off a minute ago, he looked absolutely livid now, his jaw clenched and eyes vacant.

He tugged her by the arm down the hall, away from her class. They came to an empty room at the other end of the building, and he forced her inside before locking the door behind him. "First things first, why haven't you answered any of my calls? I've barely slept all weekend worrying about you." He ran a hand through his hair, and she noticed he looked more tired than he usually did. "I'm supposed to be at the office right now, but I'm here, because you're all I fucking think about."

She had no response. His voice was loud and angry, but his words held so much passion. Passion she'd thought he was incapable of.

"Nothing to say? You think you can walk away from this, Adora?" He wrapped his arm around her waist and tugged her so hard, her body slammed against his, her books falling to the floor. "I'm never letting you go."

"Did you not hear what I said about your parents?"

He scoffed. "You think that changes anything between us?"

"They're your *parents*, Tobias."

"I'll fucking deal with them, but trust me, nothing they do can shock me. You have no idea the shit they've put me through."

"Well, they have a high-priced lawyer after me, and I don't want them destroying *my life* when I've done nothing wrong."

He cupped her face in his hands, staring at her with such intensity her breath caught. "You think I'll let them do anything to you? To our baby? They're trying to control my life, but when it comes to you, there will be no compromises. I need you to understand that."

"The lawyer threatened me, said they were powerful."

Tobias chuckled, then exhaled away his anger. "*I'm* the majority shareholder at the Bennett Corporation, not my father. I'm the one to be feared, Adora."

"I should be afraid of *you*?"

"I'm saying you shouldn't be afraid of anyone or anything ... not when you have me." He placed a hand under each of her shoulders and lifted her off her feet, his strength amazing her. Tobias pinned her against the wall, and she wrapped her legs around his hips. His hard cock pressed against her core.

He nuzzled her neck, the scent of his familiar cologne arousing her effortlessly. "It's been three days since you were in my bed."

"We can't do this," she whispered, already under his spell.

He kissed her on the mouth, his tongue demanding entrance. She forgot all her resolve, falling victim to him all over again. She needed him like she needed air to breathe. They kissed like lovers being reunited, hungry and desperate for each other. "I want to see you after classes in my office," he said.

"Your office?" She held him around the neck, wanting more of his kisses.

"I'll send a car for you. I have a heavy workload today, but I have to see you. We have a lot of unfinished business to deal with." His voice was hoarse and breathing labored.

"Have you thought about this, Tobias?"

She wanted to tell him that he'd stolen her heart. She wanted to be sure that his family wouldn't be a problem, even though she couldn't see a way around it.

"Nothing's changed. We made a deal in the coffee shop, remember? One night in my bed isn't enough reassurance that you're carrying my baby."

"Is that all this really is, Tobias? You want to

breed with me?"

His growled, his hand cupping her ass as he thrust against her, making her gasp. Tobias combed his free hand in her hair, securing her head. "There's no other woman I want," he said. He nipped along her jawline, before shelling her ear with his tongue. "I'm going to fuck you until I'm certain you're pregnant with my child. I don't care how long it takes."

She liked the sound of that, her overheated body craving his hard body all over hers. Her body had fully healed the past few days, and all she craved was more of what Tobias could give her.

The chimes for opening classes sounded in the hallway. "I have to go," she said.

He lowered her to her feet, and her entire body ached for him when he pulled away. Tobias glanced at his watch. "Three-thirty, Adora. Be ready for my driver at the front of the school."

"Okay," she said. She couldn't refuse him, didn't want to refuse him. After the nightmare on Saturday morning with his parents, she'd convinced herself a relationship could never survive. But every time she was in Tobias's presence, his confidence and commanding presence made all her worries slip away.

He adjusted his collar, then opened the door. Tobias turned to her, his dark eyes focused on her alone. "Never run from me again."

Chapter Ten

"Is this all the information you've got?" Tobias asked, looking up at the private investigator. After Maximus killed himself with an overdose, something in his gut told him he'd need some insurance in time to come. In his safe, he had every piece of dirty evidence that linked his parents to a great deal of shame and scandal.

Call girls, underhand dealings, paying off people. Even the cover up of Maximus's spiral. He was also able to obtain footage of his parents paying a man to beat an employee who wanted to expose them. The woman had left, but with a permanent limp that made employment difficult. For a long time, he'd been following their dealings, cleaning up their messes, and making sure that if there was ever a time to turn their threats against them, he'd have ammunition.

Running a hand down his face in an attempt to clear the fogginess from his mind, he knew he had to step in. For Adora's sake, he needed to put an end to it. Keep them silent.

"That's not all, sir. We've been made aware that they're speaking to Hamilton."

"What?"

"You called me on the weekend. Wanted me to include tabs on Hamilton."

"I remember." The weekend hadn't gone the way he'd hoped it would, and it pissed him off that he was searching for a way to be with Adora. Being without her wasn't an option. He nearly lost his fucking mind not having her with him. The only reason he'd stayed away was to give her a chance to deal with her insecurities, but that was all.

Seeing her today at college, feeling her body

against him, everything became clear. He started to understand what his brother meant. He'd never understood what Maximus was searching for—why would he? Love wasn't part of his life, never had been. Did he love Adora? He knew he couldn't be without her, and even though it had only been about a week, it didn't matter to him.

He'd experienced how good her pussy felt wrapped around his cock, and he wasn't going to live without that. The way his parents had looked at her, as if she was nothing but dirt, had sickened him. He'd seen the contempt they had for her mother, and he hated exposing Adora to that kind of shit.

"What would happen if half this shit was exposed?" Tobias asked.

"There would be an investigation to some business dealings of your father. Bennett stock *could* plummet, but it would depend on what aspect they control. There's nothing attached to you."

"There's enough here to keep them out of my business?" Tobias asked.

He knew his private investigator wasn't a fan of his parents, or their dealings.

"Yes."

"Excellent. Until I say otherwise, this stays between us."

Tobias watched the man leave, and sat back staring at the file. It was collateral that he would need. His parents thought they could pay off the college, get Adora kicked out of the programs. They were already pinning cheating claims on his woman, and it had been only a couple of days since they'd met her.

They crossed the line, and he was going to do everything he could to keep her safe, and if that meant taking on his parents, he'd do it. He hoped he wouldn't have to bring down the company he'd worked hard to build up, but he had a feeling his threats would have enough impact on their own.

What he wanted to know was why Hamilton was contacted. Adora didn't need to deal with this kind of shit, and he'd make sure that she didn't suffer because of his own family problems. He should have dealt with them a long time ago, but as always, he left them alone, and now his parents were taking steps to get rid of the woman he'd picked. And he'd never wanted a woman more.

Glancing at the clock, he wondered if Adora would do as he asked, or if he'd have to go and chase her down.

Seconds passed, and the sound of his personal assistant over the intercom came through.

"Sir, I know you said to notify you when Adora Garcia arrived, but, erm, I've got a Maria Garcia here," she said.

Tobias sat up. "Are you sure?"

"Yes."

What was Maria doing here?

"Send her in."

There was only one way to find out.

His PA opened the office door, introducing her again before leaving, closing the door behind her. Maria Garcia stood in his office, her hands clasped together, and looking so out of place, it was almost pitiful.

He wondered if he should just wait to talk to her when her daughter arrived. They'd never been able to share much in conversation, and he didn't want just anyone to know his business.

"I'm sorry to disturb you." Her accent was very thick, but her English impeccable. She talked a little slower, and each word was pronounced as if she wasn't used to it.

"You speak English?"

Maria sighed. "Yes. It's … not as good as Adora's, but I try."

"Does Adora know?"

The sadness in Maria's eyes was clear. "No."

He stood up from his desk, rounded it, and perched on the end, folding his arms. "Why are you here?"

"You're going to hurt my daughter, like all men with power do." She tucked some of her hair behind her ear, and for the first time, Tobias saw the woman that Hamilton had hurt. The sadness, the pain, the fear—it was all there.

"I've no intention of ever hurting your daughter."

She shook her head in disbelief. "I've been fired from my post today. Your parents' reach is … very far."

He stood up a little straighter at that.

Maria sighed. "I don't like to interfere, but I know my daughter's education means the world to her. I want her to have what I never could. She deserves it so much. They're going to take it away from her."

"I promise you, Maria, that will never happen. I would like to hire you in a permanent position." He reached back, clicking the intercom. "Get me an employment sheet." He turned back to Maria. "I was so busy focusing on how to win back your daughter that I didn't think about you. That's my problem, and I'm sorry."

His PA returned holding what he asked for. He thanked her, and waited for her to leave.

"I won't take that."

"Look, Adora is going to be mine. I've already got something in place for you, where you can live and not have to worry about another Hamilton."

He watched her pale.

"You know about that?"

"Adora knows, Maria. She knows who her father is, and what he did to you."

Maria looked away and he caught tears in her eyes. Even after all this time, she felt immense pain.

"You loved him?"

She turned back to him, wiping the few tears that had spilled down her face. "Why wouldn't I?"

"It's just that most women…"

"You thought I was after his money? I never was." Maria offered a sad smile. "My English wasn't very good when we met, and it has taken me a long time to learn. He was the love of my life, and he broke my heart, and every single promise he made me."

"I'm not like him."

"You like Adora now, but in time, she will not meet your standards. Your parents will tell you that she's an embarrassment. You'll choose money over her."

The way her eyes glazed over, Tobias saw she was reliving some kind of memory.

"He promised to be with you?" Tobias asked.

"I had a ring," she said. "We were going to get married, but he picked wealth, and cast me aside like old garbage. I saw the news of his fancy wedding. The pain was unlike anything in the world. He got to move on. I didn't. I don't want that kind of pain for my daughter. I'm sorry, but you will never love my daughter, or give her what she deserves. If you're a man of honor, of your word, you will let her go, to be with someone who'll love her no matter what."

She nodded her head and left the way she came. He didn't try to stop her.

He still held the employment form in his hand.

There was no way he could live with Adora being

with anyone else. She belonged to him, and only to him. He pondered Maria's words. She'd known him for years, and even she believed he was incapable of love. Was he that much of a bastard?

Love was overrated, he'd convinced himself. It made people do stupid things. He slipped off the desk, placing the form down, knowing his parents were slowly ruining any chance he had with Adora. Just because he wasn't capable of feeling love, didn't mean that he, himself, didn't want her falling for him.

He did.

They were messing with his plans, and time was running out.

"Sir, Adora Garcia is here to see you."

Just hearing her name make his heart skip a beat. Making sure his suit was impeccable, he let his PA know to send her in, and then not to allow for any interruptions.

Adora entered and gave his PA a sweet smile. He went to his door, and flicked the lock in place before standing in front of his woman. Adora was his woman. She'd been his from the moment he took her virginity, and had her screaming his name.

Neither of them spoke for the longest time. Just being near her made everything better.

"Your parents are going to ruin my chances at college," she said. "You have no idea how hard it was for me to make that happen."

"I'm not going to let them. You leave them to me."

She licked her lips, and her gaze landed on the floor at his feet.

"What is it?" he asked.

Finally, she lifted her head. "They're going to ruin everything, and I don't know what to do."

He cupped her face, wiping away her tears. In a

quick selfish moment, he wondered if she was pregnant. Not to annoy his parents, but because he wanted to claim her as his own. This went far beyond pregnancy for an heir. He wanted her all to himself, and he was selfish enough to get what he wanted.

****

Adora had debated coming to Tobias's office.

She knew the kind of reach his parents had. The lawyer that she'd said "no" to moments before seeing Tobias in the morning had been waiting for her as she left campus grounds. He'd let her know exactly how ugly his parents could be, and what they would do if she didn't take the money. She'd not taken the money, and he told her to think about it. What he'd said though … they would destroy her.

Any chance of the future she had planned would be completely wiped out.

"What you do," Tobias said, wiping her tears away, "is you let me take care of them."

She shook her head.

"No, listen to me, baby girl." He held her firmly, and she stared into his gaze, feeling herself once again falling for him. The feelings he evoked inside her, often made her wonder if she was crazy. They barely knew each other, but he made her heart pound and her pulse flutter. She got butterflies in her stomach, just by being close to him. Even his scent held her captive. "I know my parents. Let them think they can win. I've got everything I need for them to stay away from you. You're not going to be abandoned. I'm quite insulted that everyone seems to think that's what I'll do."

She couldn't help herself. She laughed, and he smiled with her.

"I didn't speak up for my brother, Adora. Let me speak up for you. Give me this chance to make something right between us."

"I want my education."

"They're not going to take it away," he said. "I'm already on it." He ran his thumb across her lip. "I've never asked for anyone's trust or faith in me, Adora. I'm going to ask for yours. Trust me to make this right."

The sincerity in his voice, and the need in his eyes, she knew he meant every single word, and because she didn't want to hurt him, she nodded her head.

He slammed his lips down on hers, and she melted, feeling utterly spineless. The hands on her cheeks moved to sink into her hair, holding her in place as he devoured her lips.

She moaned.

Gripping his arms, she held him tightly as her nipples budded, and heat flooded between her legs. She wanted him, wanted to be owned by him, claimed and chosen.

When he took her bag and placed it on the floor, she didn't stop him. Nor when he began to remove her coat, sliding the buttons through each loop until it opened up. He pushed it to the floor, and she fiddled with the single button that kept his jacket together. His chest was rock hard, and she teasingly ran her fingers down his shirt, feeling those ripped abs.

"We shouldn't do this here."

"I don't care what we shouldn't or should do. I only know what I want, and right now, I want to feel my dick deep inside you. Hear you scream my name."

They tore at each other's clothes, and when they were both down to their underwear, Adora failed to care. He'd seen everything already, and hadn't walked away.

Tobias lifted her up in his arms, and she gasped as he swept the contents off his desk, the clutter crashing down on the floor. He dropped her on the edge, a feral need in his eyes.

Gripping the edges of her panties, he slid them down her thighs, and threw them over his shoulder.

He spread her legs and she cried out as his fingers slid deep inside her pussy. Closing her eyes, she thrust up to meet his touch.

"No, look at me, baby. I want you to see who is touching you. Who is going to be fucking you, and who is going to be putting his baby inside you."

She opened her eyes and groaned as she saw two of his fingers thrusting into her pussy.

"Who do you belong to?"

"You," she said, without hesitation.

He pulled his fingers out of her pussy, and watched as he sucked them from her cream. "You taste so fucking good."

"You're dirty," she barely managed to say.

"Damn right." He went to his knee, and his tongue replaced his fingers, teasing her pussy, stroking over her clit, then down to plunge inside her. There were no words for the pleasure he took. She felt so exposed with the massive windows surrounding them. On display for the entire city.

She was merely his to use, and the pleasure went to the next level as he sucked on her clit. He used his teeth, creating just the right kind of pain that made it almost unbearable, and yet, she didn't want him to stop.

"Such a pretty pussy," he said, murmuring the words against her.

The pleasure started to build, her body sensitized and jolting as her orgasm neared. She knew she was going to explode, and warned him of it, not able to hold back if she tried.

He didn't give her a reprieve, and when she came, he continued to lick her pussy until she begged him to stop. Tobias pressed a kiss to her clit before standing between her thighs. "I love watching you come. I'd keep you like this all day if I could."

There were no words, as she watched him slide his rock-hard cock along her slit. Her cream coated his length as he toyed with her, teasing mercilessly when she wanted him inside her.

"Look at how wet you are."

He moved toward her entrance, and she gasped as slowly, inch by inch, he began to fill her, going deeper. His hands skimmed up her thighs, resting on her hips.

"Now that is a sight I love to see." His gaze lifted to her. "Your cunt wrapped around my dick, and it's squeezing me, Adora. It wants me inside. You want me to fuck you?"

"Yes."

He gripped her hips and slammed the last inch inside her. He hit a spot that had her screaming his name, begging for more. She was so full, so consumed by everything Tobias.

The massive oak desk stayed in place as he pulled out of her, only to slam in deep.

"You're mine, Adora. This pussy is mine. I'm going to take care of you. You, our baby, everyone." His hands stroked up her body, cupping her breasts. "Soon, they're going to be full of our baby's milk. I want to watch you feed our child."

He continued to rock inside her, and there was something in his voice as he told her what he wanted. She heard the passion, the need, and something else.

His hands returned to her hips, and she cried out as he began to fuck her, pistoning his hips like a machine. His cock slid in and out of her, pounding deep. Suddenly, he pulled out, and flipped her over so that she was bent over the desk. His fingers stroked her ass, parting her cheeks as he found her entrance once again.

She knew she was wet and heard the moisture as he slid inside.

"Look at the city, Adora. No other woman holds the kind of power that you do." He pushed some of her hair off her neck, and sucked over her pulse. "You have me. All of me."

Did she?

Could she have gotten his love even though he didn't believe in it?

The look in his eyes, the way he held her, the feel of him surrounding her, she could *almost* convince herself it was all real. Could she allow herself to be drawn in by those promises? It was all too good to believe, and yet, why not?

She gripped the edge of the desk to secure herself, and moaned as he began to tease her once again, touching her pussy, working her clit, setting her on fire with need as he fucked her from behind. The pleasure was overwhelming as she came a second time.

"Fuck, that feels so good. I love that only my dick has been inside your pussy. You're all mine, Adora. All mine, and no one will take you from me."

He rode her hard, fucking her with a passion that he'd not showed her before his parents turned up. The pleasure was almost to the point of pain.

His cock was rock hard as it claimed her over and over. The grip he had on her hips would leave bruises, she knew that, and still, she didn't care.

She cried out his name as he brought her to a third mind-altering orgasm. It rocked her entire body, leaving her a convulsing mess of post orgasmic bliss. This time, she heard his own groan as his cock pulsed inside her, the flood of his cum, filling her pussy.

The only sounds to be heard in the office was of

their heavy panting. Tobias kissed her shoulder. "When I'm with you, everything else fades away, and we're the only two people left, Adora." He turned her head, and she saw that thing again in his eyes.

Could it be love?

Could she trust it?

Tobias made her feel. He made her … yearn for him. She wanted his love more than anything else. She wanted to show him that love wasn't a curse or a disease but something to cherish, to look forward to, and certainly not to be afraid of.

When she turned around, his hand rested on her stomach. "I will take care of you and our baby. You have no idea how important you are."

Chapter Eleven

A couple weeks went by and Tobias wondered if all the sex they'd been having had the desired result. He wanted to suggest that Adora see his personal physician, but he didn't want her to think he only cared about the baby. Part of him had expected to tire of sex with one woman, but he'd only grown more and more addicted. She had infused herself into every facet of his life, and even work was becoming more enjoyable. Her fresh ray of sunshine had given light and focus to his one-dimensional life.

He didn't like the fact Adora still lived in her shitty little apartment. She was his princess, and he wanted her to have the very best. A few nights she'd slept over, and it gave him a taste of life committed to one woman. He could only speculate that her mother had talked her out of a relationship with him. But not all billionaires were the same. Well, *he'd* changed. Adora's sweetness had changed him.

Tobias adjusted his tie as he walked down the hallway of Hamilton's crown jewel. It was an architectural marvel in the downtown core. As he studied all the details in the sprawling ceilings, he thought of Adora and her natural gifts. She loved her studies, had a passion for architecture. It must have been in her blood.

That's where the similarities to her father ended. That asshole was nothing like his daughter. She was sweetness and innocence personified, and Hamilton was everything debased in the world, so similar to Tobias's own parents.

He walked into the main office and tapped his knuckles on the reception desk three times. "I need to see William."

"Do you have an appointment?"

"No, tell him it's Tobias Bennett."

She picked up her phone and within a minute led Tobias to a glass-enclosed office at the end of the hall. He walked in, taking in the sights.

"Very nice," he said, walking around the circular office. It was unique, if anything.

"You like it?"

"I can appreciate a good design. You've worked on a few of my buildings, or have you forgotten?" Tobias asked.

Hamilton leaned back in his desk chair, a pencil to his lips. "I appreciate all the business your family has given me. Your mother, especially, has excellent taste."

"And your daughter?"

William groaned, sitting straight. "What do you want from me, Tobias?"

They were close in age, both big players in the business world. Their paths were probably on the same trajectory until Adora changed Tobias's.

"My mother's been here a few times in the past two weeks. Why is that?"

He chuckled. "It's not my place to discuss private business matters."

Tobias massaged behind his neck, looking out at the view of the city. "Don't fuck with me, Hamilton. Your little girl's warming my bed, and a few whispers in her ear and you'll be looking at a paternity lawsuit so big you'll wish you'd never met Maria Garcia."

William exhaled. "It's not what you think. They don't even know she's my daughter. I'm the one who requested the face to face."

"Why?"

"Your parents went to the faculty and requested Adora be cut from all the elite lists. I put two and two together."

"I'm listening."

"Look, Adora doesn't deserve to be punished because of you … or me. I've done a lot of shit in my life, and I have regrets, but that doesn't make me a monster," he said.

Tobias wasn't buying it. "You've had twenty years to make amends, and that night at La Ballezza was the first time she'd seen you in the flesh."

"I didn't know about her."

"Bullshit."

"Does it matter? The past is the past. I can't change it," he said. "When the college contacted me, I wasn't about to let your parents ruin Adora's career. We both know how ruthless they can be."

"Don't tell me they actually listened to you."

He scoffed. "Not likely. They mentioned a baby, and wishing Adora would disappear. They said she was a gold-digging little whore."

Tobias ground his teeth together. "She's your daughter. You own up to that? The kid they want gone is *your* grandchild."

Hamilton had no balls. He always hid behind his women and money. Tobias wasn't letting him off the hook so easily.

"Since when have you wanted to settle down, anyway, Tobias? It seems unusually cruel to force Adora to live the same life as her mother."

"Don't compare me to you. I don't shirk my responsibilities. I'm with Adora because I … want to be with her. I want the best for that girl." He realized he was about to use the "L" word but quickly stopped himself.

"Then tell her to take her professor's offer to apprentice at my company. She won't even have to see me."

"She'll never agree to that. She hates you with the

intensity of the sun, and I'm not sure anything you can do will change that." Tobias wasn't on top in business for being gullible. He had a sense when someone was screwing with him, and he didn't trust William.

"It would be in her best interest."

"What about your sons? You going to tell them about their sister? Think they'll like the idea of splitting the family inheritance four ways?"

William's face dropped. "I want to do the right thing by Adora, but I'm not willing to bring my own family down in the process."

"Of course not."

"Look, people make mistakes. Nobody needs to know about any of this except you and me. I feel bad about what happened to Maria. No need for Adora to suffer."

Tobias cracked his neck to each side, his hands clasped behind his back once he reached the edge of the office. He watched the cars driving far below from his vantage point. William Hamilton was fueled by guilt, nothing genuine. Not love. Tobias wouldn't allow him to hurt Adora. If she needed a job, Tobias could give her one.

"Let me know if my parents contact you about Adora again. Otherwise, don't lose any sleep over your dirty little secret."

Tobias left the office, feeling sick to his gut. He'd take care of William's responsibility.

Once he arrived back at the Bennett Corporate headquarters, he took the elevator up to the penthouse. As he walked toward his office, his secretary rushed over to him. "Sir, I'm so sorry, I was about to call security."

"What is it?"

"There's a woman in your office. She insisted on locking herself inside."

He knocked on the door, "Adora?"

The door opened a few inches. He smiled because he knew it had to be her. Tobias turned to his secretary. "Adora Garcia has full access to my office. In the future, don't try to stop her."

"Yes, sir."

He entered the office, and locked the door behind him.

"That was a long lunch," she said.

"I had some errands to run. You're off early, no?"

Adora nodded. "It's reading week. I'll have more free time to get caught up."

He hadn't seen her too much in the past week between work and school. They'd had more date nights, but it wasn't enough time together, in his opinion. "What made you decide to stop by?" He could tell something was on her mind.

Adora shrugged.

"Will you be sleeping at my condo tonight?"

"I better not."

Now he frowned, shrugging off his jacket and placing it on the back of his chair. "Tell me why, please. Why do you insist on keeping your distance?"

"It's exactly what you're doing with me, Tobias." She ran her hands up his chest, reaching up on her tiptoes to wrap her arms around his shoulders. "You want me to give up everything, but you're still keeping up all these walls."

"I have no walls, baby."

She cocked an eyebrow. "Sure." Adora turned and walked toward the windows. Something was off about her, something sad and unsettled.

"Has something happened? Don't hide anything from me." Last week, Tobias had sent a registered letter to his parents, outlining a few of the incriminating tidbits he had on them. It was enough to get them to back off. They'd created him to be ruthless, so they shouldn't have been surprised. They hadn't expected him to turn against them. The moment they approached Adora they'd sealed their fate.

He sat at his desk chair and patted his lap. Usually she'd oblige him, but not now. Had his parents' lawyer gone after her again? Maybe he needed to up his game.

"We don't talk about us," she said.

"What are you talking about? That's all we ever talk about."

"No, we talk about the baby, getting pregnant, watching my stomach grow." She paced the office. "I mean, I realize that was the deal. This was all about the great Bennett heir. But somewhere along the line, I fell in love."

He didn't know what to say. When she looked at him with those big dark eyes, all her vulnerabilities on the surface, he became speechless. She was so damn beautiful. And young. He'd taken advantage of her when they first met because he never expected her to want anything to do with a forty-five-year-old man. To hear her declaration, a multitude of emotions took him by surprise.

"Nothing to say?" She exhaled a little breath. "It's okay, Tobias. It was my fault for thinking I could change you." Adora placed a brown paper bag on his desk. "I have to meet my mother for lunch."

She walked out. He watched her go, and for some reason stayed rooted in place, not stopping her. Her words still played in his head. This all started out with sex, using Adora to mother his baby without attachments. Somewhere along the line everything changed.

Tobias opened the bag and reached inside. It was

a white stick.

A pregnancy test.

It was negative.

****

Everything had been going so well, but the longer they were together, the more fragile she realized their relationship was. No matter how happy they were, the fact was this started because Tobias wanted a baby. If she couldn't give him what he wanted, how long until she used up her usefulness? They had sex like rabbits and no pregnancy. Adora wasn't naïve. She knew it could take months to make a baby, but the negative test made her think, make her wonder if Tobias would even want her if she couldn't give him an heir.

Dating, sex, and compatibility was great, but she needed things to move to the next level. She needed Tobias to be real, to open up to her, to emotionally commit. And she wasn't sure he was even capable of giving her what she needed.

By the time Friday came around, she missed Tobias fiercely. He hadn't called, and she assumed he'd lost interest after seeing the test. She'd wanted him to think, to consider what he wanted before they got too deep. It worked, but her heart was already starting to crack down the middle. They were supposed to go to a gallery opening tonight to celebrate one of the Bennett Corporation's newest office buildings. Since she hadn't heard from Tobias, she assumed the date was off.

Adora lay on her twin bed, reading her text book. Ever since seeing him earlier in the week, she'd wanted to kiss him, to feel his warm skin. What if she never tasted him again? How would she feel if she saw him with a new girlfriend? Maybe a model? She immediately felt for her mother. Adora couldn't imagine watching Tobias get married and seeing it plastered on the news.

Her cellphone rang, and she rolled to her side to grab it off her night table. It was him. She dropped her book, and bolted up into a sitting position. Her heart raced, a sense of peace filling her just knowing he'd remembered her.

"Hello?"

"Are you ready?" That voice. Just the baritone made her wet.

"I wasn't sure if we were still going. I haven't heard from you all week," she said.

There was silence on the line.

"Tobias?"

"I'll have a car at your apartment within the hour. A dress would be appropriate," he said. "And, Adora?"

"Yes?"

"Keep your hair out, and I don't want you wearing any panties."

He ended the call, and she sat there looking at her phone. The man was cold as ice. He was ready to continue on as normal without talking, without changing. And she was too much in love to refuse him.

Adora showered and wore a simple floral dress. It was the nicest thing she owned. She wanted to look beautiful for Tobias, to see desire in his eyes. It had been a while since he'd claimed her body, and her pussy ached for him. When they had sex, to her, it felt like bonding … like love. Even if it wasn't real, she'd take what she could get.

The drive to the downtown core was tense. She had a nervous energy—excitement to see Tobias and anxiety about the fancy event. No matter how much he reassured her, she always felt out of place in his world.

She stepped out of the car and looked up at the building. The sunset reflected off the angled glass surfaces, mesmerizing her.

"Impressive, isn't it?" Tobias's arms snaked around her waist from behind. She hadn't even seen him.

"It really is."

She twisted around in his arms and rested her head on his chest, breathing him in. Even with the distant traffic, she could hear his strong heart and it grounded her. A well of emotion took her by surprise. She couldn't imagine life without Tobias, but was she willing to sell her soul to the devil?

"You're so beautiful." He smoothed his hands down her hair. "Come on, I want to show you something."

He took her hand, and it felt like the most intimate thing in the world walking hand in hand with him. The doors were held open for them, and women with trays of champagne danced around the well-dressed crowd in the lobby. Everyone wanted to talk to Tobias, but he brushed them all off and kept leading her to the door just ahead.

Once inside the room, he closed the door. It was an office, but it wasn't his usual style.

"What is this?" she asked.

He picked up a remote control from the desk and hit a button. The built-in blinds began to lower on all the windows, blocking out the people in the lobby and the view of the street from the other side. "Doesn't matter. I just needed to be alone with you."

"To fuck?"

He frowned. "Watch your mouth, baby girl. It doesn't suit you." Tobias pressed a finger to her lips and tossed the remote on a chair. "We'll have time for that later."

"Then why are we here?"

"We need to talk. Well, I need to talk," he said.

She liked the sound of that, but didn't want to get

her hopes up. He could be telling her that it wouldn't work, that he'd find a more fertile woman to mother his heir. "Okay."

"I've been doing a lot of thinking, and you know what I realized?"

She shook her head.

"I'm an asshole."

Her jaw dropped. "No, Tobias. Don't say that." She ran her fingertips along his jaw, but he grabbed her wrist and kissed her pulse point.

"It's true. I only wanted a baby to keep my lineage going. I didn't even want to be a father or husband," he said. "I planned to ship the kid off to boarding school and maybe see him on holidays. As for the woman, I didn't want to see her once I knew she was pregnant."

She swallowed hard.

"I had everything a man could want—money, power, women. But I've learned something, Adora. Do you know what that is?"

"No, Tobias."

He smirked, holding both her shoulders, looking down at her. "None of that matters. Not once you find the woman you love."

"I don't understand. What about the test?"

"Baby or no baby, you're all I want, Adora. You've changed me. I'm miserable without you."

"What does this mean?"

"It means I want more. I want what my brother wanted, it just took me longer to figure it all out." He cupped her face and kissed her lips once. "I love you, Adora Garcia. Nothing will ever change that."

He'd actually said it, and she believed him. Not because she wanted it to be true, but because he was being sincere.

"I love you, too."

"This doesn't mean I'm not going to keep trying for that baby, just that the game plan has changed. I don't want to replay my fucked-up childhood. I want us to have a real family, Adora."

She couldn't stop the tears from slipping down her cheeks. This was better than a fairy tale, and Tobias was her unlikely hero.

Adora wanted to list off a dozen or more thing that could put the brakes on their moment, from his parents to her father, but she kept her mouth shut. Love could conquer anything.

"Now, did you do as I asked?"

She narrowed her eyes, not catching his drift. When both his hands squeezed her fleshy ass, she remembered the panties. "Yes, I'm naked underneath my dress."

"Mmmm, so obedient." He rubbed the front of his pants, and she saw his thick hard-on. "Now, while my stock holders are mingling, I want to christen this building properly."

After what he'd just said, she was ready for anything he could dish out. "Do whatever you want to me."

"I plan to."

He opened the drawer to a small table and pulled out a tube of lube. Did he think she needed that? Her juices were already leaking down her inner thigh she was so ready for his cock. He had a wicked gleam in his eye, one promising sex and sin.

He tossed his jacket on the floor. "Get on your knees, Adora."

She did as told, getting down on to all fours over his expensive suit jacket. He lifted her dress up over her back, exposing her bare ass to the air. She didn't move, but she could feel his eyes roaming over every exposed inch.

"Did you miss my cock, baby?"

"Yes."

"Are you ever going to let another man touch this beautiful body?" He smoothed his hands over the globes of her ass, his thumbs teasing her forbidden entrance.

"It's all yours, Tobias."

He growled. "What have you done to me?" he asked. "Things are going to change now. I need to see you more than a couple times a week." She heard the spurt of lube, and his moist finger slowly entered her asshole. "Next time you visit my office, I want you on my desk with your legs open while I work. I want to use you as a pen holder."

His filthy mouth combined with his forbidden touch, made her whine and wiggle, an orgasm right at the surface.

"Talk to me, baby. Tell me what you want."

"I just want your love," she said.

He chuckled, a dark, delicious sound. "Adora, you already have it."

Chapter Twelve

Two months later

Tobias's parents finally agreed to keep their distance. Not only did he have it in writing, but he also made them aware that the moment they got near Adora, he'd release the information he had, and when they thought their life couldn't get any worse, he'd do the same all over again. They were not going to get in the way of his life anymore. They'd ruined his brother's short life, and what he had with Adora, it was worth fighting for.

Her father, William, also agreed to keep his distance. When he tried to arrange a meeting with her, Adora was the one to shut him down. She didn't want to know the man, and from what he knew, Maria had also refused to see him. His future mother-in-law had also started dating, which was new. Adora had been so worried about her mother going out with someone.

He'd spent the entire night with her, convincing her everything was going to be okay, and it was.

In the past couple of months, he'd changed. He didn't want to be the cold bastard that his parents had created. Adora had showed him there was nothing wrong with falling in love, or showing that woman exactly how much she was loved. His woman told him every single day. If she stayed with him, she would wake up, kiss his lips, and whisper her love in his ear. If she didn't stay the night, she'd text or call him, letting him know exactly where her heart lay. He also got to prove to her that they could make it work. That she could study and spend time with him.

He wanted her with him every single minute of every single hour, but he'd take what he could get.

For two whole months it had been perfection, and

what started out as a breeding had now changed for him. His love of Adora only got stronger with every passing second. He'd not even wanted her to take a pregnancy test. All he cared about was having Adora with him, loving him, and so he could take care of her.

"Penny for your thoughts?" Adora asked.

He'd stood at his bathroom mirror, washing his face. She wore one of his shirts, which fell to mid-thigh, showing off a great deal of leg. His cock instantly thickened, and he wanted inside her again.

Turning toward her, Adora's cheeks heated as she caught sight of his rock-hard cock. "Wow."

"Do you really need me to tell you what I was thinking about?" he asked.

She giggled. "Not at all." She leaned back, her hands touching the doorframe. The angle she stood pushed her tits right out, the hard points of her nipples clear to see. "I've been thinking about you, too."

Her seductive side had certainly grown in the past few weeks. It was no longer him initiating sex. Adora had a way that made his dick hard without her even trying.

Leaning against the sink, he folded his arms, staring down the length of her body. Tonight, he intended to propose. At first, he was going to take her to a big fancy restaurant, but he'd come to see that she didn't need all that. All Adora cared about was his feelings, making him happy, and knowing that she made him happy.

He couldn't believe at times that he'd gone from being a block of ice, to a man who shared everything. She wouldn't have it any other way, and he liked that. He loved sharing everything with her.

"Open your shirt."

One of her hands moved down, and began to slide

it open. She wasn't wearing any underwear, so she stood before him, completely naked. Her bottom lip sucked between her teeth. When the shirt was open, she placed her hands above her head again. "Like what you see?" she asked.

He shoved his pants down and grasped his aching cock. The tip was already slick with his cum. He smeared it all over the head, making himself nice and wet "Spread your legs." She opened her thighs, and he groaned. The angle was all wrong.

"I think we should take this into the bedroom," she said.

Tobias didn't dispute her, and followed her in. Adora lay on the bed and opened her legs wide. "Is this better?" she asked.

The lips of her pussy were swollen, her entrance nice and slick. He groaned. "Touch yourself. Put your fingers on your pussy."

Two fingers slid between her slit, sliding across her clit, then down to plunge inside. He couldn't contain the groan as she pushed them up to the knuckle before pulling them back out. Working his cock from root up to the tip, he watched her, his arousal heightening.

She pulled her fingers out, and stroked them over her clit. He stepped closer to the bed, released his cock, and took hold of her fingers. Taking both of them into his mouth, he licked the cream right off her. She still tasted fucking amazing to him.

He couldn't get over how much he loved this woman. How much she made him ache, and drove him crazy with need. At times he felt possessed with the emotions she stirred up inside him.

The rest of the world could disappear as far as he was concerned, and all that remained was the two of them.

"Give me more," he said.

She ran her fingers over her pussy, slid the fingers inside, and presented them slick to him once again.

It wasn't enough.

He needed more. Gripping her hips, he pulled her up, and slid his tongue through her creamy slit, plunging inside her before pulling out, and swirling across her clit. She cried out, screaming his name as he fucked her with his tongue. He felt the tightness within her cunt as she gripped him, but it wasn't enough. When it came to Adora, nothing was ever enough. He let go of her hips, gripped his cock, found her entrance, and watched as her cunt swallowed him into her tight heat.

Pinching her clit, he stroked her, feeling each little flutter as her pussy squeezed his cock.

Tobias stayed perfectly still, watching as she tried to fight him, but he wanted to feel her orgasm, and he wasn't going to let her go.

"Please," she said.

"Fuck, baby, I love watching you," he said.

He stopped teasing and finally brought her to orgasm. It took every ounce of his control not to fill her with his cum. She drove him crazy, wild even. Only when she came down from her peak, did he hold onto her hips and begin to fuck her, going a little deeper. When the angle didn't work and he couldn't quite get deep enough, he pulled out of her heat and flipped her over, putting her onto her knees and sliding in deep. Her ass nestled against him as he held her tightly, fucking her harder than before.

Turning her toward the mirror, he made her watch as he fucked her.

"Look at your face, baby. You love having my cock so deep inside you? You love me fucking you?

Taking you. Making you mine all over again."

"Yes, Tobias, I'm yours. I'm all yours."

He reached between them, and teased her pussy again. He wanted another orgasm from her, to feel her come on his cock.

"And I'm yours, baby, always will be yours." There wasn't any other woman he wanted. His love for her had no bounds. He wanted everything. The love, the family, the future. He didn't want to end up like his parents, hating life or the woman he married. He wanted to stay with her.

She came a second time, and he rode her hard, watching as her tits bounced. He went from staring at her in the mirror, to watching his slick dick filling her.

Her cream soaked his length, and he groaned. The pleasure began to build, and his grip on her hips tightened to the point that he knew he'd leave bruises.

Tobias growled her name as his orgasm spilled from him, filling her tight pussy. He didn't let her go, pressing kisses to her neck and shoulder as the pleasure continued until it finally ebbed away, but he didn't let her go. They collapsed on the bed, and he moved so he didn't hurt her, but with his cock still deeply inside her.

"I never get tired of you doing that," she said, her ass wriggling against him.

He chuckled. Taking hold of her hands, he kissed her neck, and he couldn't think of a more perfect time.

"Marry me."

She tensed up and turned her head suddenly. "What?"

He stared into her pretty eyes, and a deep calm settled over him. She was the love of his life. "I want you to marry me. I know I'm a bastard, and I don't deserve you, but I love you more than anything else in the world. I want you to be my wife."

"But … the heir—"

"I don't give a fuck about an heir or getting you pregnant." He cupped her face. "It's you I love. This isn't about anything other than letting the world know that you're mine. I don't want to hide you like some dirty fucking secret. I love you, Adora Garcia, daughter of a cleaner, father unknown." He gave her a wink, which made her smile. "I want the world to know that you're my wife. That you picked me, and that one day, you will be the mother of my children. I won't hurt you. I *can* guarantee I'll piss you off."

"You're a man. It's in your DNA."

He kissed her lips.

"Your parents?"

"They don't matter, and won't matter. It's just us, baby. You and me." He pulled out of her pussy, and grabbed the ring he'd stored in his bedroom. When he turned toward her, he saw his cum spilling from the lips of her pussy.

Stay focused.

Moving to where her hand was, he slid the ring onto her finger. The perfect fit.

"What do you say?" he asked.

The smile on her face told him all he needed to know.

****

Adora held her books close to her chest and couldn't wipe the smile from her face. She and Tobias were going to get married, and she had the best news for him as well. Standing at the edge of campus, she took a deep breath, and couldn't believe how lucky she'd gotten.

Her mother was finally moving on, and had admitted to her that she was in love with this new man of hers.

Tucking some hair behind her ear, she waited for Tobias to come and pick her up.

"Adora?"

She turned toward the sound of her name being called, and was shocked to see her father, her real father, approaching her. Tobias said he'd handled him, but he kept trying to get in touch with her. Turning toward him, she watched as William Hamilton approached.

"What do you want?" she asked.

"I've ... spoken to your mother," he said.

"My mom spoke to you?"

"Yes."

"Wow." She pushed some hair off her face, feeling a little nervous about being near him. "What did she say?"

"She gave me a piece of her mind, which was long overdue. She's also moved on."

"You broke her heart. Why are you here?"

"I wanted ... you know it's easier not knowing about you than it is to know about you. Since Tobias paid me a visit I just ... I want to make things right with you."

She stared at William, and felt nothing. "You don't owe me anything. I don't want anything."

"Are you in love with Tobias, or is this something else?"

"Are you asking me if I'm a gold-digger?" She snorted.

"No, no. The Bennetts—"

"Are not your concern," Tobias said.

She felt his hands on her shoulders and closed her eyes as the comfort of his touch surrounded her.

"What are you doing here?" Tobias asked. "I told you to stay away from her."

"I was just making sure..."

"I don't need you to pretend to take care of me.

My mom doesn't want you, and I don't want you in my life."

"You heard my fiancée, Hamilton. This is the last time, understand? You come near her, and I'll make sure everyone knows what a lying, cheating, bastard you really are."

William nodded, and she watched as he left.

Turning in Tobias's arms, he cupped her face, and she kissed him back. "I missed you," she said.

He took her books, and they walked hand in hand toward his car. "I'm sorry I was late. A meeting ran over."

She leaned against the car, and smiled at her. "Don't worry about it." She twirled the ring on her finger, and bit her lip. "There's something I want to tell you actually."

"Okay."

She was tempted to tell him now, but decided to wait. "I'll tell you when we get home." He took possession of her lips, and she moaned, nearly caving to him.

Her pussy already wet, desperate for him.

Climbing into the car, she went to grab the belt buckle, but he stopped her. "That's the first time you've called it home," he said, taking her lips once again.

Cupping his cheek, she stroked her thumb across his skin. She'd moved in with him after he'd proposed. There was no way she'd marry him and keep her apartment. "It's our home."

"That's right."

He kissed her again, and she giggled as he groaned. "I've got to get you home."

Once he climbed into the car, she turned toward him, and watched as he pulled out into traffic.

He took hold of her hand, locking their fingers

together. She stared at their hands, and marveled at how different her life now was.

"I don't even get a hint of what it is you want to talk about?" he asked.

"Nope. Do you love me?" she asked.

"Now that's an easy one. Yes, I love you." He glanced toward her, and she smiled. "More than anything, Adora."

She felt the change inside him, and knew he spoke the truth. He'd done everything that he could to make her feel safe, protected, keeping his parents away from her as he did.

The drive didn't take that long at all, and in what felt like a matter of minutes they were inside their sitting room in his penthouse suite.

Removing her bag and jacket, she turned toward him, and took a deep breath. "I didn't want to fall in love with you."

"Okay, that's not how I anticipated this going," he said.

"I thought you were like my father. A rich boy used to getting what he wanted, and I didn't want to be just another person that you could have. I wanted to be more than that. I tried and failed to fight off these feelings you inspired inside me. It was kind of scary at times." She licked her lips and took a deep breath.

He moved toward her. "Baby, what's going on?" He rubbed her shoulders, and she saw the concern in his eyes. "I love you. I was an asshole in the beginning, I know that. I didn't know what to do. I only knew I wanted you."

She licked her dry lips, and pulled out of his arms, going to her bag. "I've been sick every single morning I've woken up." She handed him the pregnancy test. "And so after you dropped me off today, I decided to get it checked."

They'd not spoken about pregnancy in a couple of weeks, maybe even longer. She knew what he wanted though.

He stared down at the test. "I don't know what this means?"

"I'm pregnant, Tobias." She took another deep breath. "We're pregnant."

His gaze widened, and he looked back down at the white stick. "We're pregnant?"

"Yes."

The smile on his face had her heart pounding. He picked her up in his arms and swung her around. "We're pregnant, baby." He put her down on her feet. Kissing her lips, he then bent down. "That means we've got to keep an eye on Mommy now, and we've got to make sure she rests and eats right." Tears filled her eyes as he stood up. "Why are you crying?" he asked.

"I didn't know if you'd be happy about this. Everything is different now."

He wrapped his arms around her, gripping her ass, and squeezing the cheeks. "I still want you pregnant, Adora. I know I'm going to be an ass, so having kids will make it easier for you to stay with me."

"You're going to use your kids as bait?" she asked, chuckling.

"I've got a feeling I won't have to." He rubbed his cock against her stomach. "When did I get so fucking lucky?" The love she saw in his gaze lightened the weight in her chest.

He loved her. She had no doubt.

"I'm the lucky one," she said.

"You know what this means, right?"

She shook her head. "What does it mean?"

"It means that we've got to go to Vegas and get

married. Then we've got to start hunting for a house because no kids of mine are being born in a penthouse suite."

"You want a mansion?" she asked.

"Nope. A small place out in the country with a garden, a pool, a couple of bedrooms for all of our kids. Don't forget you've still got to graduate from college. Just because you're having my kid, that is no reason to slack off. I expect amazing grades, impeccable results."

She began to laugh. Tobias believed in her. He believed in their future, and the potential she had.

"Let's not forget the pool table," she said, remembering one of his desires of fucking her on a pool table.

He groaned. "I've already got the one I want picked out."

"You're insatiable."

"You make me that way, Adora Bennett."

She paused, staring at him. That would be her name soon.

"It sounds good, doesn't it," he said.

"It sounds ... okay."

He gripped her ass even tighter, and he lifted her up in his arms. "You're a little vixen when you start."

"Can I ask for one favor before you take us to Vegas, and we have to start planning for the baby?" she asked.

"You can ask me for anything. Name your price and I will give it to you."

"I want you to make love to me tonight in every single room of this place. I don't want you to go anywhere without thinking of me."

He sank his fingers into her hair, ravishing her lips, and she wrapped her arms around his neck.

"I already think of you every second of every

single day, but what my lady wants, she will get."

She wanted Tobias's heart, and she had that. She loved him more than anything in the world, and she knew this was the start of something incredibly special. Adora was now a true believer that opposites could attract.

The End

BRED BY THE BUSHMEN

Breeding Season, 2

Sam Crescent and Stacey Espino

Copyright © 2018

Chapter One

Caleb White tapped his fingers on the steering wheel as he waited for his brother to finish collecting their mail. He hated coming to town, but once every couple of months, they made the long trek from their cabin back to civilization. They had to buy food supplies for their pantry. In another three months they'd make the same damn trip but it would be to stock up for a lot longer as they were forecast to have a rough winter.

Damon was taking too damn long, and it was starting to piss him off. He nodded at the townsfolk and played the polite card, when in truth, he couldn't give a shit about what people thought about him. The only reason he played along was so it made life easier.

Their parents had decided to live off the grid before they were born, and it had been the only life they knew. When their parents got killed in a bear attack, they'd been shipped off to the city to live with their estranged uncle.

Going from complete freedom to living within boundaries, and constantly being told what they were doing was fucking wrong, it had gotten tired real fast for him.

They'd done their time in the city, going to college, building a business, and finally, selling up, and returning back to their old life, which Caleb loved.

At forty years old, he'd finally found the life for him. His brother, being two years younger, felt the same way. The only problem? They were … lonely. It had been an unexpected variable. When they were kids, living off the grid was perfect. They never thought about women, too busy helping their father build and farm.

It didn't take long after moving back home as adults to realize something was lacking. But they didn't just want any woman.

It would have been easy to phone up an escort, meet her in town, and then go back to their life, but they didn't want that.

They both wanted a woman to share, and who'd love to live their life with them outside of the parameters of society where they could make their own rules. What woman would want that life? He doubted they'd ever find the woman for them.

"Come on, Damon," he said, starting to lose his patience.

Finally, his brother came out of the shop, carrying their letters with a huge smile on his face.

"Took you long enough," Caleb said the moment he got in the truck.

"Stop your whining. If you've got an issue with how long I take, next time you go in, and stop fucking riding my ass." Damon chuckled. "She was flirting with me, and so I was flirting back with Dana."

"She's married with three kids."

"And I'm this strange guy from the wilderness. Give me a break, will you?" His brother sat back. "I heard they're doing one of those self-discovery camping trip things again."

Caleb cursed. "Why do they fucking bother?"

"It's big money. A bunch of rich people pay to think they're one with nature," Damon said.

"Most of the time they end up lost and we're the ones that have to find them, and I don't want to be the one to have to deal with that."

"At least they're not doing it in the dead of winter this time. I nearly froze my dick off because of them last year," Damon said and rubbed his crotch.

"We don't have time for a bunch of people who are out of their depth. We've still got to finish canning the fruit."

"Please, do not say canning while anyone can hear. I don't want the guys in town to know that while they were chasing women, we were learning the dangers of canning the wrong way."

Caleb burst out laughing. Even though they'd been with their uncle, he'd known he was going to go back to his parents' way of life one day, and so he spent every available second learning what he could. He remembered a lot from when they were teens, but hadn't paid attention to many of the important elements of survival.

"Maybe there'll be a woman in this group, and we can, you know, lure her into our cave. Convince her that being around us is better than the whole world, make her fall in love, and we can have lots of sex and babies."

Even though Damon tried to make a joke, Caleb still heard the yearning in his brother's voice. They both wanted a woman together. To love, to cherish, and to fill her with their child.

They'd shared women in the past, and it felt right to the both of them to have a woman between them. They hadn't found one worth keeping.

"We'll find her, Damon," he said.

"Yeah, we will."

Each time they came to town, his brother lost a little more hope along the way. Caleb hadn't lost hope yet. He did truly believe there was a woman out there who'd like to live their lifestyle.

Neither of them spoke for the rest of the drive, arriving back to their cabin, and working in silence.

They carried out the large abundance of cans, tubs, dried pasta, rice, and everything that would keep them going.

Once their pantry was full, and organized by date, he liked to keep everything in its appropriate spot. Then he headed out into the garden to finish harvesting potatoes while Damon got the canner ready.

For a couple of weeks, they harvested the ripe fruits and vegetables from their garden, and preserved them with their canner.

He loved this life more than anything else, leaving the smallest footprint possible, but each night he fell asleep holding on to a pillow. He'd remember his parents and the love they shared. They were taken away too soon. Now it was just him and Damon.

This was what he wanted, but he'd not planned for the loneliness, or the need for a woman's touch against his skin, or the sound of her laughter filling the air.

He couldn't give up hope, otherwise he'd failed his brother. Even though there were only two years between them, his father always told him to take care of, and look out for his brother, and he'd keep doing that.

They'd find a woman, and then their dream would be complete.

****

"You're too fat, Opal. You need to lose weight.

There's nothing you can do about being ugly, but you should lose the weight. Are you thick or stupid?" Opal Clark held on to her hiking bag as she made her way through the forest, wondering if she actually was thick and stupid. At least talking to herself made her feel less alone.

She paused near a tree, leaning against it and wiping the sweat from her brow. She didn't believe coming out to the wilderness would help her in any way. All of her life she'd been told what a waste of space she was, how useless, and pathetic, and annoying she was. That she'd never be good for anything, and it had all taken her to the edge that one Friday night. She'd gotten drunk and started to take some pills. Only they hadn't worked fast enough, and so, slamming her fist in her bathroom mirror, she'd grabbed a shard of glass, and placed it against her wrist.

For thirty minutes, she'd sat poised and ready to end her miserable life.

Then, through her thin apartment walls, she'd heard the subtle sound of a baby cry, and something snapped inside her.

She'd cleaned up the glass, tossed the pills and alcohol out, and entered into this camping trip that helped people shed off the layers of control from modern day society. She thought it would be a really great way of finally finding herself, but right now, she just felt miserable as she grabbed her bottle of water.

I spent my life's savings on this?

So for the past two weeks, she'd been around a bunch of strangers, who happened to be wealthy men and women, who were looking for a good time. Trying to pretend their wealth meant nothing to them, when the truth was, they'd never had to go a day without anything in their lives.

There was no way she was bonding with people who didn't understand what real struggle meant. They were spoiled and arrogant, and made her feel worse about herself.

Why was she alone right now? Well, she'd been able to afford the hiking, and soul-searching part, just not the scenic plane ride. While the rest of the group left to go and have that life-altering experience, she'd been told to wait, and a pickup would be along shortly to collect her. That had been two days ago, and now she was trapped in the wilderness, where everything looked exactly the same.

"I won't cry. I will not cry. This is the whole process. Being at one with nature, and learning to thrive in an environment I'm not used to. Everything is going to be okay. I'm fine. I'm not going to die a miserable death because no one cares if I'm here or not." She breathed in deep, drank another sip of her water, and tapped the tree. "You look exactly the same as all your brothers and sisters. Got to keep moving, and talking to myself, because that is totally fun, right?"

When did she become the kind of woman who talked to herself?

"Only twenty-two, and already going loopy. What was I thinking? Sure, Opal Clark, find yourself in the wilderness, it'll totally make sense. I should have just phoned one of those stupid lines that offers to hel-ahhhhhh…" She screamed as she suddenly tripped over a root of a tree, and rolled down the hill, coming to a stop right next to a rock, hitting her head. She pressed a hand to her suddenly aching head, and came away with some blood. "Ouch." Rolling over, she went to stand up, and squealed as pain rushed through her ankle, making her collapse in a heap. Staring down at her boot, she couldn't make out any damage, but she had heard trying to take your boot off was dangerous. She leaned against the large rock that she just hit her head on, and winced. Taking several deep breaths, she paced herself, and finally tried to lift up but nothing was happening.

Dropping back on the ground, she glanced around and saw nothing that could help her.

Reaching into her bag, she found her cell phone, and it was indeed dead as well. No miracles tonight. And only one jerky left.

She rested her head on the rock as panic tried to take over. "Don't panic. Don't worry. Everything is going to be fine. You waited an entire day in that spot they told you to stay at, and now you're in the middle of nowhere with a really bad ankle, and a throbbing head. It could get worse."

As if someone was determined to mark her words, she heard the thunder, followed by a sudden flash, and rain began to fall.

"Seriously! Right now? You're going to rain? Like I don't have enough on my plate without you mocking me at every damn turn." She slammed her hand on the ground and growled. "Give me a damn break."

The rain didn't let up, and as she couldn't move, she grew wetter. She wrapped her arms around herself, feeling the chill seep into her clothes. Tears filled her eyes as the true extent of her circumstances settled in.

She was alone.

No one knew where she was.

She didn't have a working cell phone.

Her ankle was either sprained or broken.

No one was coming for her.

The hours passed, and she watched the sun go down until it disappeared with the last of her hope. The rain still fell but more in a light drizzle. When she heard the howl of a wolf, that was it. She let out a scream, hoping that somewhere, someone was as crazy as her, and wanted to spend time in the wild.

****

"What is it, Bear?" Damon asked, watching his St. Bernard's tail wag as he looked off toward the forest.

"He's getting old. He probably heard a rabbit or something," Caleb said, standing in the doorway.

Bear patted his foot then rushed toward the edge of the forest, and came back to him.

"I don't think it's a rabbit," Damon said.

He'd been the one to train Bear after they'd saved him from a rescue center five years ago. He was a huge dog, and being out in the middle of nowhere was the perfect place for him.

"It's dark."

"Yeah, and I don't care. I don't like the way he's acting. What if someone's hurt?"

"Ugh! Fine. Let's go and see what's wrong with your damn dog." Caleb grabbed two flashlights and handed one to him. They'd explored the forest surrounding them so many times that they knew all the dangerous spots where bears liked to hunt.

He had no intention of being eaten by bears or by wolves.

Caleb had also grabbed one of their shotguns as well.

"Come on, boy, go on, go find it." Damon followed Bear's trail. The dog sniffed at the ground.

"You know if he brings home a rabbit, I'm not eating it," Caleb said.

Damon laughed. His brother didn't like killing and eating rabbits, but then, neither did he. Maybe he was lame, but he'd rather have a big pot of vegetable soup than have to kill a fucking rabbit. Their father never killed a rabbit, and they actually kept them to eat the scraps. They had yet to purchase some, and were using the scraps to help make compost.

They'd been out in the forest for a good twenty minutes when Damon was tempted to head back.

Caleb was moaning, which was what he liked to do. He figured Caleb was lonely, just like him. They'd gotten the life they always wanted, the only problem was, they didn't have the woman, and they both wanted one.

They wanted to start a family, keep their family name alive.

The right woman would have to live away from society *and* share her life with the two of them. It was more of a dream than an expectation. It would be a miracle for that to ever happen. What worthwhile woman would want to live out in the middle of nowhere with two very demanding men?

None came to mind.

He was just about to tell Caleb they should head back when he heard the moan. A feminine, pain-filled moan.

Bear whined, and as Damon shined his torch toward his dog, he saw him standing next to a large rock, and leaning up against it was a woman.

"Holy shit," Caleb said.

They both rushed toward her.

Damon tried not to shine the light in her eyes, but she moaned, and her teeth chattered from the cold. Removing his coat, he wrapped it around her shoulders, and immediately began to check her over.

"What's your name, sweetheart?" Caleb asked.

"It's Opal. I was … part … of the … thing."

"The thing?" Damon asked.

"The camping trip thing."

Caleb asked her questions, and Damon held her hand as they discovered something was wrong with her ankle, and also, she'd banged her head pretty good against the rock. "We've got to move you, baby. You're in good hands now. Nothing bad is going to happen to you."

The moment Caleb lifted her up, she gave out a cry and then passed out in his arms. His brother gave a little grunt as he moved her into a more comfortable position.

"Damn, I didn't expect her to slump down like that."

"Do you have her?" Damon asked.

"Yeah, I've got her. We're going to have to call the doctor to come out here and have a look at her. Go on ahead, Damon, we've got to make sure she's okay."

Damon followed Bear, who led the way back to their cabin. After opening the door, he was met by the warmth of the fire.

With the light, he saw the raven-haired beauty was covered in mud but beneath that, he saw a really beautiful woman.

Caleb placed her down on their sofa and stared at her ankle.

"What is it?"

"I don't want to take that off in case something bad is going on."

"You think it could be a break?" asked Damon.

"It's something. The pain was enough to keep her ass sitting there in the rain, and when I lifted her she passed out."

Caleb grabbed a couple of blankets, and Damon went to their supply closet to grab the thickest ones they could find.

"How long do you think she's been out there?" Damon asked.

"A couple of days now. The camping trip left,

remember?"

"Why would they leave a girl out there on her own?" Damon started to get angry. He was pissed off. If they hadn't shown up, he had no doubt she'd be dead by morning.

He and Caleb had warned the organizers of the camping trips that they were fucking dangerous, and at every single turn they were thwarted. Not this time. This woman could have died out there, and no one had even sent out an alert of a missing woman.

"Call the doctor. Get him out here. I don't want to risk moving her in case she's taken a fall or something more." Caleb reached out and slowly moved some of her hair off her face, which covered a large cut against her forehead.

"That doesn't look good."

"I have a feeling she tripped, fell against the rock, and hurt her ankle in the process. Anyone who's not used to these forests can hurt themselves pretty easily." Caleb cursed. "I'm making some tea."

Grabbing the phone, Damon sat on the wooden coffee table, watching her as he waited for the doctor to answer his call. He gave him a rundown of what happened and hung up.

Without waiting for instructions from Caleb, he dialed the camping trip organizer, and didn't give a fuck that it was nearly eleven at night. The moment Rich answered, Damon quizzed him.

"Do you have any fucking idea that you left a woman up in the forest? She's fallen, you asshole, and was so far off the trail she could have died if it wasn't for my dog!" His anger began to build as he thought about this poor woman out there all alone. They didn't live in the suburbs. Their cabin was nestled in the most rugged wilderness one could find, thousands of acres of old-growth forest.

He held her hand tightly, knowing he wouldn't let anything or anyone hurt her. As he did this, he also wondered where his possessive feelings had come from.

Chapter Two

Caleb strained out the tea leaves from the pot and filled a mug with the homemade concoction. He couldn't help but remember when their father used to make tea for their mother every evening. He'd never seen a couple more in love, even after decades of marriage. He aspired to have that kind of love. Something he'd lost hope of achieving once he celebrated his fortieth birthday earlier in the year.

At least he had enough good memories to carry him through the rest of his life. He was big on tradition and hoped his parents were proud when they looked down on their sons. They'd done everything right … except carry on the family blood line.

The doctor had arrived a few minutes earlier, busy examining their sleeping beauty. He didn't dare voice his feelings because he could already see the glint in his brother's eyes. Damon was so damn desperate for a woman, he couldn't think straight.

As Caleb entered the room, the doctor was finishing up, adjusting his stethoscope around his neck. His patient attempted to peek open her eyes, then she'd drift away again.

"What's the verdict?" he asked, setting Opal's tea on the coffee table.

The doc tidied up his medical bag, the same old one he used when they were kids. "She'll live," he said. "Just a sprain and mild concussion. Nothing some rest won't cure."

"Thank you for coming so quickly," said Damon, shaking his hand.

"You're lucky. I was nearby checking on Blackwoods's pregnant wife, otherwise it would have taken me hours to get way out here."

"Everything okay with them?"

He nodded. "Nothing out of the ordinary."

They walked the doctor out to his truck in front. The moon was just a sliver in the sky, the cloud cover nearly blocking it out completely. At least the rain had settled.

"Drive safely," said Caleb.

The doctor put his black bag in the passenger seat, then turned and placed a hand on Caleb's shoulder. "You want me to call the authorities, have someone come out and get the girl?"

He immediately shook his head. "No, we'll handle everything. Like you said, she needs rest."

"Just a few days and she should be good to walk on that ankle."

"Yes, sir."

They watched him drive off, the cones of light disappearing into the forest. The roads were only roughly carved out between the trees, barely wide enough for their truck. When they'd moved back home after decades away, it had taken weeks of brush removal and clean-up just to reach their cabin.

"Now what?" asked Damon, once they were alone on the front porch.

He shrugged. "It's only a few days. We have enough supplies to feed another mouth."

Damon exhaled, leaning against one of the support beams. "That's not what I'm fucking talking about and you know it."

"Don't start," he said.

"You telling me you're not attracted to her? Because that's bullshit, Caleb."

It was true they both had the exact same taste in women. They preferred a woman with meat on her bones, curves that overflowed in a man's hands. Opal had an innocent beauty, all fresh and natural. He could imagine her ripe with their child, but he immediately pushed those thoughts away. Obviously, Damon wasn't doing the same.

"Even if I was, it doesn't matter. We don't even know a thing about her. She said a few words before passing out."

"Well, I can feel something," said Damon.

"It's called blue balls. Get over it," said Caleb. "Besides, a woman like that is likely married or at least taken. And don't forget how women run the other way when they find out we live off the grid."

"You're so damn negative." Damon wrenched open the door, the screen slapping back into place. Silence settled around him once alone. He didn't want to grow old and bitter, but he didn't want to delude himself either. Mostly, he didn't want Damon to get hurt. His brother was ready to put his heart on the line for a complete stranger.

He took a few cleansing breaths, then returned inside, locking up behind him. Damon was sitting on the coffee table, ogling their guest.

"You're up," Caleb said. "How do you feel?"

"Like I rolled down a hill into a pile of rocks." She chuckled and tenderly touched her head.

He passed her the mug of tea. "Drink this. It'll make you feel better and warm you up."

"Thank you." She cupped the mug in both hands. "I didn't think I'd make it."

"You're safe now. Why weren't you on the plane with everyone else?"

She finished taking a sip of tea. "I couldn't afford it. I spent most of my saving just to go on my little adventure."

Caleb was well aware the nature trips were

targeted for the rich, people with so much money they didn't know what to do with it. Damon and Caleb had done well for themselves in the city, starting their own construction company. It only taught him that money couldn't buy happiness.

"I hope this experience didn't give you a sour taste for country living," said Damon. "Once you're feeling better, I'd be happy to show you just how beautiful the land really is."

Caleb scowled at his brother, but Damon ignored him.

"I'm surprised your boyfriend didn't come along with you on the trip. I know if I had a woman like you, I wouldn't let you out of my sight."

Fuck. Couldn't Damon keep his big mouth shut for two minutes? He was putting their guest on the spot when she was most vulnerable. His manners were shot to shit.

Caleb wasn't a monster, and he had dreams and desires like any other man. He just didn't believe in forcing himself on a woman. A relationship had to be stoked slowly, brought naturally to a flame. Damon wanted to skip right to the damn baby-making.

Opal bit her bottom lip, likely feeling awkward. "I don't have a boyfriend. I was doing this for me."

Damon smiled, glancing over at him with an evil smirk. Just because she was single didn't mean she was ready to hook up with two bushmen. But Caleb couldn't help but feel a trickle of hope.

****

Opal had woken up to the warmth of blankets and the crackle of an open fire. She thought she was dreaming, her mind creating a merciful fantasy in her dying hour. When she opened her eyes, the kind face of an old man looked down on her. A stethoscope hung around his neck, and she immediately felt the burden of survival slipping away. She was out of the elements and in the hands of a doctor.

She was half in a daze, studying the wooden plank ceiling above her and the different shaped knots in the wood. As her faculties returned, she focused on the two men still in the room, and she remembered the sequence of events—well, bits and pieces. Those men had saved her, brought her to this place in the woods. She tucked her hair behind her ears, imagining she looked worse than shit. The last thing she should care about was her appearance, but those men… They were tall and built, all burly muscle, rough hands, and worn jeans. The one with the blue eyes sat on the table, his elbows resting on his knees. His shoulders were massive, the red flannel shirt hugging his muscles.

The one with the short beard had dark eyes, the eyes of a predator. He'd look at her, but instead of smiling, the corners of his eyes would crinkle. He acted like she was an unwanted house guest, and she supposed she'd already put these men through the ringer tonight.

When he offered her the tea, her nerves settled slightly. "I'm sorry for putting you both out."

"Don't worry about us," said Blue Eyes. "You just worry about getting better."

"I don't know your names," she said.

"My name's Damon, and this is my brother Caleb."

They both sat on the coffee table in front of her now, two perfectly rugged specimens of the male form. She didn't want to stare, but they were very nice to look at. "Who lives here?"

"Just the two of us," said Damon. He ran a hand through his mop of dark hair.

"And you said you're brothers?"

He nodded. "Caleb's two years older, but a lot of people mistake us for twins."

She found it odd that two grown men lived alone together, no family, no wives, or children. Opal wanted to know so much more, but didn't want to insult them or open up any old wounds. Maybe one of them was a widower.

"Who's waiting for you back home?" asked Caleb. He didn't talk as much, so he had her undivided attention.

"I live alone. I have a little studio apartment above a discount store." After she spoke, she wondered if she should be telling these strangers that no one was waiting for her return. Maybe they lived alone because they were crazy axe murderers. She tensed up, countless horror flicks scrolling through her mind again.

"A city girl?" asked Caleb.

"I've lived in the city all my life. It's where the jobs and public transit are. Only people with money get to live in the suburbs."

"What do you call this?" asked Damon, waving an arm in the air.

"Well, it's far from the suburbs." She smiled. "I can't even imagine living way out here. How do you two survive?"

Caleb didn't look impressed with her question and kept quiet.

"I guess it's something you get used to. Or addicted to. Once you get away from all the noise and bustle, you don't want to go back," said Damon.

"I'd never make it on my own."

Damon wet his lips, distracting her. "You just need a man to take care of you," he said. "Or two."

Caleb stood up and stormed off to the kitchen. She heard cupboards banging, then the water running.

His quick escape had stolen her focus for a minute, but had she heard correctly? Had Damon hinted at something kinky? She must have misunderstood.

The hot tea and roaring fire had warmed her, bringing back her sensibilities. She looked around the cabin. It must have been built by hand, with a lot of history. The log walls were well insulated, the interior cozy and rustic. Big colorful rugs adorned the floor and the stone fireplace flickered with red, orange, and yellow flames. It was the type of place perfect for a retreat, a getaway for the mind. Maybe a few days holed up with Caleb and Damon in this little piece of paradise wouldn't be so bad after all.

She'd started this adventure to heal herself from the inside out, to give herself a chance at life after she'd almost taken her own. Her entire life had been a struggle. The bullying first happened in grade school and never let up. She'd always been teased for her weight, and she found out adults could be just as cruel as kids. Opal didn't want to grow old alone, in fact, it terrified her. But so far, men kept their distance. And loneliness nipped at her heels.

"Is everything okay?" she asked.

Damon leaned closer, and she took a good look at him. His eyes were an unusual blue, and she imagined they'd be even more stunning in the sunlight. He had scruff on his face, a straight nose, and strong jaw. There was something about the brothers, something different than the men she'd seen in the city. Their untamed quality lured her in, made her conjure up impossible fantasies in her head. What she wouldn't give to feel Damon's strong arms around him, see lust in his eyes. This was every woman's fantasy—trapped in the wilderness with two irresistible hunks. Too bad they were way out of her league.

Opal was used to being ignored or cast aside. It was just the way things were for her.

"Everything's fine. If you're worried about Caleb, don't be. He's old-fashioned and doesn't believe in going after what he wants."

"What does he want?"

He smirked, and it was the sexiest thing she'd ever seen. "You."

****

Damon didn't give a shit if Caleb wanted to live in self-denial. He planned to take what he wanted, and he wanted Opal—wanted her as his wife and to carry his child. He knew damn well Caleb felt the same way, but it would take some convincing before he agreed to take a chance on her.

She looked young, maybe too young for them, but he knew they'd be able to take care of her properly. Damon didn't like the sadness in her eyes, or the fact she'd been barely living. They didn't have much in way of material possessions, but that was by choice. They had money in the bank, but that was where it stayed. As long as they had an abundance of food, supplies, and firewood, they were happy.

"You're wrong," she said. "Men don't like me in that way."

"In what way?"

She bit her lower lip. "You know … as a girlfriend or wife."

"I'm not following, sweetheart. Why on earth wouldn't a man want you? I feel the same way as my brother. Finding you was a saving grace, like you'd been dropped out of the sky just for us."

"Us?"

"We share everything." He left it at that. Caleb had a point about scaring her off too soon. Describing all the delicious things they'd like to do with her in bed would be a bad start. They'd never found a woman special enough to be the mother of their children.

Opal was that woman.

She attempted to move her leg and winced. It was late, so it would be best to get her to bed. Rest was the answer to most things. He stood up and leaned over to scoop her up into his arms.

"Careful, you'll hurt yourself," she said, clutching his shirt.

"I'm a big boy." He carried her to his bedroom. There were only two in the cabin. He set her down on his patchwork quilt as tenderly as possible. The doctor had already removed her boots and socks, and he noticed the injured ankle was dark and swollen.

"Where're you going to sleep?" she asked.

"I'll take the couch."

"This is your bed? I can't take your bed from you. You've already been too good to me."

He sat down beside her, the mattress dipping slightly. "Did you know the townspeople are afraid of us? Apparently nobody wants to fuck with the White brothers. I can't blame them, exactly. We don't always tend to react with our heads, and one thing for certain, we're very protective of what's ours."

She swallowed hard, looking at him with those big doe eyes. He wanted to make it clear that she wasn't going anywhere. Damon planned on keeping her, fucking her, and filling her with his baby. His brother wanted the same thing, so he'd only fight him so long. And this little lamb might protest, but she'd soon learn how good life could be as their woman.

"You should get some sleep. It's late and rest will help you heal faster. I'm only a shout away if you need anything," said Damon. She looked perfect in his bed, and he had to pull himself away. Their home had lacked a female presence for too long, and until Opal showed up, he didn't realize just how much he needed her. Before he closed the door behind him, he said, "You're safe here. I wouldn't let anything bad happen to you."

He closed the door and then crashed on the sofa, resting his forearm over his eyes. He felt exhausted and invigorated at once. They'd found the most beautiful treasure, the woman they'd both been praying for. It was too good to be true.

Caleb brushed his legs aside and sat next to him. "You're fucking nuts," he whispered harshly.

"What did I do?"

"It's a small cabin. I could hear almost everything you said to that girl. You're trying to scare her into staying."

He shook his head. "You're crazy. I just want her to know how far I'd go to protect her, to keep her."

"You're going to push her away."

"She's not going anywhere," said Damon. "She's ours, you'll see."

"She's not a toy, she's a woman. You can't make someone love you," said Caleb.

Damon bolted to his feet, running his hands through his hair. He didn't want to hear this. He needed love, deserved it. The only person he had in his life was his brother. Yes, Caleb meant the world to him, and the thought of losing him terrified Damon, but he needed more. He craved the love of one woman. Wanted a real life, a family, a home filled with laughter like when they were kids.

He didn't want to hear Caleb's negativity, even though his own doubts threatened to bring him down. They weren't getting any younger, and when would the perfect woman fall in their laps again? He had to prove to

Opal that they could give her everything she needed.

"Love takes time, and I have all the time in the world," said Damon.

"And once her ankle heals, and she wants the hell out of the boondocks?"

He frowned. "She won't want to leave. If you'd help me instead of trying to sabotage me, maybe we could actually make this work."

"Don't get your hopes up, that's all I'm saying." Caleb sat in the old rocker in front of the fire. Damon was tired of seeing his older brother slowly lose his zest for life. They were going through the motions, but needed so much more. Opal had to be the answer for both of them.

Chapter Three

Caleb knew more than his brother. He'd gotten his hopes up one too many times, and he refused to allow it to happen again. Damon always lived in a world where everything was possible. There were times Caleb was sure his brother believed in miracles, Santa Claus, and even the tooth fairy. No, he knew his brother didn't believe in those things, but he always had so much hope.

Women didn't want to live out in the middle of nowhere, and from what Opal told them, she had a life in the city. The horrible, smelly, polluting, city. There was no way a woman would want to give up the ease to living out in the wilderness. He loved it here. When his parents were taken from him, he'd hated the city. Hated the people. They were constantly asking questions as if they had a right to know the answer to them, and it pissed him off.

He'd always been a private person, and talking about his feelings never worked for him.

The following morning, he was the first one up, and made Opal some of the tea he'd made her the night before, along with some toast and their best homemade jam. Making his way to the bedroom, he was surprised to see her already sitting up in bed.

"Morning," he said.

She offered him a smile. "Morning."

"Did you sleep well?"

"Yes. I slept amazingly. Thank you so much."

"I've come with goodies." He placed the tray on her lap, and then took a seat, bringing it closer to her.

"You really don't have to do this," she said.

Her stomach chose that moment to growl, and he laughed. "I don't mind making you up a tray. You need someone who can help you out right now. It's time to heal. Don't worry about a thing."

He saw her cheeks heating, turning a pretty pink. "This is the first time I've been brought breakfast in bed."

"Until your ankle is better, get used to it."

He watched as she took some of the jam on her knife, and spread it over the toast. The moment she took a bite, her eyes closed. "This is amazing. What flavor is it?"

"Wild strawberry. They grow in abundance around here, and Damon and I are always picking them."

"This is your jam?"

"It is."

"You actually made this?" she asked, taking another bite.

"You kind of have to living out here. We go to the main town to pick up enough supplies, but for the most part our pantry is filled with our own stuff." He liked it that way. Being self-reliant, keeping close to nature, it meant a lot.

There were always too many additives and pollutants in store-bought food. He didn't like anything that had a warning or an ingredient he couldn't pronounce.

"I've never met anyone who actually preserved before. That is new for me."

"It's a totally manly thing to do," he said, thinking about what Damon would say. He gave her a wink. "You're from the city, anyway."

"Yeah, the city…"

He saw the smile on her face drop. "You came out to the wilderness to find yourself?"

Opal nodded. "I was surrounded by a bunch of people attempting to get back to nature, wanting to know what it felt like to be poor, and to go without."

He heard the sadness in her voice. "You know what that's like?"

"Being poor? Can't you tell? I spent everything I had in order to find out who I was, and now I feel like I've lost everything, and I don't even have money to pay for the medical bill." She placed her toast on the plate, and pressed the palms of her hands against her eyes. "And I still don't know who the hell I am."

"You don't need to worry about the bill. The doctor, he likes getting some of our preserves. We've already got a box ready for him." They also had plenty of money to pay for her bill, but he didn't want to talk about dollars and cents. It was the root of all evil, in his opinion.

"I don't like taking charity. I can deal with it. As soon as I'm able, I can work, I'll pay you back."

His heart went out to the woman on the bed.

Taking her hand, he pulled it away from her face, and moved a bit closer. "We won't take your money, Opal. We're not monsters. Just get well, and let us take care of you. That's all you need to do."

When he looked at her, he saw the same beauty that Damon talked about. He also felt that yearning, the need to claim her, to make her theirs. It had been so long since they'd been with a woman. Sex had become an empty action, meaning nothing to him. He didn't want sex to mean nothing. Or his life.

He wanted love, connection, and of course, rough dirty sex.

Staring at Opal, he imagined her naked, spread between him and his brother, taking their cocks, begging for more, and they'd be more than happy to give it to her.

His cock hardened at the thought, and he knew he had to get out of the room. Before he could say or do anything, his brother came in.

"Morning, everyone." Damon moved to her other side before dropping down unceremoniously on the mattress. "Now, Caleb's grumpy ways haven't upset you, have they?" His brother reached forward and wiped the tear away.

"Caleb made me breakfast and tea. He also listened to me moan about how crappy my life is. He's more than fine." She squeezed his hand. "Thank you, to both of you. If you hadn't come to get me, I could have died. I don't want to die, and thank you so much for making me realize that."

He didn't like what he was hearing. To Caleb, her words could mean a great many things. One of them meaning that there was a time Opal had wanted to end her life, and that didn't sit well with him.

****

Over the next few days, Opal got used to seeing Caleb and Damon. Both brothers had a rustic appeal and homegrown muscles—she couldn't stop sneaking peeks. They were so caring that she yearned to be their woman. How crazy was that? There was no way those two men wanted a woman like her. She'd been told many times over the years that she was too fat to ever be wanted. It was one of the reasons she'd wanted to end it all before coming on the retreat.

Pushing those thoughts aside, she decided that even though they would never want her, she'd enjoy their company and make the best of the situation. Both men were totally different. Damon was the fun one who liked to joke, and of course, flirt, while Caleb always seemed serious. He rarely joked, and he didn't flirt.

There were many times when she'd catch Caleb looking at her in a way that made her think of sex, and all the dirty things she'd love to do with him. Even with her injury, she wanted to be with them, and that was completely crazy because she'd never been drawn to men in that way. Even at twenty-two she was still a virgin, and had expected to stay that way until she died.

"So, how does your ankle feel today, princess?" Damon asked, entering the room. He yanked open the curtains, the dust motes dancing in the sun rays. She loved when he sweet talked her, even though she assumed it was how he talked to every woman. The positive attention was new for her, and she thrived on it, craved it.

It was getting colder, and she'd heard them talking about a snowfall warning. Her ankle wasn't broken, and the doctor said after a few days' rest she should start to move around. It looked like that day was going to be today. Damon and Caleb had been carrying her to their bathroom so that she could use the toilet and wash. She needed to push for her independence if she wanted to get well.

She looked forward to a shower or even better, a bath.

Opal wiggled to the edge of the bed while he gathered her dishes. She lifted up off the mattress and took a step. There was a little pain but nothing to complain about. A big weight lifted off her shoulders knowing she was almost good as new.

"I think I'm fine." She turned to find Damon staring at her. The sun shone through the window and when she looked down at her body, she saw that her night shirt had become transparent. Quickly covering her body, she offered him a shy smile. "I hope I don't sound rude, but do you think I could have a bath?"

"You can have whatever you want." He cleared his throat, and the playfulness was gone. She wanted the moment to mean so much more, but nobody could want her the way she needed. He just wanted no-strings sex.

Her nipples tightened as he turned away, his shirt stretching across his shoulders. Both men were ripped, all hard muscle, and from what they'd both told her, they worked the land by hand all the time.

They lived an amazing life.

Peace, tranquility, freedom.

She didn't miss the city. Every time she listened, she heard the birds singing, or the sound of the trees rustling in the wind. Back in the city, it was all about cars honking or people shouting. The air was always thick with pollution, and everyone was always pissed off. Her old apartment had thin walls—babies screaming, people having sex, and lots of yelling and cursing. She hated that life, and never wanted to go back to it. But what choice did she have?

Damon and Caleb had both been lucky to get away. The lifestyle they chose was one she'd love to be a part of. It would be a dream come true, one she hadn't realized she had until staying with the brothers.

"I'm going to get washed up." She escaped to the bathroom, desperate to get away from the feelings Damon inspired in her. A man like him could destroy her because she knew it wouldn't take much for her to fall in love. Closing the door softly behind her, she ran some water into the bath. Everything was simplistic and plain, exactly what she'd expect in a small cabin home. It was perfect.

Damon had told her before to make herself at home, and she tried to do so without outstaying her welcome. Stripping off her clothes, she noticed the bruises on her skin, which still hadn't faded. She sighed. Opal had tried to find herself, and all she'd succeeded in doing was nearly killing herself. Once she sank into the water, the warmth seeped into her bones, relaxing her.

Running a hand down her stomach, she thought of Damon and Caleb. When it came to the brothers, she found it next to impossible to think about one without the other. They were opposites but also one. Her body came alive. Heat flooded her pussy, and her nipples tightened as she imagined both men touching her, loving her. It would feel so good to have their rough hands all over her curves, their lips caressing her flesh.

She hadn't misheard Damon the other day about what they wanted. He'd been honest with her. They shared their women. Everything in their life, they did together, and even though she tried to fight the fantasies those words conjured up, she couldn't. Touching her tits, she toyed with her nipples, biting her lip as a moan built up inside her. She didn't release it, and kept it down, not wanting to be heard. The last thing she wanted was for Damon to know what she was doing.

Would it be such a big problem?

She didn't know if she wanted to answer her own question.

Her thoughts were all over the place.

Opal slid a hand down her body, touching her pussy, cupping herself. She'd been overly sensitized since first seeing the brothers in the morning. Rubbing the palm of her hand against her clit, the pleasure was instant, and she gasped as it went through her entire body, hardening her nipples. What would it be like to have to men worship her? For them both to want her body.

Damon and Caleb were sexy men, with a no-holds-barred vibe that pulled her in. They were both so different and she liked them together, like two halves of a whole.

Moving her palm up, she slid her fingers across her clit, and closed her eyes, thinking of their lips on her body. She imagined them touching her, placing her on the bed, and each of them kissing her body. They'd suck on her breasts, not one part of her left untouched or unwanted.

That was what she craved more than anything, to be wanted. No one had ever taken the time to get to know her, and just the thought of the brothers wanting her filled her with hope.

She came with a few strokes against her clit, and the orgasm wasn't exactly thrilling. It never had been. Her orgasms were a release of the pressure, but nothing special. She had a feeling Damon and Caleb had the experience to show her a thing or two about being taken, being fucked. Unfortunately, they could have any woman they wanted, so why would they settle for the ugly duckling?

****

Hearing Opal's lackluster orgasm pissed off Damon. All he wanted to do was take her from the bathroom, spread her on his bed, and eat her pussy so she knew what a real orgasm felt like. Instead, he had to listen to the little moan, and even the finale was pitiful.

This woman hadn't had a man's touch, and he wanted to change that, to show her how good it could be with two men. He'd been with a lot of women, so it didn't take long for him to peg her as a virgin. The thought of claiming her, breeding her, owning her was too much. He'd been pent up since she showed up, but he refused to let it affect his mood. Damon's only outlet was physical punishment, so he left the cabin before he did something he'd regret.

Bringing the axe down on another plank of wood, it shattered in two, and it didn't help his mood at all. Caleb was pissing him off with all of his serious man bullshit, and right now, his desire to be fucking selfish was riding him high. What was wrong with taking Opal as their own? It wasn't like he planned on using and discarding her. She'd be their woman. Their everything.

He'd seen the pleasure on Opal's face as she listened to the quiet sounds of the wilderness surrounding the cabin. By her own words, she was poor, which meant her life back home was nothing to covet. She probably lived in a rundown apartment building that was more suited to being demolished than refurbished.

Damon had explored the city at great length. The poor parts and the wealthy parts. Their uncle had asked them to try to involve themselves in city life, and to make a go of it.

From the start, he'd done what he'd been asked to do, and what he found hadn't enthralled him. It had turned him off. The city was a cesspool, and he was just as eager to escape as his brother.

Caleb thought he lived in a fucking fantasy land for being hopeful. He wasn't naïve to the evils in the world, but he chose not to dwell on them. Pushing the bullshit and pain away made life tolerable. He'd learned that once his parents died.

"Any reason you're attacking our firewood?" Caleb asked, leaning against the porch railing.

He ignored his brother and placed another log on the tree trunk, lifted the axe, and brought it down.

Before they died, their mother would often watch their father chop wood, doing all the manly chores that living in the wilderness demanded of him. Their father taught them almost everything they knew.

"Why do you think our parents decided to live out here?" Caleb asked.

Chopping another plank of wood, he lifted the axe out, and stared at his brother. "We know they were wealthy. Money was never a problem."

"No one would accept our mom," Caleb said.

"What?"

"I asked our uncle that question one night, and he told me that the moment Dad saw her, he wanted her. She was some waitress or something. Our grandparents didn't approve. They wanted someone from wealth to marry their son."

"How did I not know this?" Damon asked.

"Did you ask?"

He shook his head. "No, I didn't ask." He placed the axe against the tree trunk, and sat down, not caring about the uneven surface. Damon took a deep breath, calming the beast within.

"Is this about our mom and dad, or is this about a certain woman who's cleaning up our home?"

"I heard her in the bathroom," Damon said, running a hand down his face.

"You heard her what?"

"I heard her touching herself. She was trying to give herself an orgasm." He chuckled. "Well, I wouldn't call it an orgasm. She gasped at the end but that was about it." He shook his head. "I know you want to wait, and you don't think she's the one, but I'm telling you, she is."

"I never said she's not the one, Damon. I've asked you not to get your hopes up because I don't want to see you sad. You're my brother. My little brother. You see the world as sunshine and rainbows."

"I know the world is a fucked-up mess, Caleb. I know our way of life isn't understood by a lot of people. Even our uncle never understood why our parents did what they did. We do, and we know this is what we want." He stepped up close to Caleb. "Tell me that when you look at her, you don't imagine her pregnant with our kid. That you can't imagine her coming apart as we touch her."

"Damon, don't. It's not that simple."

"Life isn't simple, but this doesn't have to be so fucking complicated. What is it with you constantly being Mr. Negative?"

"I'm trying to protect you."

He shook his head. "You can try to protect me all you want, but I'm not going to end up lonely because of it. Don't ruin this for us."

Brushing past his brother, he entered their home, and went straight toward the kitchen where he found Opal sitting at the kitchen counter. She wore one of their shirts, and it looked good on her. Her pale features now had a little color in them. She smiled the instant he entered the room, and that smile, it went straight to his cock, and made him think all kinds of dirty thoughts. He wanted her, fuck the consequences.

Something told him that Opal was different from a lot of women. His brother would think he'd gone crazy, but the moment Damon saw her, he knew she was the one.

She'd been on that trip to find herself, and he knew she'd tried to end her life, or at least thought about it once. This woman was screaming for help, but no one was listening.

He didn't say a word, tongue-tied for the first time in his life. Damon grabbed some slices of bread and started to make himself a sandwich.

"You have an amazing home," she said.

He watched as she glanced around the room with a childlike wonder. "Have you only ever lived in apartment buildings?"

"Yeah. Cheap ones. Most of my neighbors have been cockroaches."

He saw the sadness in her eyes, and he was done.

Life was about taking chances, and he was about to take one for all three of them.

Chapter Four

Opal felt fresh after her long soak in the bath. Her head was clear, and her energy had returned. It was the day she'd dreaded, the day she *should* ask for a drive to town because she was no longer bed-bound.

Damon's mood had been off since this morning. There was an energy between them, but she didn't want to disappoint herself and believe it was intimacy. For all she knew, he had grown impatient with her slow recovery.

"Hungry?" he asked.

"I'm fine." She'd already had breakfast in bed, thanks to Caleb. "I'm trying to watch what I eat, anyway."

"Why?"

"Because I'm fat."

He dropped the butter knife on the counter with a clang and turned around, his face stoic. "You shouldn't talk about yourself like that, Opal."

"Why? It's just the truth."

"Eat to be healthy, not to change yourself." He stepped closer and pulled another wooden chair from the table and set it in front of her. Damon sat down and took one of her hands between both of his. Damn, he had big hands … her thoughts wandered to forbidden territory again. "You're perfect the way you are."

She shook her head. Opal was a big girl. She was used to the negativity and insults about her looks, so she was past living in denial. "If I had money, I'd definitely get a reduction."

The horror on his face took her by surprise. Had she gotten too personal? Grossed him out? She wished she could take back her words and just eaten a sandwich. "It's a good thing you don't have the money," he said.

Damon stared at her, only a breath away, their knees touching. She could feel the blood pulse in her hand, very aware of his touch. "Not many women are as blessed as you. I'd hate to see you change one thing about those beautiful tits."

Her jaw dropped.

"You've been a temptation since the moment we found you in our woods. I've been telling myself to behave and mind my distance, but the truth is I'd give anything to keep you."

"Keep me?"

Her mind was a whirlwind of thoughts. She wanted to refute him, tell him he was full of shit, but she'd never seen a man more sincere. Damon, this Adonis of a man, was actually attracted to her. What did it all mean? Did he want a one-night stand? A prisoner?

"Man wasn't meant to be alone, Opal. Even the Bible says so." He ran the backs of his fingers along her jawline, a look of complete devotion in his eyes. "Would it be so bad to live here? With us?"

Was she dreaming? She wanted to pinch herself, but knew this was all too real. "You don't even know me. I've been here less than a week."

Opal wanted to ask why they hadn't chosen another woman by now. Who on earth could refuse them? Should *she* refuse them? Maybe they were alone for a good reason.

"You're a woman—gorgeous, sweet … innocent." He licked his lips after saying the last word. Her pussy tingled, as if sensing his thoughts, experiencing his need.

"Caleb doesn't even like me." She wanted this, but couldn't just jump on board without a backward glance.

Damon chuckled. "He fucking loves you, darling.

He's just stubborn and afraid you'll reject us." He ran his free hand through his dark hair, the sunlight accentuating his blue eyes. "Tell me I'm not wrong. Tell me you want to stay."

Her anxiety grew by the minute. She pulled her hand away and bolted to her feet. This couldn't be happening. Good girls didn't just run off into the wilderness with two bushmen, never to be seen again. What about her apartment? Her job? Her spoon collection? Opal braced both hands on the counter as she looked out the window above the sink. A few lazy snowflakes drifted down, the wall of evergreens in the distance a reminder of how far she was from civilization.

A hand rested on each shoulder from behind and she jumped. She turned around, craning her neck to look up at Damon. She didn't realize how tall he was, his presence larger than life. "This is crazy," she said.

"You have a man to go back to?"

"No, but I have a life in the city. I can't just uproot and play house with you." What kind of life did she have back home? One she needed to escape from. Her apartment was shitty, her job hell, and she'd been lonely. So lonely. Her hopes and dreams had been tied up in romance novels and the very slim chance her prince charming would show up one day. It wasn't much of a life, so why was she fighting this?

He took a step back, his chin up. The man was sex on a stick, strong jaw, broad shoulders. His red-checked shirt was unbuttoned, his white wife beater clinging to his hard chest. "Your heart is in the city." Damon nodded once. "I can't force you into our way of life. Living out here is extreme, I know that."

What had she done? His disappointment was palpable. She hadn't said "no" to him, but replaying her words in her head, she'd been rude. Opal supposed she was looking for more reassurance, confirmation everything would work out if she decided to stay, but she'd gone and insulted him.

She believed people could learn to fall in love. In her case, she was halfway there, already carrying a massive crush for both brothers. But there were so many variables, so many chances for disaster.

Opal watched Damon leave the kitchen and heard the front door close behind him.

****

Caleb had been stacking wood, preparing for the coming storm. A bitter wind chill had already blown in and a light dusting covered the land. He adjusted his toque and did the top button up on his padded jacket.

When the front screen door slapped shut, he turned to catch Damon storming out of the house.

Damon paced in circles, kicking at the kindling left on the ground. "You were right," he said. "Don't bother gloating because I already feel like shit."

"What are you blathering about?"

"I asked her to stay. Asked her to be our woman."

Fuck. He should have expected this, but he thought his brother would listen to his advice to take things slowly. He'd jumped the gun and scared her off.

"What she say?"

"That she has a life in the city. I don't think there's a woman alive who'd want to live out here." Damon yanked off his shirt, balled it up and whipped it in on the ground. "She was perfect, Caleb. I thought she was the one."

"You'll catch your death of a cold. Get inside," said Caleb.

"No, I need to run."

Caleb watched his brother walk off in just a tank top and jeans. He didn't bother trying to stop him. This was exactly what he feared, watching his brother lose hope.

He tugged off his work gloves and made his way to the porch. Their little guest was done playing games. He'd stayed out of his brother's courting, taking the road of caution, but now it was time to intervene. Time to set their flighty dove straight.

Once he entered the house, silence settled in immediately. He wasn't good with emotions. Where Damon usually wore his heart on his sleeve, Caleb kept his walls firmly in place. Ever since their parents were killed, their lives had been a whirlwind. He'd closed his heart off the best he could, the only way his fourteen-year-old self knew how to cope with so many devastating changes. His only constant had been Damon, and it killed him to watch him suffer.

"You're feeling better?" he asked when he spotted Opal standing near the fireplace. The fire had petered out, only the red glow of ashes left behind.

"Yes, thank you." She wouldn't look at him, still glancing down at the embers.

He hung up his jacket and then grabbed his supplies near the door before kneeling in front of the fireplace. "Storm's coming. I'll keep a good fire going so you stay nice and warm." Caleb added some kindling, blowing slightly, building the fire back to life. Within minutes, he was ready to add full logs to the flames.

"It smells so good," she said.

He stood back up, brushing some ashes off his jeans. "The best smell." It reminded him of family, Christmas, and happiness to name a few.

She swallowed hard, finally looking up at him. *Such pretty green eyes.*

"Maybe I should leave before the storm. Will a taxi come way out here?"

"There ain't no taxi service out here, Opal. Take a look around. We own thousands of acres and there are countless more surrounding that."

"How will I get home?"

He shrugged. "Looks like you're stuck."

"I can't stay forever," she said.

Caleb moved forward, forcing her to back up against the wall. "How old are you? Twenty?"

"Twenty-two."

He was almost twice her age, and he didn't give a fuck. Caleb may not announce it to his brother, but he wanted Opal and planned on keeping her. Every day he grew more and more attached, convinced she'd meld perfectly in their lives. She was young, innocent, a blank slate … perfect for their mate, the mother of their children.

Damon was passionate, cutting her loose too easily. He'd swooped in fast but backed off without a fight. Caleb knew better. They needed to seize what they wanted in life or it would pass them by. He wasn't sure what game Opal was playing, because he could read her like a book. When she thought he wasn't looking, he could see the way she sized them up, desire in her eyes. She wanted them just as much. They could give her everything she needed, likely more than she had roughing it in the big smoke.

"You're young," he said. "You need a man to take care of you."

"Is that you?" she whispered, looking up, daring him with her eyes.

"It's me *and* Damon." He stated the fact, waiting for her to protest, but she didn't.

"How can you protect me here? Everything probably wants to kill or eat me," she said.

Caleb shook his head. "You'd be surprised. With

a little common sense, we all get along just fine. The only danger here, like the city, are people, not animals. But don't worry your pretty head, because we'll protect you from them, too."

Besides the usual issues with squatters and drifters, they had relentless loggers pushing them to sell a good-sized chunk of their land on the west end. It wasn't going to happen.

"This is fast and crazy and doesn't make sense." She was rambling, trying to make excuses when he knew what she wanted. Why did she have to complicate something so simple?

He braced a hand against the wall close to her head. Caleb leaned in, brushing his lips against her ear. "If you leave, you'll destroy my brother. He thinks he's in love."

"Did he say that?"

"He asked you to stay, no? You refused. I've never seen him this broken—not since our parents were killed. He's usually abnormally upbeat."

"I'm sorry about your parents … and Damon. I wasn't trying to hurt him," she said. "I'm not going to fix anything by staying. He hardly knows me. I'm just a woman."

"That's all we want, baby doll. Life out here is rough, but it's perfect. Almost perfect. We need that missing piece, a woman to share, a mother for our children."

"And if you'd found a different woman in the woods?"

He smiled. Her insecurities were endearing. "We would have driven her to town so she could get the help she needed."

"How am I different, Caleb?"

The sound of his name on her lips made his cock

strain in his jeans. He'd been pent up for years, starting to feel like a monk rather than a man with base needs. Somewhere along the line, he'd given up hope. It was Damon who kept them together, convinced their day would come. To see him give up, his zest fizzled away, tilted everything off its axis. Caleb had to fix this for all three of them.

"I'm not one for fairy tales and such, but surely you've heard of love at first sight?"

She frowned, unconvinced. "Love? If I had to guess, I'd say you hated me. I hardly ever see you smile."

He couldn't keep his hands to himself. Caleb ran a hand through her dark hair, still slightly damp from her bath. She didn't pull away. "Just protecting myself. No sense giving you my heart if you plan to run away."

"And if I stayed?" She wet her lips—plump, pink lips.

"We'd take care of you, love you … pleasure you. Me and Damon have been on our own for a long time. Too long. It would mean everything to have a family again."

****

Damon had blown off some much needed steam. Getting deep in the heart of nature always seemed to calm him. He wasn't sure why Opal got to him on such an elemental level. He'd fucked around with women alone and with Caleb and he'd never looked back. Never cared once they parted ways. But their dark-haired beauty had gotten under his skin. Something about her called to him, demanded he claim her as his woman.

But she didn't want him. She wanted her life back.

He took a deep breath, determined not to be an asshole for the rest of her stay. It was his father who'd taught him how to treat the opposite sex, and his mother who'd taught him to take a breather rather than speak out of passion. On days like today, the advice came in handy. It looked like the storm was picking up, and Opal would be stuck with them at least another couple days, depending on the roads.

Damon kicked the snow off his work boots and entered their cabin. Every knot in the wood, every nail, held memories. The warmth of the fire made his face tingle, the familiar scent welcoming him home. He closed the door and rubbed his arms. It was a stupid to take a run without an overcoat with the bitter chill, but his mind had been elsewhere.

When he glanced around the room, he caught sight of Caleb and Opal. His brother had her pinned to the wall by the fireplace, his hand on her hip. *What the fuck?*

"Something wrong?" he asked once beside his brother.

Caleb didn't take his eyes off their guest. She looked so tiny and vulnerable next to his brother. They weren't small men by any standard. "She doesn't realize it yet, but I guarantee you our little dove wants to stay with us."

It couldn't be true. She'd made it clear she had a life in the city. Or maybe he'd been too quick to judge.

"Your arms are so red," she said, looking over at him.

"Yeah, it's not smart going outside half naked in this weather," said Damon. "I'll survive."

She reached out and rested a palm on his bicep, her little hand doing more than warm his frozen skin. "You're freezing!" There was genuine concern in her voice, and a deep caring in her eyes. It felt good to have a woman dote over him.

"How about you warm me up?" he asked without thinking. Why couldn't he keep control like his brother? Their uncle always said he lacked a filter on his mouth.

She didn't looked insulted. Instead, she moved closer, running a hand up and down each arm, trying to create warmth from friction. After a while, she started moving slower, her fingers tracing his muscles. The moment felt intimate, his cock harder than oak, straining in his Wranglers. When she reached up high to rub both shoulders, he couldn't hold back. He took her waist, ducked low, and kissed her on the lips.

How long had it been since he'd kissed a woman? Even during one-nighters he never kissed. Opal's lips were softer than silk, and she melted against his mouth with no hesitation. He pulled her closer, his cock pressed to her stomach. She smelled like clean soap, and all woman.

When he pulled back to gauge her reaction, her lips were swollen and parted, her chest heaving. Fuck, he wanted her on his bed, but for once, he fought for control. The last thing he wanted to do was scare Opal away. He didn't want her for sex—well, not only sex. Damon was in this for the long haul if she'd give them a chance. Judging by her kiss, she was open to the possibility.

"I feel warmer already," he said. Damon ran the pad of his thumb along her lower lip. He stared into her green eyes, wondering if she could see all the way to his soul. She was beautiful, intense, and had more curves than most men could handle. He wanted to love every inch of her body, memorize every beauty mark and detail.

"I've never had a boyfriend," she said, her tone colored in shame.

"Nothing wrong with having no experience," said

Caleb, moving in from the other side. "In fact, there's nothing more attractive."

A virgin. An untouched peach. He wanted to eat her pussy until she begged him to fuck her. He wanted her marked and claimed, so full of their cum that every man would know she was the property of the White brothers. Just like with their land, they were very territorial.

"Stay," whispered Damon. "Take a chance on us." He kissed her temple.

"I'm afraid. Of everything," she said. "What if you change your mind once you get to know me?"

He scoffed. "This isn't the city, sweetheart. We play for keeps. Once we make this official, we'll be a family."

She smiled, but quickly hid it. "How do we make it official?" Opal bit her lower lip. Was their little virgin teasing him? She was playing a dangerous game.

Chapter Five

There was nothing back home in the city. Opal hated to admit that to them. They had so much living off the grid. A beautiful home, peace and quiet, and she saw how much they cared about each other. The love and bond that she'd always heard about between brothers was real. She wouldn't know how that felt.

All of her life she'd been unwanted, and a lot of people had made that clear to her. She was nothing but a waste of space, and it was the reason she ended up on this trip. It seemed fate had interrupted her plans, and put her straight in Damon and Caleb's path.

Damon's arms were so powerful as they enveloped her. The way he held her, she never wanted him to let go. He drove her crazy with need, and she closed her eyes, feeling Caleb step up behind her. She felt surrounded, overwhelmed in a new, exciting way.

"If I didn't know any better, brother, I'd think our little minx was trying to get us to take things to the next step."

She didn't have a clue what she was doing, but hoped they'd know what she needed. Although she didn't have experience with men, she had a vivid imagination. It had been on overdrive ever since showing up at the brothers' cabin.

Damon released her, and going purely on instinct, she slid her hands up the base of his neck, refusing to let go. He felt so good, his skin firm and warm, all male.

Caleb placed his hands on her hips, holding her steady. His firm grip brought her body to life. His touch made her ache. Luckily, it didn't look like she'd have to beg.

Both men scared her with the power they held over her. She couldn't control the range of emotions bombarding her. Although her first instinct was to run, she had to follow this through. Had to trust. She'd never wanted anything from anyone in the past, but when it came to these two men, she wanted it all. The moment felt magical, and she never wanted it to end.

"You can tell us to stop at anytime," Caleb said, taking her ear lobe between his lips, teasing her erogenous zone in just the right way. She exhaled with a little moan.

"We can stop. We can go slow. We can do whatever it is that you want and need," Damon said.

"I want to feel everything." Should she be saying this? It wasn't a lie. She wanted to give herself over to these bushmen, give them free rein over her heart and body.

In the moment, she didn't care what was real or not. The only thing she cared about was getting their hands on her. Men had always stayed away, so this was her chance to seize a fantasy—one she prayed lasted longer than one night.

Caleb teased her waist, his rough fingers slipping beneath the shirt, touching bare skin. "So soft. Let's help her out of this."

They lifted her shirt up and over her head. Beneath was another layer. With it getting colder, she'd had no choice but to put on layers so her body didn't freeze. With the warmth of the fire, though, along with two large bodies on either side of her, she was in a furnace. Not that she minded. She'd never been a big fan of the cold, and loved to be warm.

The other shirt she wore was pulled up over her head and tossed to the ground with the other. The bra she wore was gross, but she had to keep her breasts secure otherwise they bounced, and drew way more attention than she liked.

Feeling a little bold, she lifted up Damon's shirt and tugged it over his head. Seconds ago he'd been cold, whereas now, he was so warm. His hard muscles were pleasing to her eyes, all defined from old-fashioned hard work. Their sheer strength made her feel safe and protected.

Why run when they made you an offer you don't want to refuse?

Even her own protests sounded stupid to her ears. She wanted both men, and they were offering themselves up to her. It was a dream come true.

With the flick of the catch, her bra followed her shirts on the floor.

She stood before them now with her breasts completely bare. A moment of vulnerability kept her frozen in place. They could touch, look, do anything. Were they impressed with what they saw or was she too big for them to handle?

Damon pulled back a little. His hands resting just above Caleb's on her waist, and the heat in his eyes made the answer clear.

No one had looked at her like that.

He looked like he wanted to eat her.

Relief cascaded through her just knowing he accepted her body as it was. She'd never be thin, and for once in her life, she wanted to be loved for her own body, explosive curves and all.

Caleb's hands moved higher, and she gasped as he cupped her tits, offering them up to his brother. "I think she'd like us to have a taste."

Damon didn't complain. Leaning forward, he took one of her nipples into his mouth, and pleasure shot straight through to her core. It was oddly titillating that two men could share her so naturally, no competition, no awkwardness.

It was instant, hot, and she couldn't help but moan. He sucked hard on the tight bud, and while he teased one, Caleb pinched the other. There were hands and lips everywhere.

Leaning back against Caleb, she took his support. Damon placed his hand across the top of her breast, holding it in place as he licked and sucked at her tit.

She pressed her thighs together, feeling the heat begin to burn brighter than anything else she'd ever felt. Opal gasped for air, feeling like she was coming undone.

"I bet he's hard as a rock for you right now. You've never been with a man before, baby, and you're going to be in for a right treat. You see, not all men like to take their time. Damon and me, we'll be taking our sweet time with you—get to know what makes you moan, what drives you to want to fuck." Caleb kissed her neck, licking across her pulse as he continued to hold her tits up like an offering to his brother. "We'll show you to heaven and back. Treat you like a queen, because to us, that is exactly what you are."

Damon kissed across her chest, going to her other breast. His hands went to her sweatpants, and he began to jerk them with force down her hips. She didn't mind.

Closing her eyes, she felt Caleb's breath across the back of her neck.

You're with two men.

She didn't care. She wanted this more than anything else.

Damon moved down her body, his massive frame lowering in front of her as he slipped her pants off each foot. She tentatively smoothed her hands over his shoulders, along the corded muscle, then combed her fingers into his thick hair. He looked up at her with adoration in his eyes, and she swore she fell a little more in love.

As he stood back up, his fingers skimmed along her thighs. He got rid of her panties with a simple yank. She bit her lip from the sharp streak the thin material left behind. These men were rough and unforgiving. She was in for a wild ride.

Heat flooded her pussy, and she didn't want to stop. Never wanted this to end.

Whatever they were offering, she'd take it.

The past week had been amazing, and the truth was, she didn't want to leave. All of her life she'd been made to feel like a nobody. These brothers made her feel alive for the first time. Now she had a feeling she'd never want to leave.

****

Caleb adored her softness. She was a complete contrast to their hard muscle. Opal was all curves, and pure woman. Her tits were huge, her hips rounded, and her stomach soft. Her body could take a hard fuck, but before either of them could show her how good a nice hard fuck could be, they had to prepare her. Opal was a little virgin, so they had to bide their time.

The last thing he wanted to do was to hurt her, or for her to not want to be with them.

He intended to get her addicted to them, just as they'd grown addicted to her.

It almost made him smile at the thought of her leaving. Did she really, for a second, think he'd ever allow that to happen? Her trek into the woods was a one-way trip. She belonged to them, and now they'd make it official—marking her, claiming her, breeding her.

When Damon stood up after stripping her naked, Caleb saw the heat and the love in his brother's eyes. Opal was the right woman for them, and he'd told her the truth. They weren't just after any woman. They wanted the right woman. The woman that would crave this life, love the both of them, and give them children.

The last thing he wanted was someone selfish.

Opal wasn't selfish.

It wasn't hard to see that she'd been deeply hurt in the past, and that made it hard for her to trust. That was fine, though. He was going to make her forget everything.

"I want to taste her," Damon said.

The fire was set, and there was plenty of room in front of it. Helping Opal to the floor atop a large bear pelt rug, he quickly removed his clothes. Caleb wanted to be naked and ready.

She watched them in silence. For now, she tried to cover her body, but in time, he intended for her to let them see every single inch of her. She was a beauty, and he didn't mind spending the rest of his life showing her how fucking sexy she actually was.

Once they were both naked, Caleb gripped his erection. He was long and thick. They had good DNA, both blessed with above average cocks.

As he wrapped his fingers around the length, Opal watched every move. He wondered if it was her first time seeing a man naked. They would certainly be her last. She licked her lips, her chest rising and falling rapidly.

The sensuality was there, burning inside her. He'd teach her how to unleash her desires, to ask for what she wanted.

All she needed were the right men, and he and Damon were the right men.

"I don't know what I'm doing," she said. "I might be no good."

"That's not possible," he said, reaching out to stroke her cheek. "We can show you everything. Just trust us. You won't be sorry."

"If you don't like anything we're doing to you, just say," Damon said. "We'll stop."

"I know. I do trust you. I know you both won't hurt me."

Caleb saw the trust in her eyes, but he wouldn't allow himself to think anything more of it. Trust was one thing, but he wanted her love.

He wondered why she denied them at first.

Why she tried to run back to the city?

Whatever the answer, he'd find out, and he'd prove to her that leaving them would be a big mistake.

They were large, hardened men, but they were capable of love. In fact, he knew without a doubt.

"Are you ready?" Damon asked.

"Yes."

Caleb sat back and watched as Damon pressed her back against the floor, making her lie down. He saw her nerves showing through, so he moved to her side. Caleb had a great view of Opal's pleasure.

He didn't have a problem with watching. In fact, he loved to see his woman come apart, especially as he knew it was also taking care of his brother. Since their parents died, they'd only had each other. Caleb committed himself to Damon, and his brother's happiness meant everything to him.

Damon spread her thighs wide at the knees, then caressed the lips of her pussy. She shivered, her fingers combing into the bear rug on either side of her. Caleb saw her sweet clit, swollen and ripe.

"Look at that sweet pussy," Damon said. "You're so wet, baby. So wet, so perfect."

"Taste her, Damon. How does she taste?"

Opal moaned, arching up, whimpering as Damon sucked her clit into his mouth. Reaching out, he cupped one of her breasts, pinching the nipple. His cock was so hard it ached, but he ignored that, focusing on Opal and making her first time memorable.

While Damon ravished her pussy, Caleb cupped her face, titling her head to look at him. She was such a beautiful woman. Sweet innocence.

He knew he was falling for her already, and it didn't matter how many times he tried to fight it, she'd gotten under his skin.

Running his thumb across her lips, he couldn't wait to see them wrapped around his cock. Tonight was about her, though. They were going to take her to a heights she'd never even dreamed of, and then keep her there.

Leaning forward, he took possession of her lips, and felt her moan. He flicked his tongue across her mouth, and she opened up. Plunging inside her, he felt her tongue press against his, and he closed his eyes, becoming lost to the moment.

She wasn't fighting either of them.

The entire room was thick with desire, the pleasure intense.

Wrapping his fingers around his dick, he stroked himself in an effort to ease the ache, but it didn't work.

Opal was like fire in his arms, and he wanted her.

Pulling away from the kiss, he stared into her eyes. "Have no doubt, Opal, we want you. How does she taste, Damon?"

"So fucking sweet. So ready. She's wet for us, Caleb. She wants us."

And he wanted her.

"Have you done any of this with other men, Opal?" asked Caleb, a new level of possessiveness taking him by surprise.

"No. I've never had a boyfriend."

"Good girl." He took a nipple into his mouth,

teasing the other, and she cried out both of their names. They drove her closer and closer toward orgasm. Neither of them let up, wanting her to come. It would be easier for her later if her body was well prepared.

He loved her softness and the fact no other man had ever been with her.

She was all theirs.

His and Damon's.

To love, to fuck, to breed.

Shit, just the thought of her swollen with their kid was enough to make him ache for more, dream of forever.

He couldn't get over how perfect she was, for the both of them.

For the rest of their lives.

****

Opal's pussy tasted like sweet peaches. Damon felt like a greedy bastard as he didn't want to share. Why should he have to? Well, he would.

He should have known Caleb wouldn't let her go that easily. They'd seen the way she looked at both of them. After witnessing the yearning in her eyes, he wondered why she wouldn't take a chance to stay with them. They weren't bad men, nor would they ever harm her.

Damon knew he'd already fallen in love with her, but he'd spent so much time getting to know her. He'd made her laugh, and seen her through pain. He'd even heard her orgasm in the bathroom, and even though it hadn't been by his own hand or his brother's, he'd still found it sexy to hear. For over a decade, he'd been living in suspended animation, craving love and family. He'd started to lose hope, then Opal appeared as their saving grace.

Damon took his time, spreading the lips of her

pussy to get a better look. Her little cunt was pink and swollen, her thick thighs opened wide. Opal had a light patch of pubic hair, all natural. He couldn't stand the modern women who waxed everything off to look like a pre-teen. Opal was perfection. He sucked on her clit, sliding down to tease against her entrance, but he didn't penetrate her.

No, that pleasure would be on one of their cocks, claiming her as their own. He was excited at the prospect of having her in his bed.

Resting one of his hands on her stomach, he looked up to find his brother watching them. They both wanted to fuck her, to breed her. To get her swollen with their heir.

His cock ached, pre-cum already leaking out of the tip.

He needed to get himself under control, otherwise he was going to blow his load, and he wasn't about to spoil her first time.

Caleb was older than him. He had way more patience, and Damon knew that it would be Caleb to take her virginity. There was no way he'd even make it enjoyable, whereas Caleb would be able to hold himself back, to give her time.

Sucking her clit into his mouth, he used his teeth to create enough pressure to cause a little pain, but combined with the pleasure, it would take her to new heights.

She screamed their names, and the sounds echoed off the walls—sweet music to his ears.

He was tired of waiting.

Flicking his tongue back and forth, he drew her orgasm to the peak, and this time, he thrust her over the edge, loving her release as she came with abandon. There was no control inside her. Her body convulsed, her pussy spasming against his mouth. It was beautiful to see their woman completely vulnerable, trusting them in the most intimate way.

He took his time, and only when she couldn't handle his touch anymore, did he finally pull away.

Licking his lips, he relished her taste, knowing that he was going to love her pussy many more times.

"That was amazing," she said. Her hand went to her face, then stroked down her body as if calming the burn inside her. "I wasn't expecting it to feel that good."

"Do you want us to stop?" Damon asked. "Or would you like Caleb to take this sweet pussy? To make you ours?"

"There's no going back once you take my cock," said Caleb. "This. You and us. It'll be a done deal."

"Yes, yes, I want it," Opal said.

He stared at his brother, seeing Caleb's eyes flare.

Damon shook his head, hoping his brother saw that he didn't have the control to take her. He knew that Caleb wanted him to be the first, but Damon couldn't do it. Moving from between her legs, he climbed up toward her head, taking her lips.

"You've given me the sweetest gift letting me taste your pussy." He took possession of her lips. "Thank you."

Opal held onto the back of his head, pulling him down. Out of the corner of his eye, he watched as Caleb moved between her thighs.

Caleb stroked her pussy, making her cry out as he teased her sensitized clit.

"Are you sure?" Caleb asked. "Do you want this? You wanted to leave just a while ago."

Damon glared at his brother. This wasn't what he wanted.

When he'd come home, he'd seen the look in

Opal's eyes. She didn't want to go. He didn't understand why she'd try to leave, but he also didn't want to make it easy for her to go. He loved her, dammit, and the last thing he wanted was for her to leave.

"No, I don't want to leave. I want this, Caleb. I want to at least give it a try with you and Damon. Or until you get fed up with me."

This had Damon's full attention. Turning back to look at her, he shook his head. "We'll never get fed up with you." It was taking all of his control not to tell her how much he loved her, and scare her off.

"I know I'm not anything special. I've never been wanted before in my life. I know I can be a giant pain in the ass."

Caleb growled. "Have you been told this before?"

"Yes. It seems I was a burden to everyone. No one wanted me to be born. It's fine. I know I was a big mistake, and that people have been trying to get rid of me. It's fine."

And there he saw the problem.

Opal was used to being pushed aside. To not being wanted. Was that why she left the city? So they didn't get rid of her, and she didn't have to feel that rejection again? They may have lost everything, but before the accident, their family had been perfect. Damon couldn't image coming from a family that never really wanted him to be born. It could break a man. It had broken Opal.

Damon felt like an asshole. He'd ran because he thought she was like other women, too fickle to commit. She wasn't like other women at all. Opal didn't know what it was like to be wanted, to be loved unconditionally.

"You're not unwanted, Opal. Anyone who told you that bullshit in the past is asshole." Caleb moved between her thighs so they were both looking down at her.

Damon's heart pounded as he saw the tears shining in her eyes. He wanted to hurt every single fucking person who put that look there. This was why he didn't want to be part of society. Too many people had too much fucking power in hurting others, and he was over it.

There was no way he'd ever let anyone hurt their woman again.

"You're our woman, Opal. We'll protect you, care for you, and we'll give you everything your heart desires. All you've got to do is give us a chance to prove it. We're not like other people, and I promise you, we won't break your heart," Caleb said.

Once again, Damon and his brother were on the exact same page.

Chapter Six

Opal couldn't believe this was happening, that she'd had the nerve to give in to both brothers. It was impossible to say no to either of them. When they'd enveloped her by the fire, closing in on her with their rock-hard bodies, she was ready to commit—body and soul. She knew whatever they offered would be memorable, but not this damn good.

Damon's eager mouth had devoured her pussy, bringing her hurtling to the best orgasm of her life. When she'd pleasured herself in the past, it had always been a lackluster release of pressure, nothing more. With Damon suckling her clit and Caleb worshiping her tits, it had been too much. She exploded against Damon's tongue, her orgasm rocking every cell in her body.

Caleb looked down at her, his dark eyes hungry and intense. "I can't do this," he said. He stood up, then leaned down to effortlessly hoist her into his arms. His strength shocked her. "Your first time is going to be in a proper bed."

He carried her into his room. It was dim and smelled like his cologne. Damon followed behind them.

Caleb laid her down on his quilt, standing at the side of the bed. He raked his gaze over her nude body, the light from the fire outside the room giving enough light to see even her most intimate parts. A wave of insecurity washed over her. As she attempted to cover herself with the corner of the blanket, Caleb shook his head.

"I'm not sure why such a pretty thing like you is still a virgin, but I'm not complaining," said Caleb. "I don't take this honor lightly."

He braced one knee on the bed, the mattress creaking. When he ran the backs of his fingers along the outside edge of her breast, she shivered. Her pussy still tingled from Damon's attention, but her nerves of going all the way—with two men—stole some of her inhibitions.

"Relax, sweetheart." Damon sat at the head of the bed. "Caleb will take good care of you." It still shocked her that no jealousy existed between the two brothers. They must have a strong bond, something she knew nothing about. It relaxed her somewhat, gave her a sense of peace.

"Nothing to be afraid of," said Caleb. "Your body was made for fucking." He crawled over her body, his hard muscles flexing as he positioned himself above her. Caleb leaned down and kissed her on the lips, a gentle brush.

When he parted her thighs, his fingers circling her sensitive clit, she closed her eyes. These new experiences were addicting.

"I just love her tits," said Damon. "Big and juicy. I'll never get enough."

"Well, she's ours," said Caleb.

Opal may not admit it, but their possessiveness, their claim of ownership of her gave her a thrill every single time. Being wanted was a beautiful feeling, something she'd sought all her life. There was no way she'd walk away from this. She just hoped she hadn't pegged the brothers wrong—her heart couldn't take it.

Damon gave her breast a squeeze. She'd always felt her huge chest was a hindrance, making her look fat and sloppy, but both men seemed enthralled by her plus-sized figure. It gave her confidence a much-needed spike. There really must be someone out there for everyone, as the old saying went.

"I'm going to go real slow. For tonight," said Caleb. His finger slipped inside her pussy. She was so slick, there was no resistance. Then he added another, finger fucking her with two fingers. He was rough and gentle at the same time. "She's nice and tight, Damon. She'll feel like heaven around my cock."

"I don't think we've ever had a virgin, have we?"

"She'll be our first," said Caleb.

Heat built in her pussy, rising to fill her entire lower stomach. She felt so surrounded, so wanted.

"How's that feel, sweetheart?" asked Caleb.

She licked her lips in order to speak. "I like it."

He frowned. "I'm not trying hard enough, then. I want you to love it, want you begging me not to stop."

Opal swore she'd orgasm again and they hadn't really started. His shoulders were corded with muscle and she couldn't keep her hands to herself. Every time she touched him, he reacted, giving her a sense of power. The same he wanted over her.

He removed his fingers and replaced them with the smooth head of his cock. She gasped, uncertainty making her nerves flare. Damon made a hushing sound in her ear, before suckling her erogenous zone.

Caleb swirled his thick cockhead around her overflow of moisture, then pressed in an inch. Opal gasped, her nails raking his back.

"Easy, baby. I'm not going to hurt you." Caleb stopped dead, giving her a kiss to make her forget her worries. His short beard rubbed her cheek, reminding her of his virility. His dick throbbed inside her, hard and swollen, and she knew he was holding back for her sake. It felt amazing that he put her first, cared about her experience.

"Keep going," said Damon. "Just go slow."

She knew Damon was pent up and eager for his turn. It excited her, made her feel desirable. His older brother complied, pushing in bit by bit. She held her breath as her body adjusted to his size. She felt so full, so completely claimed.

"Shit, you're tight." His cock was fully seated. Her heart raced, the initial fear turning into a new dirty desire. She wanted to be fucked, to experience everything they had to offer.

****

She was only twenty-two. A virgin. And she was his.

Caleb gritted his teeth as he sank in deep. Her virgin cunt was hot and tight, pure heaven. It had been years since he'd bedded a woman, but Opal was worth the wait. He wanted to go slow, to make her experience gentle and painless. But having the busty beauty under him, her receptive body squirming and throbbing, was putting his control to the test.

Damon trusted him to lead, so he had to keep his head.

"How's that feel? Do you like my dick inside you, baby?"

"Y-yes," she stuttered. Her breathing was heavy, her eyes hooded. He had her just where he needed her, on the verge of begging.

He pulled back slowly and eased back in, savoring the feel of her pussy hugging every inch of him. "This is yours now. Whenever you want it," he said. "There's no other woman for me now."

Damon whispered in her ear. "Ours."

It sounded good to hear such happiness in his brother's voice. There was already life in their little cabin now that Opal was there. Things were changing for the better. Soon they'd have her ripe with their child. It wouldn't matter which seed impregnated her because they would all love the baby unconditionally. The rest of society could go fuck itself. All they needed was Opal.

Caleb began to work her, pumping his hips in a smooth rhythm, careful not to push too hard. She was hot and slick, driving him crazy. "Such a perfect little pussy," he said. He picked up the pace, dropping his head to kiss her on the mouth. From the corner of his eye, he could see Damon fisting his cock, anxious for a turn with Opal.

As much as he'd love to double-team her tonight, he'd save that for another day, but they wouldn't be able to wait long. There was nothing better than filling a woman completely full of cock.

"More," she said between kisses.

She'd be the death of him. "I'm trying to go easy for you, sweetheart."

Opal shook her head, thrusting her body up, trying to claim more of him. She was ripe and wanton, and he had no plans of letting her suffer. Caleb pushed up on his arms and got to his knees, tugged her up under the thighs. With his cock deep inside, her body arched up and on display, he got a good grip of her hips and gave her what she wanted.

He watched his erection pull out and disappear over and over, glistening from Opal's natural juices. Damon collected her arms above her head, holding her wrists in place with one hand. His brother engorged himself on her tits, moving up to her neck, loving every inch of her.

As Caleb fucked her, he circled her clit with his thumb, eager to feel her milk his cock.

"Caleb, I can't take any more."

"Let it all go. Don't hold back," he said. She was new to sex, and they had a lot more to show her. Opal needed to learn how to embrace her sexuality, to give in to the pleasure rather than fight it.

Damon pinched her nipples, and within seconds,

she called out, making the sexiest moans he'd ever heard. Her pussy clamped down hard, squeezing him mercilessly. Only once he'd emptied every last seed inside her did he pull out and move over for his brother.

They swapped places, and Opal was in such a post-orgasmic daze she didn't even seem to notice.

"Can you handle yourself?" asked Caleb.

"I'm good. So is she by the looks of it."

Opal twisted on the bed, her eyes closed, and her beautiful tits thrust up as she reached down to touch herself. "Ah, ah, ah. That's mine," said Damon.

He dropped down over her, supporting all his weight on his forearms. With one positioning thrust, he was fully inside her. She gasped and then squealed, wrapping her arms around Damon's shoulders. "Oh God, Damon…"

"Fuck, you feel like heaven."

Caleb crashed down beside them, watching his brother pound her lush body. The springs protested and the headboard pounded against the wooden planks. She was perfect for them. Their woman, their sex toy, the mother of their children.

****

Damon had been waiting for this moment. He'd had countless women in the past, but they'd meant nothing. What he needed and wanted was a woman to love, not just fuck. Opal was that woman.

Her pussy was nice and tight, Caleb's semen leaking out as he pistoned in and out of her cunt. He trusted his older brother to prime her right, and Caleb hadn't disappointed. Opal was eager for his cock, nipping and sucking his shoulder, prodding him with her heels. Both he and Caleb were well hung, and their little wild cat took both of them with no problem.

"I'm going to come again," she whispered next to

his ear.

"I could keep going all night long," he said. It was the truth. His body was at its prime, and after what felt like a lifetime alone with Caleb, he appreciated having a woman in his life. "But you go ahead and let go, baby. Come all over my cock."

"Damon…"

Her body stiffened, then she exploded. She convulsed, her pussy squeezing him. Her feminine panting was music to his ears. He combed his hand into her long, dark hair as his own orgasm barreled to the surface. Damon tugged her head back, wanted to see her face as he flooded her with his release.

"Fuck." The power of his orgasm surprised him. He was thirty-eight, not eighteen, but sex had never been like this.

She was such a beauty, her big green eyes glazed over, her pink lips swollen.

He knew all about lust.

Damon was in love.

****

The next morning, Damon woke up to unusual sounds. Living this deep in the wilderness for so many years made him sensitive to noises that were out of place. There was a trespasser.

He looked down on the floor. Bear was still asleep, but he was getting old, not as alert as he was years ago. At least the old dog had brought Opal to them. Caleb and Opal were still asleep on the bed, a comfortable warmth enveloping them. Damon reluctantly snuck out of the quilt, his feet hitting the cold wooden floor. He'd have to toss some logs into the fireplace to get the house warmed up before Opal woke up.

Damon already loved his new life. They'd make breakfast, learn more about their woman, and teach her about life in the wilderness. It was the lifestyle they learned from their parents, and nothing was more peaceful or rewarding.

He grabbed some socks and tugged on his jeans and flannel. Before leaving the house, he had a padded jacket, toque, and his rifle. The morning air was bitterly cold, a spray of snow falling down from the roof as he stepped on the porch. For a moment, he savored the silence and sight of the fresh snow on the evergreens. Then he heard the noise again.

He ventured off the steps, the deeper snow nearly reaching the rim of his boots. Damon followed the sound of hammering, and he knew damn well it wasn't animals. They owned the land far beyond what the eye could see, so people were on their land. Having Opal in their home made him more territorial than normal. He wouldn't tolerate drifters who could potentially be a danger to his woman. The type of men they'd caught before had been unsavory, the kind lacking any morals, hygiene, or human decency. The city wasn't the only place with a dark side. If they wanted to live their dream, they had to defend their land and their values.

He eventually saw color between the trees in the distance. Damon had his rifle cocked and ready as he closed in. He counted two, so he wasn't too outnumbered. It was stupid to come out this far without backup from his brother.

"Can I help you?" he said. Damon always tried to give people the benefit of the doubt, but he didn't give his trust easily.

The older man stood up straight and just stared.

Damon's peripheral vision caught the younger blond reach for something under a tarp. He turned and pointed his rifle. "Keep your hands where I can see them," he warned.

"I ain't doing anything wrong," said the blond, holding up his arms at the elbows. He had a missing front tooth and greasy hair. Damon had a bad vibe from both of them.

"That's real good," said Damon. "Why you both way out here in this weather?"

"Are you the law?" The old bastard was pushing his luck. "I thought this was a free country."

"You haven't heard of the *stand your ground* law? I find that real hard to believe," he said. "Considering this is *my* fucking land, and my gun is loaded, that's not looking good in your favor."

"We didn't know anyone owned this," said the blond.

He pointed to the quickest direction off his land. "As long as you move along, we won't have a problem."

Damon had evaluated everything in those few minutes. They were setting up a rudimentary campsite, and he wasn't sure why. He didn't like it. Blue tarps, propane heaters, a snowmobile with sled and supplies. He'd ask what they were up to, but they'd only give him lies.

He waited as they packed up their gear, leaning against one of the trees. They didn't mind the odd extreme camper or hiker traveling through. Even the backpacking groups like Opal had joined were tolerable. These lowlifes were up to no good, and he wanted them gone. If Caleb had been there, he wouldn't have been so gracious.

Almost an hour later, he was hiking back to the cabin. This time, he took the opportunity to enjoy the beauty—the birds singing, and sunrays trying to peek through the clouds. He hoped Opal could learn to love this land the same as him. It would take a while before his insecurities would die down. He was terrified she'd tire of their lifestyle, eager to get back to the thrill ride of living in the city. After having a sample of life with a woman, he couldn't go back to just living with his brother. It would destroy him.

Before his hand touched the doorknob, Caleb wrenched open the door. "I heard an engine. Where the fuck have you been?"

He knew Caleb wasn't pissed, just worried. They'd had run-ins with drifters, squatters, and loggers over the years. Sometimes things got ugly. Damon's greatest fear had always been losing his brother, and the fear went both ways.

"Some piece-of-shit squatters," he said. "I scared them off."

Caleb frowned, taking the rifle from him and clearing the chamber. He set it on the rack by the door. "You shouldn't have gone out alone."

"I know. There were just two of them, though."

"Doesn't matter. You know better," said Caleb.

Opal padded into the living room in just one of their oversized John Deere t-shirts. Her hair was lightly disheveled, but she looked like an angel.

"What's wrong?" she asked.

"Nothing, baby. You sleep okay?" Caleb diverted to a new topic. They were on the exact same page—they didn't want to scare her off. This was the honeymoon period, and she could either fall in love with living off the grid, or learn to resent it. It was important to make her experience a positive one.

Caleb already had the fire roaring, and Damon smelled oatmeal and the sweetness of brown sugar. He hung up his coat and set his boots on the tray.

"You're all wet," Opal said, reaching up to brush the moisture out of his hair. "You should get dry before you catch a cold."

He wrapped his arms around her waist and lifted her off her feet, giving her a little whirl around. She giggled, and the sound filled the room. "Yes, ma'am." It felt good to be cared for by a woman. Addicting, even.

Soon they'd claim her together, marking every inch of her as theirs. Now he just wanted to enjoy her, love her, protect her.

Chapter Seven

Opal had never been addicted to sex. Why would she? For so long she'd always been overlooked. No one wanted her. The fat girl. Pushing those thoughts aside, she watched as Damon and Caleb went about their business around the cabin. They were fixing things, preparing everything for the next lot of bad weather, and she sat down with a warm cocoa, watching quietly.

Not only that, she was desperate for them. Watching them was not helping her at all. In fact, her pussy was slick, and she hoped one of them initiated sex soon. She didn't want to come across as the woman so desperate she'd do anything for their attention. Biting her lip, she couldn't keep her gaze away for too long. As they mulled around the cabin, she wasn't even paying attention to what they were doing. They were both so in charge, so masculine.

"How are you doing, sweetheart?" Damon asked, coming to stand in front of her. He'd already dried off from his trek outside.

She'd also noticed his apprehension, and the fact they were securing more bolts to the doors, and locking up the window shutters. Something didn't feel right, but she wasn't about to ask them what.

"I'm doing good. Are you better?"

"Never been better before." He took a seat beside her, placing an arm across the back cushion. Leaning against him, she smelled the great outdoors, the freshness that always made her feel so good being around him.

Opal liked living in this cabin at the edge of the world, being away from the city, and now knowing how good it felt to have the brothers make love to her—she didn't want it to ever stop. They were both amazing men.

Sipping at her hot chocolate, she pressed her

thighs together, and offered him a smile. Damon's gaze had dropped to her legs, and his hand followed. He was so much bigger than her. He made her feel on the smaller side, which was crazy considering her size.

Slowly, Damon teased her thigh, moving up and down her leg, and each new sensation drove her crazy for more.

"I liked watching you come apart for me," he said, his lips trailing down her neck. She still held the hot chocolate in her hands, and she didn't know what to do. "Are you feeling sore?"

She felt a little sore but not so bad that she didn't want them both again.

"I'm fine."

His hand moved to cup her pussy, and she arched up against him, needing more. She'd never been so wanton in all of her life, but there was something about Damon and Caleb that made her forget herself.

"Let me take that from you," Caleb said, taking the mug before she spilled it all over herself. That wouldn't be good.

Damon eased her down on the sofa and moved her so that he sat between her thighs. She stared up at him, aware of the intensity in his gaze, and knowing exactly what he wanted. She wanted him more than anything else.

He teased the zipper of her pants down, and pulled them off. She wasn't wearing any panties, so the moment they were gone, she was naked from the waist down, apart from a pair of thick socks.

The position she was in also meant she was spread open for them both to see. It was oddly titillating rather than embarrassing.

"Her pussy is so fucking tight, so beautiful," Caleb said.

She turned her head to find him sitting on the coffee table, staring down at her. During her first week, she could have sworn Caleb hated her—now she knew better.

"I know it hasn't been long since we last had you, but I need you again," Damon said. He stroked the hard ridge of his cock, and all she wanted to do was touch him.

His hand moved between her thighs, and he teased her slit. His thumb stroked her clit before gliding down to press inside her. It wasn't enough and it only served to drive her crazy, making her need stronger. She didn't want him to stop. He pulled his thumb from her, and replaced it with his fingers.

He pumped two inside her, and she was so wet she heard the sounds of her own arousal.

She wasn't embarrassed though. Seeing the excitement on their faces, she didn't think for a second she could ever be. They were entranced, staring at her pussy with a feral need.

"I have to taste you," Damon said.

He slid down the couch and she gasped as his mouth latched onto her clit, sucking it inside. Closing her eyes, she arched up as his fingers continued to fuck her. He continued to tease her nub but his fingers moved from inside her. The dual stimulation brought her to new heights. The angle exposed her ass, and he trailed his fingers back, coating her anus with her own cream.

"One day, baby, we're going to fuck you here," Damon said, releasing her clit long enough to talk. The forbidden idea drove her need higher. They were so filthy, and she loved every minute of it.

"Please," she said.

"What do you want, baby?" Caleb asked.

She turned her head to look at him once again and

was surprised to see that he no longer had his pants on. His cock was already rock hard, and he was working it up and down. The tip leaking copious amounts of pre-cum, and she wanted him in her mouth, to taste him, to feel him explode on her tongue.

Licking her lips, she stared at him, not knowing what to say for him to understand what she wanted.

"You want my dick, baby?" he asked.

"Yes."

"You want it in your pussy?"

She shook her head.

"Where?" he asked.

Her cheeks heated, and it wasn't just because of arousal. This was new for her. It felt foreign to ask for what she wanted, especially when it was so naughty.

"I don't know what you want unless you tell me."

She cried out as Damon bit down, causing her a little bite of pain that took her breath away. The pleasure far outweighed the shock.

"Come on, Opal, I want to hear you say the words," said Caleb.

"I want to taste you," she said. Maybe she was afraid of rejection, that they'd think she was a whore for speaking her mind. She was wrong.

The smile he granted her was well worth any embarrassment she felt. He stroked her cheek. "That wasn't so hard."

He stood up, and moved toward her head. The tip of his cock grazed her lips, and she closed her eyes, sucking him into her mouth.

His pre-cum exploded on her tongue, and the taste of him only served to drive her need higher for him. His cock was hard, like silk over solid wood.

One of the brothers shoved her shirt up, and tore her bra from her, exposing her tits. She didn't care. With

Damon teasing her clit, and Caleb caressing her nipples, she was in sensation heaven.

She couldn't understand why any woman would turn these men down. They were both amazing, and right now, they wanted her.

Opal didn't want to think about what would happen when they were done with her. They wanted her, and were convinced they wanted to keep her, and so she'd bask in that, and deal with the fall out, if it even happened.

"Fuck, baby, your mouth is so fucking good," Caleb said.

She smiled around his cock, and stared up at him as he hit the back of her throat. It felt good to see him coming apart with her mouth alone.

****

Damon was already addicted to the taste of Opal, and also to how responsive she was. She was a dream come true. Just being near her and seeing the arousal building—he was a sucker in her hands. He wanted her, all the time. From the moment he saw her, looking so lost and hurt, he'd known he was never going to be able to let go. Caleb had proven difficult but even he was falling under her spell.

He watched as she sucked on Caleb's cock. Her lips looking so pretty as she worked it. His own dick pulsed with a fresh wave of need, and he wanted her lips on his. For a virgin, she was willing and quick to learn.

"Let's take this to the floor," Caleb said.

Moving the coffee table out of the way, they all removed their clothes, and the moment they did, Damon moved between her legs. Sliding his cock along her outer folds, he bumped her clit, watching her come apart with each move.

She moaned, thrusting her hips up to meet him,

and he couldn't wait for a single second more to feel her cunt wrapped around him.

With the tip at her entrance, he pushed inside her.

Damon gripped her hips, slamming all the way to the hilt, loving every ripple as her pussy tightened around him. Opal wrapped her fingers around Caleb's cock, taking him back into her mouth, and it felt so fucking right to be sharing her.

Running his hand up her body, he cupped her tit, pinching her nipple. He watched her response, getting acquainted with what she loved, and what seemed to drive her arousal higher. He wanted to spoil her with pleasure, and to show her what she could get by being loved by both of them.

Some women may not be able to handle two men, but Opal needed the two of them. She'd been alone for too long, and he hoped that it would help their cause to show her attention, to prove to her that this could be their happy ending.

Once she grew accustomed to his length within her, he paused, loving every second.

"How does she feel?" Caleb asked.

"So hot and tight. Her pussy was designed to be ours, Caleb." He pulled out of her, only to slam back inside. "How's her mouth?"

"Heaven." Caleb stroked her hair back from her face, and he saw the love his brother had for her. She wasn't a quick fuck. She was everything. The future.

It hadn't taken neither of them long, but these feelings were rare, and he wanted her desperately. He wanted this to work so damn much. The thought of being alone again was unbearable.

Driving inside her, he watched her suck Caleb's cock, and her tits bounced with each thrust. Holding himself inside her, he stroked his fingers along her slit, teasing her clit.

She'd been so close that he knew with only a few strokes she'd come apart, and she rewarded him. She thrust up to meet him at the same time as sucking Caleb deeper into her throat.

Watching her lose control was almost as good as feeling her cunt squeeze him like a fucking vise.

Everything was so fucking perfect.

Riding her hard, he filled her to the brim. As his release stirred, he didn't pull out. Filling her pussy with his cum, he closed his eyes, hoping that one of them got her pregnant soon so they could be a family.

He heard Caleb moan his arousal, and once they all reached their peak, the scent of sex filled the air. He didn't pull out of her straight away, and instead, moved beside her. Caleb moved to her other side, and Damon pushed some of her hair out of her face.

"A girl could get used to this," she said.

"I was hoping you'd say something like that," Damon said. He saw that there was still doubt in her eyes about their proposal. She must have been hurt so badly that no matter what either of them said, she still didn't completely believe them.

Caleb cupped her cheek, and turned her head toward him. His thumb caressing over her bottom lip. "Will you trust us?"

"I do trust you. I trust both of you." She looked at both of them, biting her lip. He loved it when she did that. Caleb tugged her lip out from between her teeth.

"Don't hurt yourself."

"Is someone on your property a bad thing?"

The change of conversation surprised both of them, but he didn't mind. She was uncomfortable with talking about her feelings. He'd noticed every single time they talked about it, she tried to find something else to say or at least change the topic.

"It's fine, and you don't have to worry about it," Caleb said, taking the lead.

It wasn't good. Damon had a bad feeling, and now that he thought about it, the look in those drifters' eyes haunted him.

"Let's go and get you cleaned up," Damon said, easing out of her.

"I'll go run a bath," Opal said.

He knew she was already in love with their large bath tub, and Damon watched her go. "We're not going to tell her?"

"Look, you saw two men on our land. Fine. I'm going to try and see if they were lost."

"They may not be lost, Caleb. You know the risks," Damon said.

"I imagine we've got more chance of being eaten alive by wolves and bears than we do being attacked by poachers or thieves." Caleb slapped him on the shoulder. "Don't worry about it."

Damon had lived with his brother his whole life, and right now, Caleb was trying to get him not to worry. It only meant one thing to him—Caleb was concerned but he was doing the older sibling thing where he tried to take the stress away from him.

Wasn't going to happen.

They were in this together, and he made a note to keep a gun in all areas of the house just in case of an attack. He wanted to be able to protect their woman.

****

With Opal asleep in their bed, Caleb let himself out the backdoor and stared out at the forest and the stars littering the dark sky.

Damon's instincts were rarely wrong, and he always made sure he listened. If those two men were a concern to Damon, then they worried *him*. He didn't know why the men were on their land, but it wouldn't be hard for them to kill them, and try to steal everything they had. He'd heard of it being done before, and no one had been any wiser. It was a tradeoff for living in the remotest part of the country.

He held a shotgun in his hands, and their dog sat waiting for whatever instructions he had. Nothing seemed out of place to him, but he wanted to be sure regardless. Tomorrow he'd go and check everything out. There was no way he'd leave Opal alone. He didn't want to leave Damon alone, either, but there wasn't much choice in the matter right now.

Their chance of a future together was in their grasp. Every passing second, he felt the walls around Opal's heart melting. She'd been hurt a lot, and he figured she'd suffered a great deal of pain. Maybe not physical pain, but words could still hurt.

She didn't trust them completely, nor did she trust their need for her, and he was fine with that.

They'd win her over, he had no doubt.

"If you think this is nothing, why are you out here right now?" Damon asked, coming up behind him.

"You need to go back to bed," Caleb said, without turning around.

"You can't keep doing this, Caleb. You can't keep shutting me out. We're in this together, and that means we fight together to protect what's ours."

Damon stepped out into the cold, and it pissed Caleb off. His father had always told him to take care of his brother, and he'd be damned if he'd let anything happen to him. It was the only thing his father ever asked of him.

"Get inside before you get cold. I need you to protect Opal."

"We'll protect Opal together. I'm not going to let you get hurt. It's not happening. You can be a pain in the ass about it all you want."

"What's going on?" Opal asked.

They both turned to look at her. She'd pulled on a large jacket, and Caleb cursed as he saw her shivering, her bare legs exposed to the elements. Her hair was tied up at the base of her neck, and it had gotten loose with sleep. He didn't know how it was possible, but she looked even sexier like this.

He also noticed she was still wearing large socks.

"Why are you carrying a gun?" she asked. "Is there an animal?"

"It's nothing."

She frowned. "I know I'm from the city but even out here, a shotgun is really out of place. What's going on? Is this about those men Damon was talking about?"

Neither of them spoke.

He didn't want to concern her, and he knew Damon felt that way as well. If she got a scare in her, she may want to leave and never turn back.

She snorted. "Look, I know you guys think I'm some helpless female."

"We did kind of find you hurt, alone, and helpless," Damon said.

"Yes, but I'm not. I'm strong enough to handle whatever you're going to tell me, so stop treating me with kid gloves, and maybe I can help."

Caleb stared at her. "You don't even think we're being serious about a relationship with you," he said.

"Caleb," Damon growled his name, but he didn't care.

The last thing he wanted right now was for Opal to be worried about her safety, and if that meant exposing her own fears, so be it. Out of the two of them, he wasn't supposed to be the nice brother. He was the practical one.

She stared at him. He expected her to look away but she didn't.

"You can't deny it," he said.

"I'm not." This shut any protest up from Damon. "I'm not used to this, okay. How do I know I'm not going to be passed over when you find another woman?"

Caleb shook his head. "That's not going to happen."

"I'm used to it, okay, and I know what you're trying to do," she said.

He raised a brow. "What am I trying to do?"

"You're trying to turn this on me when the real problem is those two damn people that trespassed on your land. I get it. I've done it my whole life." She held the coat around her even tighter. "Give me time," she said. "I'm not used to ... meaning anything to anyone."

Damon stepped up toward her, and Caleb felt so much pain for how she must have felt.

"We want you, Opal. We're going to take care of you for the rest of our lives."

Taking one last look at the forest, Caleb entered their home, locking the back door after their dog. "Let's go back to bed."

Chapter Eight

Opal didn't miss the city one bit. After over three weeks of roughing it in the wilderness, she had no regrets. And roughing it was a loose term. The brothers had a fully stocked panty, wood stockpile, generators, and everything to make life comfortable and secure. They had a little piece of heaven out here.

The brothers hadn't tired of her, and she actually believed they were growing closer to each other by the day. Caleb promised to teach her how to make maple syrup early in the new year, and Damon was going to show her how to keep bees. It was such a simple, beautiful way to live, and she never wanted things to change.

"It's chilly out there," said Damon after pushing open the front door. A gust of cold air rushed in the cabin, making the flames in the fire flicker. He hung up his toque and coat and ran his hands up and down his arms. "I've chopped enough wood for the week, so we're good." He winked at her and butterflies fluttered in her stomach. He always made her feel like a princess when she was used to being the ugly duckling growing up.

He leaned over and kissed her lips on his way to the kitchen. There was hot cider on the stove, the scent of apples and cinnamon infused in the air. She heard him getting a mug from the cupboard. Life was beyond comfortable, like she'd known the White brothers her whole life.

She heard them talking in the kitchen. "One of the solar panel batteries just died. We'll need a new one soon if we want hot water," said Caleb.

"The weather will only get worse. I can get to town on the snowmobile. They always have a stockpile of batteries."

Opal turned around on the sofa to see Caleb shake his head. "If anyone's going, it'll be me."

"I won't even argue with you," said Damon. "But if you go, get some stuff women need. Check out the general store, too."

"Way ahead of you." Caleb clapped Damon on the shoulder, then headed to the bedroom.

Once Damon was sitting next to her with his cider in hand, she waited for him to fill her in. When he said nothing, she couldn't hold back. "Do you think it's a good idea for Caleb to travel all the way to town in this weather?"

"This isn't bad, sweetheart. We're used to much worse." He took a sip of his drink.

"But he'll be alone. On just a snowmobile. What if something bad happens?"

He smiled at her. "Trust me, he can handle himself."

She exhaled, trying to feel the same confidence. Was he going for batteries just so she could have her regular hot baths? If so, she could certainly do without that luxury. Opal left the living area and slipped quietly into the bedroom. Caleb was just in his long johns, rooting in his drawers for clothes.

"Don't go," she said softly.

He stood to his full height, turning to face her. A long-sleeved thermal shirt dangled in his hand. "I'll be back tonight. Nothing to worry about." He cocked his head, staring at her with such intensity. Why did she feel her eyes well up with unshed tears?

Everything was so perfect it scared her. She didn't want to lose what she had with the Caleb and Damon. What if Caleb was killed like his parents? They were hardcore survivalists and still didn't make it during an animal attack. So many things could happen so far off the grid, especially with such cold temperatures.

Her life had been a struggle, and she wanted to grab hold of the brothers and never let go. She didn't want her fairy tale to end.

She shrugged. "I get nervous."

He came toward her, tossing his shirt on the bed. Caleb wrapped his arms low on her hips, holding her close. "What happened to you?" he asked. "You can't keep the truth locked up forever." Caleb wiped the moisture from her eyelashes.

He spoke slowly, his words filled with kindness. Caleb was right, of course. She couldn't expect them to open up while she closed off her darkest secrets. It was embarrassing to tell the truth.

"You wouldn't understand."

"Try me."

She swallowed hard. "You know I've never been with a man. That wasn't entirely by choice. Since I was young, I was told I was fat and would never amount to anything. That brainwashing really took its toll on me." Opal looked down, feeling shame. "Before I came here, I tried to take my life, to end everything. I really believed that death was the answer, the only way to escape the pain and depression."

He used a curled finger to tilt her head up. "Thank God you didn't go through with it because you've saved us, Opal. You're everything to us—you have no idea. Both of us were barely hanging on. Even though we had each other, we were empty and lonely. You changed all that."

She smiled at him, a tear slipped from her eye.

"And I couldn't have chosen a better women to get lost in our forest. You're gorgeous, baby. Perfect. Neither of us can get enough of you."

He kissed her forehead, then her lips, a soft

promise. She rested her head on his chest, closing her eyes and listening to the strong beat of his heart. "I don't need warm baths, just you," she said. "Don't worry about the batteries."

"It's more than just hot water. We need the batteries for just about everything, but I promise I'll be in bed with you tonight. Damon will be here to take care of you."

"Okay." She reluctantly agreed, but still didn't have a good feeling.

****

Caleb had found a treasure in Opal. Their beautiful, young virgin was a godsend. He sure as hell enjoyed spoiling her. It seemed they'd been waiting for her their entire lives. Now that they had her, they'd never let her go.

Since she'd finally opened up to him, they could move forward. He'd continue to show her how important she was, and just how beautiful he found her. All her insecurities needed to be laid to rest.

After dressing in multiple layers of thermal clothing, he packed a backpack with emergency supplies and loaded up the snowmobile. He strapped on a container of extra gas and secured a rifle to his load.

"I'm heading out. Lock up until I get back. Keep the fire stoked," he said.

"I know," said Damon. "You've told me ten times already. I'll take good care of Opal."

He knew his brother was capable. Caleb was just stalling, worrying about leaving them alone while he took a run to town. There were plenty of daylight hours yet, so it would be an easy ride to where he was going. The drive home may be a bit more precarious.

"Be careful," said Opal. She grabbed a handful of his overcoat. If felt good to have a woman waiting for him when he returned. He had purpose, something to look forward to in life. Soon she'd be pregnant with their child. He leaned down and gave her a quick kiss, not wanting to indulge himself too much. It would be all too easy to succumb to Opal and push his trip too late into the night.

"Promise, I'll be safe," he said. "Damon can break out the trunk of board games if you get too antsy."

He left the cabin, the cool breeze hitting his bare cheeks. The day was clear, so he was anxious to get going. If he never had to leave his property, he'd be a happy man, but they were reliant on supplies from town on occasion. He'd be sure to pick up some nice things for Opal. They weren't used to having a woman in the house, and they weren't prepared for her sudden appearance.

After getting comfortable in his seat and pulling his coat closed tight, he revved the engine and took off toward the path. It wasn't much of a path now, but he knew the direction well. He'd been using the trail since he was a kid, and they'd expanded it once they returned back from the city as adults.

He'd been through a lot with Damon. They'd been thrust into city life as teens when all they'd known was rural living. Their parents had been their rocks, their mentors, and then it was just the two of them. They manned up because they had no choice, but returning back to the family cabin was a given.

The past few years had provided a new problem. The fucking loneliness. It wasn't natural for a man to live life without a woman. That constant craving for sex, family, and love was overpowering. He'd started to give up on his own happiness, but he couldn't stand to see Damon suffer. His younger brother yearned for that connection only a woman could provide. But not just any woman would do, so they were still alone until Opal showed up.

Now Caleb was determined to make things work, to provide for his family and live the same life his parents had shown them by example.

He smiled to himself, feeling a sense of completeness he hadn't known for a long time. Things were finally coming together for the White brothers.

After traveling for hours, he pulled into a clearing to fuel up and give the snowmobile a break. He unfastened his leather side bag and pulled out his water bottle. As he drank, he studied the area. There were other tracks.

He stood up and stretched his legs, scouting the immediate area. Another snowmobile pulling a sled had been through today. Since it had snowed last night, he could pinpoint the time accurately. His father had taught him the art of tracking.

Caleb's concern grew as he tried to piece everything together. He hadn't passed anyone on the way, but there were multiple trails leading to his property. Were trespassers heading to their cabin? Was there another nature party getting underway? He didn't mind people hiking or snowmobiling on his massive property. But this far off the grid, it was difficult to tell friend from foe, so they preferred their privacy close to home.

He'd come too far to turn back now. He needed to get their supplies and get his ass home. Caleb was likely being paranoid. It was in his nature. Besides, Damon was a thirty-eight-year-old man and just as skilled in survival. He needed to stop treating his brother like a child.

****

"You've hardly eaten," said Opal.

They'd made a hearty vegetable stew earlier.

They peeled and cut the squash, potatoes, and carrots together. And the entire cabin was filled with the delicious scent as it simmered in the old cast-iron pot. He loved spending time with Opal, even to do everyday tasks. He'd never felt so comfortable with anyone besides Caleb.

He sat back in his chair, running a hand through his hair. "I think I did too much picking when we were cooking." Damon smiled at her, leaning over to tweak her nose. He didn't want to say he was worried about Caleb. His biggest fear in life was losing his brother.

"I told you," she teased. "You were eating faster than I could peel." She took another spoonful of the thick stew. He loved her innocence, and the fact she trusted them and didn't think anything could go wrong. Damon wanted to keep it that way. No sense for her to worry too. Hopefully, he was just blowing things out of proportion, and Caleb would walk through the door soon.

"I won't let it go to waste," he said. Living off the grid, they learned not to throw anything out, especially food.

"You're thinking about him, aren't you?"

He narrowed his eyes.

"You're not hiding anything from me. I know you're worried," she said.

"Everything will be fine. The town's a long ways out." He was trying to convince himself as much as he tried to convince Opal.

"He'll be home soon." She stood up and came around to the back of his chair. Opal began to massage his shoulders, her small hands working magic. After all the wood cutting he'd done earlier, his body was full of aches.

He moaned. "That feels amazing, sweetheart."

"You're too tense."

"Well, you're making me feel a whole lot better." He closed his eyes and savored the feel of her skilled fingers working his muscles. Damon loved the attention of a woman—his woman.

"Are you sure you're good with all this? Sharing a woman, I mean. It doesn't seem fair to either of you."

He scoffed. "You don't know me and Caleb. We need each other, but we need a family just as much. You're perfect for us, Opal."

She combed her fingers through his hair, and he couldn't help but moan.

"I think I'm ready then."

He turned in his seat. "Ready for what?"

She bit her lower lip, that sexy little habit she had when she was nervous. "What you've both been hinting at. I want you both to share me."

Was she saying what he thought she was saying? "We have been sharing you."

"You know what I mean."

Fuck, he wanted her to say it. "Not really, baby girl."

He patted his lap, and she sat down, her plump ass making his cock harder. "Really sharing," she said.

Damon couldn't hold back. He kissed her hard on the mouth. He lost himself right away, loving her taste and playful tongue. He slipped his hand under her shirt and ran his hand over her breast, giving her a firm squeeze. "Explain yourself. Tell me."

"I want you both to take me at the same time, not just taking turns."

His jaw clenched as he attempted to control his raging libido. "You going to let me take your ass, Opal?"

She nodded, her full lips parted.

He wanted Caleb home. Now. She was driving him crazy. He couldn't wait to double-fuck her, claiming her properly. "You shouldn't tell me these things when we're alone."

"I've been wanting to tell you both, but…"

Damon held her closer. "Don't be shy with us." He ran the backs of his fingers along her cheek. Fuck, he was in love with her. "I like it when you tell me what you want."

"I'm a bit scared, too."

"Don't you worry, baby, nothing to be scared about. We'll go nice and slow. Before long you'll be begging us to double-fuck you."

They kissed again, the urgency between them growing by the minute. Opal was addicting. "I feel safe with you," she whispered against his lips. Those few words meant the world to him, and he'd spend the rest of his life living up to her expectations.

"Thank you," he said, leaning back to get a good look at his woman.

"For what?"

"Not running away. For giving me and Caleb a chance."

"I have nowhere to run. This is where I belong," she said.

He gave her a kiss on the forehead and then urged her to stand. "You finish up your dinner. I'm just going to tarp the wood outside."

Damon stepped out onto the porch, closing the door behind him. He needed a breather in order to keep behaving himself. Opal drove him crazy, but he'd wait for his brother so they could share her properly.

It had been almost four hours since Caleb left for town. It was just a normal trip, one they'd made countless times, but he had a bad feeling. Ever since those squatters had been on his land, he had a sick sense in his gut. They'd had many trespassers, but these ones were shady as fuck.

He listened for anything out of the ordinary, but it was only the usual calming hush of the forest in winter. Damon looked up at the sky, a hint of color warning of the coming darkness. He took a deep breath, trying to push away his worries so Opal didn't get scared.

When he opened the door, Bear ran out, barking up a storm, disappearing into the woods. He grit his teeth, getting tired of the old dog acting out of character.

"Baby, I'm going to get the dog. I'll be right back."

He zipped his coat up and followed Bear's trail. Even though he was a pain in the ass, it would tear him apart if he got himself killed. Bear thought he was young and invincible, but it would only take one wolf or wild cat to show him otherwise.

The light from the house faded away the farther he walked. The forest was all dark shadows. He could hear Bear ahead, so he kept trudging through the snow. When he heard a gun cock, he froze. He knew the sound well, having grown up with all sorts of firearms.

He cursed under his breath, pissed off with himself. How had he not noticed someone in the underbrush?

"Where's your brother at?" asked the man. Damon guessed he was a heavy smoker, his voice raspy. The sound made his skin crawl.

"Gone. Who's asking?"

"Don't worry about who's asking. I need an answer or we'll have a problem. A real big problem."

Damon briefly worried if Caleb was already in trouble. His only comfort was believing his brother was safe if this asshole was asking about him. "He's gone to town. He could be gone for days."

"Fuck." The second voice came from his right. "I

told you something would go wrong."

"Shut up already," said the man with the gun. "We'll wait for him at the cabin. I'm freezing my ass off."

A jolt of fear raced through Damon's veins. He didn't care about himself, but Opal was alone in the cabin. These animals had at least one gun. How would he protect her from them? The possibilities terrified him.

"What do you want with us? Money? I'll go to town with you and give you the little we have." Damon needed to keep them away from the cabin at all costs. He didn't want to showcase how much money they actually had, but if it came to it, he'd give it all up for Opal. There was no price for a good woman.

"We're not going anywhere. Start walking." The first man shoved him, but he didn't budge. "Now!"

Damon's mind raced as he complied. He was built larger than most men, and he knew he could take down both men if he had to. But the unknown kept him from acting. He didn't know what kind of weapons they had, how willing they were to use them, and if there were more than the two of them on the property.

Why couldn't these lowlifes leave them alone? They lived off the grid because they wanted to get away from people and all the bullshit of society. All Damon knew was he'd take a bullet before he let either of these men put a hand on Opal.

Chapter Nine

Opal didn't like that Damon was taking way too long. She nibbled her lip and paced the length of the sitting room. Why did the men have to go and do these things? Running fingers through her hair, she tried to think about everything she'd been taught during her trip, the whole survival of the fittest. Moving toward the kitchen, she filled up the kettle, about to make another drink when movement out of the window caught her eye. She gasped. There were a couple of men shoving and pushing Damon along.

"Shit!"

Pulling away from the window, she ran to the bedroom where it was dark. In the past few weeks, she'd found the boards that were creaky. Moving toward the window, she saw Damon walking so slowly. Every now and then, someone shoved him, trying to get him to move faster. There was a small gap in the window, and she could hear them.

"What the fuck do you guys want?" Damon asked. "We don't have any money here. We just live a simple life."

"Not interested in your simple life, pal." Another shove, and this time Damon fell to the snowy ground. She knew how sturdy he was, and in control, and knew instantly that he'd done that on purpose. No one could bring down a mountain like Damon.

He was slowing them down. Did he want her to escape? What did he want?

"We've got nothing of any value in there, so why don't you boys just move along," Damon said.

"When did your brother leave?"

"A couple of hours ago. He'll be back soon," Damon said. "Maybe not."

Caleb had been gone a lot longer.

"Anyone else in the house?"

"No."

He didn't want them to know she was there. God, she didn't want to imagine what that could mean. Her heart raced as she envisioned the horrific scenarios.

"Let's go and take a look."

Seconds later, she heard the door bang open, and she moved toward the bedroom door, slowly closing it. Looking around the room, she found a couple of guns. She was very much aware of how much her two men loved their guns. They wouldn't be anywhere without them. Why didn't Damon have a gun with him?

This was not what she was prepared for. Guns, danger, threats. Sure, there was lots of that in the city, but she wasn't the kind of woman that got exposed to this kind of threat. When the streetlights came on, she was usually safe in her little apartment.

They were out in the middle of nowhere here. Even if she was to put a call through to local law enforcement, it would be hours before they made the trip up here, and those men could have killed Damon by then.

She was surprised they hadn't killed him already.

Tears filled her eyes, and she sat on the bed, holding onto her stomach.

Everything will be okay.

Caleb will come.

Until then, she needed to stay alive, and to keep Damon alive as well. Staying in the house wasn't going to work. Staring at the window, she knew she had to get to safety. If she could get out of the house, and find Caleb, or at least intercept him, she could give him a heads up, and give Damon some time.

Shit! Everything was going to hell, and it was only because Caleb had to go and get some supplies.

Hot water wasn't worth losing either of them.

She loved them, dammit!

Even as she thought it, she covered her mouth at her own revelation.

She loved Caleb and Damon White. The two bushmen who'd saved her. Not only had they saved her, she'd fallen hard for each of them. This crazy life that they had set up for themselves, she wanted it more than anything.

To be their woman, to share each of them, to give them both everything they desired. To have a family with them. That was what she wanted so much, a family of her own.

She found a bag that she could carry on her shoulders, and in it she placed a gun and ammo that she found in the bedroom closet.

"I have to be the kind of girl that falls in love with men who have a thing for guns." She whispered the words, and once everything was in the bag, she heard movement outside of the bedroom.

"You know, are you two faggots or something?" one of the men asked.

She quickly dived into the closet, and closed it just as the door to the bedroom opened. "Two men livin' alone is sure a weird thing. Do you fuck each other?"

"We're brothers, asshole," Damon said.

"You're not in a position to talk back to me." The man flicked the light on and Opal held onto the bag she was holding a little tighter.

Her heart pounded inside her chest.

"You want to see what we've got?" Damon asked, entering the room. "We've got nothing to hide."

"Two brothers, and no woman here at all."

"No woman here," Damon said.

From the crack in the door, she noticed his gaze

kept looking around, and she wondered if he was looking for her. There was a gun trained on him. She stayed perfectly still even as the man stood in front of the closet. She closed her eyes, knowing that if they caught her, they'd hurt her and Damon would die trying to save her.

"I bet you fuck each other to pass the time. No woman, living in the middle of nowhere, it takes all sorts to deal with those urges."

Damon didn't say a thing. He simply shrugged.

"Come on, I'm bored, and I'm hungry."

They left the bedroom, and she waited several minutes to make sure they weren't coming back. She didn't know why they were waiting, only that they were. Opening the closet, she moved toward the window, easing it open. Caleb had shown her an escape route in case of any danger. Holding on to the frame, she eased out, shuffling toward the end of the raised window ledge. At the time, she'd moaned to Caleb about the practice. She hated heights, and would do whatever it took to avoid them. The raised bungalow wasn't too high, but high enough. When she next saw Caleb, she was going to hug, kiss, and tell him exactly how sorry she was. The moment her feet touched ground, she wanted to kiss it, but didn't waste any more time. Moving toward the forest where she saw Caleb leave, she ran, trying desperately to follow the tracks. She didn't have much choice but to pull out her flashlight. She only hoped none of the men would see her and that she was far enough away from the house.

****

Caleb didn't like the bad feeling he was getting. After loading up his truck, he glanced around the parking lot, seeing that it was surprisingly quiet. Taking the snowmobile back to the bay, he saw Rich, one of the guys that helped out at the guide parties.

"You okay, Rich?" Caleb asked.

Rich looked up from typing on his cell phone. "Yeah, yeah, surprised to see you out so late. We've got a bad storm heading our way."

"I heard. I was just grabbing a few supplies."

"Could you send our apologies to Opal? There's a gift basket at the office, complete with women's supplies, cards, and also a couple of coupons. I can't believe the guys forgot to pick her up."

She couldn't afford the excursion flight, but he couldn't understand how they forgot the one who stayed behind.

"Damon found her, so no worries at all. She's perfectly fine." He looked around again, wondering why he felt uneasy. "I wanted to ask, do you have another guide tour or something wandering through the forest?"

Rich snorted. "Not since Opal's one. We've had to cancel the last three tours due to bad weather. Even though a bunch of people want to get back to nature and see what they're missing, we have to do everything by the book, and if we can't guarantee safety, we can't allow it to happen."

"Huh," Caleb said. He didn't like that. "Has there been any word on anyone being up near my end of the forest?"

Rich rubbed at his chin. "No. We've had a couple of tourists coming around, but that's not unusual. They've asked a bit about your land. We've not said anything about anything, though. Is everything okay?"

"Yeah, I've got to be heading back." He said his goodbyes and rushed toward his vehicle. No one talked about his land, and he didn't like the bad feeling he was having either.

Those tracks he found were fresh, as in a couple of hours fresh. Some person was wandering around on his land, and if it wasn't someone from the tours, then he wanted to know who the fuck it was.

Putting his foot to the floor, he rushed out of town, and was already on his way home. The time seemed to stand still for him. He'd been gone way too long, and he tried to think of all the reasons why someone would want to step foot onto his barren land, or even why they were asking about it. They had no gold or mining of interest. Just their little cabin and thousands of acres of nature.

Nothing came up, and that fucking pissed him off. Slamming his hand against the steering wheel, he was ready to kill.

Damon and Opal were at home all alone. They were the only two people who mattered to him. Damon could take care of himself, but he also wasn't as good when it came to shooting shit as he was. He didn't care about hurting someone and asking questions later. Damon needed a good reason to hurt someone. This was just one of the many reasons that made them different.

The drive felt longer than normal and he was trying to hold his shit together. All the time he couldn't help but think that Opal and Damon were in danger. The past three weeks had been pure heaven. He couldn't recall a time when he'd been so happy. Having Opal in his arms was the dream he always wanted.

He'd give anything to share his life with that woman.

Loving her came naturally to him. Seeing her smile was a blessing, and he couldn't lose her.

"You don't know anything is wrong. It could all be fine, and you're worrying for nothing."

His father had told him to always trust his instincts, that when he needed them most, they'd help him survive.

Time passed, and with it, his anxiety grew.

As he made his way through the forest, going along the regular path, he paused as a flashing light waving up ahead distracted him. Fucking trespassers.

Back and forth it moved, and he came to a stop. Reaching into his glove compartment, he grabbed his .44 Magnum. After stopping the snowmobile, he climbed off, keeping the motor running. Raising the gun in front of him, he waited.

Someone rushed toward him, and then gasped.

The instant he saw it was Opal, he lowered the weapon and exhaled the breath he held.

"What the fuck are you doing out of the house?" he asked, stepping toward her.

She threw herself into his arms. She was panting hard. "Some strange men came. I don't know who they are. I hid and they have Damon. They asked about where you were. They had a gun. I didn't know what to do. I needed to warn you. I left Damon … shit … I left Damon all alone."

He cupped her face, and he saw the fear and panic in her eyes. "Calm down, baby, I'm right here." She wasn't dressed for the weather. He didn't like any of this.

"We've got to go back. We've got to go and help Damon. I can't believe I left. It seemed like a good idea at the time. What if they've shot him or something? Oh no."

He slammed his lips down on hers, doing anything he could to distract her. The panic rising up inside her wouldn't do either of them any good.

"Did they see you?" he asked.

She shook her head. "I climbed down the escape route you showed me. I was so wrong about that. It is the best plan to have. Thank you." She kissed him back.

"They didn't shoot Damon on sight?" he asked.

"No. I don't know why they're there either, Caleb. They seemed interested in what you guys did. Where *you* were. Damon told them you were only a few hours out. I don't … everything's a blur right now. I can't think."

Her hands were shaking.

"You did good coming to me, Opal. You're going to have to stay—"

"No, you're not leaving me behind. I can't … no, I'm coming with you. I've got to be there for Damon. I have to know he's okay. I'm sorry. I can't just leave like this." She pulled the bag off her shoulders. "I've got guns and ammo. I figured you'd need them. Please don't make me stay here."

She looked at him with her big eyes, and he was a goner. There was no way he was going to be able to say no to her, and he cursed.

"Get on."

He didn't know what he was going to do, but whatever it was, saving his brother was high on the fucking list.

****

Damon was going to kill the guy who kept the gun trained on him. He didn't like being on the end of something that could kill him. If this guy slipped, then his face was going to get blown off, and that wouldn't be pretty.

"You know, I'm starting to think you guys have a bit of a crush on me and my brother," he said.

He didn't know their names and so he referred to them as Asshole and Bigger Asshole. Bigger Asshole was the one who held the gun on him, and it was really pissing him off.

"Shut up," Asshole said.

"I don't get it. I mean, come on, guys, you're

holding me at gunpoint right now. We've been waiting for what, an hour? What exactly are you wanting? Because it's clearly not my death. You wanting my ass?" He stood up, bent over, and showed it to them.

"Sit the fuck down, queer!" Bigger Asshole growled the words, and Damon couldn't help but chuckle. These guys had a laundry list of issues.

Caleb had warned him many times that he had too big of a mouth, and one day it was going to get him killed. He wasn't going to go down without a fight though.

Opal had been hiding in the closet, and he'd also heard the shuffling of her getting out of the window. He and Caleb had practiced it enough that they knew the sounds. Their parents had done the same thing with them as kids in case of fire or predators.

He hoped she'd gone to find Caleb. He also hoped that she hadn't gotten lost in the forest. That was the last thing he needed right now.

Everything was riding on her finding Caleb.

When she did, and his big brother saved the day, Caleb was so going to kick his ass for going out without some kind of weapon. It was a rule they lived by, but he only expected to chase after the dog for a minute. It proved he could never be too cautious.

No one was going to berate him more than himself, and right now he was so fucking pissed off. He'd put Opal at risk because of his stupidity.

"You know, you seem to have a real issue with homosexuality. You ever thought about talking to someone about that?" he asked.

Again, no one said anything.

Asshole came out of the laundry room, and he held a pair of Opal's thongs. Dammit. "I thought you said there was no woman here?"

"They're not a woman's, they're mine." He couldn't think of anything else to say, and he was cursing himself a million times over right now. "Let's be real for a second, and forget my weird taste in lingerie. Let's talk about why you're on my land. You've got me here, in my very own home, at gunpoint. Don't you think that should warrant … I don't know … an explanation?"

"You live in a beautiful place," Asshole said. "There's a lot of land, a lot of trees. You know, a lot that can be … done with the place."

Damon stared at him as everything clicked into place.

He smiled. "Wow."

Bigger Asshole frowned. "What's wow about it?"

"Let me guess, you're two hired thugs that have been given the job of taking my brother and myself out of the equation. This land belongs to us. Our family. We're dead, we've got no one to hand it down to, and so it goes up for sale."

"Where it will sell for the cheapest price, and make a shit load of money."

Their uncle had warned them both about certain land purchases, and how companies would do anything to make a quick buck. The logging industry was ruthless and in desperate pursuit of old-growth land.

Sitting back in his chair, he stared at the two men. "I don't get it. You can kill me now. What are you waiting for?"

Before they could answer, the sound of an engine out front had Damon cursing.

What the hell had happened to Opal?

His heart raced, and from the position he was sitting in the living room, he couldn't see who had arrived.

This was not how he wanted his life to end. He

didn't know why the two men hadn't killed him, unless they just wanted them both to suffer. Whatever the reason, he couldn't let them attack his brother.

Caleb needed to get out of this alive. He'd be able to care for Opal.

He glanced around the room, looking for a weapon. His brother always stashed them around the house. When someone knocked at the door, he used the distraction to his advantage.

Running his hands across the cushions, he moved toward the end of the sofa, and leaned down. Now that he knew what the hell was going on, all they needed to find out now was who the company belonged to, and also, who hired them.

Reaching beneath the sofa, he felt the edge of the gun strapped underneath. Bigger Asshole chose that moment to look at him.

"What the fuck are you doing?"

He didn't answer.

"Get back in your chair or I'll tie you to it!"

The door swung open as he sat back down.

"Damon, baby, I'm home." The sound of Opal's voice from the front porch had him gritting his teeth.

What the fuck was going on?

"I thought you said there wasn't a woman here?" Asshole said.

Before he could say or do anything, Asshole opened the front door.

"You're not Damon."

"I'm Damon's friend," he said. "Who are you?"

He heard Opal giggle. "You're Damon's friend? I don't think he has a lot of friends. Except these."

He didn't know what she did but from the moan that came out of the other man, he had to figure it was something sexual.

"Opal, what the fuck are you doing?"

"Damon, baby, are you not coming to the door to invite me in? It's our special time, and you know how I love it when you're all mean and rough to me. Where's Caleb? Doesn't he want to join in the fun?"

He had to be in some kind of fucking dream right now. He didn't have a clue what was going on.

First, he'd never heard Opal speak like that, and second, she knew the trouble they were in. With a gun trained on him, he was having a harder time thinking than normal.

Had she found Caleb?

Did they have a plan?

Dammit!

Chapter Ten

Opal's heart was beating like a freight train. She had to keep up a cool exterior even though she felt like crumbling to pieces. The men inside the house were worse than she imagined—dirty, savage, and cold. The one who answered the door had a beer gut, a filthy beard, and yellow teeth. It took all her resolve to follow through with their plan of seduction. She wanted to be sick.

"We all like to have fun, little lady. Come on in from the cold." The drifter held the door open for her to enter. She cautiously stepped inside. Damon was sitting in a chair, not moving to get up. The other drifter stood awkwardly to the side, trying to hide his rifle, but she noticed the barrel peeking out from behind his leg. She put on her best acting job and pretended to be oblivious to everything.

"It's nice and warm in here," she said.

"Sure is," said the man with the gun. "You come here often?"

"When I feel like having a little fun. The men in town are too boring for my taste. What about you two? I haven't seen either of you before, and I'm sure I'd remember if I did." She pretended to flirt, and was shocked when they actually seemed to believe the lies coming out of her mouth.

What she needed to do was stall. To give Caleb enough time to save them all. He had a plan to make things right, but he needed a distraction and as much time as she could give him.

She just didn't want him to take too long. What if one of these pigs expected her to follow through on her promises? The thought of either of them touching her made her want to retch, but she'd do whatever it took if it meant saving Damon's life.

"You weren't supposed to be here," said Damon through gritted teeth. He definitely didn't want her there.

"Well, I decided to visit earlier. You should be happy."

"Damn straight you should be happy," said the big man. "Hell, I thought you was gay."

"Three's a crowd," said Damon, looking over at the two men.

The big man shook his head. "That's not up to you, is it? I think our guest is more than happy to see us."

"It is kind of exciting," said Opal. "I like all the attention."

The older man with the gut stepped closer, and she had to stop herself from moving backwards. "You're a pretty one. What's your name, gorgeous?"

"Rose," she lied.

"Can we be your friends too, *Rose*?"

Opal walked around the room, trying to take in the weapons and get a handle on the situation. Damon wasn't tied up, so he could act if necessary. She'd rather him sit in his chair than risk getting shot.

"If you be good boys like Damon." She leaned over and kissed Damon on the lips. Then whispered in his ear. "Caleb's outside. Don't do anything stupid."

"Shit, don't compare us to him. You're in for the time of your life. A big girl needs a capable man." From the corner of her eye, so noticed the closer man set his rifle on the dinette table. The butt of a gun peeked out from the waistband on the big man near the door. She had to be careful.

Last month she was working her minimum wage job, falling asleep alone in her shitty little apartment. She'd been one swipe of a blade away from ending it all.

Now she had so much to live for.

Everything became clear. Thrust into this life-

and-death situation put everything into perspective. She belonged with Damon and Caleb. They healed each other, broken pieces brought together to make a whole.

Thinking she could lose Damon or Caleb gave her the realization that she wasn't just in lust with the men, but in love. They'd changed everything, gave her hope, love, and a new reality. Damon and Caleb were the first men, no, first people, to make her feel she had value. They made her feel special when she'd been drilled with negativity her entire life. The brothers were her treasure, and she couldn't afford to lose them.

They spoke about family, and an heir they could raise with the same homestead lifestyle. She wanted the same thing. Opal never imagined herself as a mother, but they'd put that idea in her head, and there wasn't anything she wanted more than to give the brothers the baby they dreamed of having. She'd give their son or daughter the love she'd never been shown. Opal would love it unconditionally.

"You want a drink, honey?"

Opal bit her lip. She wasn't a drinker, but the woman she was playing probably was. "Sure. It'll help warm me up."

"Hey, Huckleberry, where you keep your stash?"

Damon frowned. "We don't drink."

"Ah hell," said the big man. "Go get me the moonshine from the sled."

The other man grumbled as he zipped up his overcoat and headed to the door. She liked the odds now … if only guns weren't involved.

Opal shrugged off her coat when the man started looking suspicious. She didn't need to plump up her cleavage when her cups were always overflowing. He stared at her tits and licked his lips.

"What are you doing?" asked Damon.

"You shut up," the man shouted. "She's done with you."

Caleb needed more time. She ran her hands through her hair, sashaying around the room. "If Caleb gets back, there'll be four of you and one of me." She bit her lip provocatively.

"Thems good odds," he said. The old bastard was practically drooling. "Come over here."

She swallowed hard and walked toward him, glancing to where his gun was kept. "What is it?"

"How about a little kiss?"

"What about my drink?"

"It's coming. Don't you worry about that. Trust me, you don't need liquor to warm you up." His twisted smile made her shudder. He reached for her, hooking his arm around her waist to pull her closer. She leaned back, desperate to keep away from him. His body odor was overpowering and she felt alone and helpless.

Damon and Caleb were worth the sacrifice.

****

He felt like a caged beast, pacing back and forth in his mind, waiting to strike. Opal said Caleb was outside. His brother was capable, but Damon refused to sit back and let his woman get manhandled. Growing up, Caleb had always been stronger and able to get things done. Damon had a soft streak and would rather keep the peace than speak his mind. All bets were off when it came to Opal.

Damon had played nice, allowing these assholes to force him back to the cabin in order to give Opal time to escape. Then he'd sat on the chair with his mouth shut, biding his time. The second that nasty fuck put his hands on his woman, Damon was out of his seat with his arm around the fucker's neck faster than anyone could react.

"Damon!"

Opal cupped her hands over her mouth and nose, fear blazing in her eyes.

"It's okay, baby," he said. "See that gun on the table? Bring it to me."

She did as told while he increased the pressure on the man's neck. His coarse beard prickled Damon's forearm. At any minute his buddy could walk through the door, so time wasn't on his side. Luckily size was.

The bastard started to gurgle, clawing at Damon's arms.

"Get the gun from his belt," he said, keeping his voice calm and controlled. He didn't want Opal more spooked than she was. Seeing her vulnerable and scared turned something primal on inside him, something fierce and protective. She was more than sex and companionship. He loved her, needed her, and wanted to build a family together. Her safety was his personal responsibility.

Once the man was stripped of his weapons, Damon's desire to kill was still strong. He wanted to gut the bastard for touching Opal and trying to steal from them.

"Damon, you could have been hurt," she said, touching his shoulder from behind.

He shook his head. "Nothing can kill me, sweetheart. Get me that twine hanging by the door."

When she gave him the twine, he got the old man bound securely to the wooden chair. "Not one fucking word out of you, got it?"

He nodded.

Damon exhaled, the rush of adrenaline washing away. He turned to face Opal. She looked pale and shaken. He held out his arms, and she didn't hesitate to rush into his embrace. Damon held her tight, holding her head to his chest, loving the feel of her soft curves against his hardness. He never wanted to let her go. Her quiet sobbing shook her body. "Everything's going to be okay. I'm here, baby. I'll never leave you."

She looked up at him, her eyes shimmering with tears. "Promise?"

"Promise," he said. "The White men don't take commitment lightly."

They'd moved to the edge of the world it seemed, but they couldn't escape trouble. Why couldn't people leave them the fuck alone?

When she'd calmed, her breathing regular, he leaned her back. "Where's Caleb?"

"He said to distract the men for a little while so he could figure things out."

"You did real good. He wouldn't have sent you if he thought they'd hurt you," said Damon.

"I know, but I'm worried about him now."

The other drifter still hadn't returned with the moonshine, so something could be going down outside. He grabbed the handgun, checked to be sure the clip was full, then placed it in Opal's hands.

"What? No."

"Like this," said Damon, training the gun on the man in the chair. He maneuvered her fingers and hands in the right position. "If he moves, shoot him."

It was time to finish this, to take back their home and their land. Damon peered out the windows, then quietly slipped out the front door.

The air was frigid, the outdoor floodlight creating a cone of light over the snow out front. It sparkled like a million diamonds. He gritted his teeth, pissed off that these criminals were trying to steal his peace and happiness.

He listened for sounds, but only the hush of the evening and low howl of wind could be heard. It was too quiet for comfort. Damon trudged through the heavy snow along the side of the house, creeping into the shadows. He saw the outline of their snowmobile and sled, but no sign of the other man.

Where the fuck was Caleb?

When he heard the brush of fabric behind him, it was too late. The bottle came down full force over his head, the bitter sting of hard liquor raining down over his face. He dropped to his knees, his head swimming. He fought to keep conscious, but he couldn't get his bearings long enough to focus. Damon slipped in and out of a dream-like state, memories from the past playing in his head.

He remembered the day Caleb had found him drunk at sixteen. Damon needed to dull the pain of losing his family, and alcohol seemed the easiest choice.

"You think this is the answer?" asked Caleb.

"I don't care."

"Well, you fucking need to care. You're all I have, Damon!"

"I'm not strong like you. I have feelings. I just want to forget everything."

Caleb grabbed him by the scruff, bringing his slumped body straight. "I'm not strong. I'm a mess, Damon. But I keep going on, and do you know why? Because of you. I'm being strong for you!"

He looked at his brother. Really looked at him. In all his pain, he never considered his older brother and the same loss he'd endured. Damon had been selfish, only considering himself.

"What do I do?" Damon asked, feeling like a shell of his former self.

"You keep going. One day at a time. We'll do it together," said Caleb. "But no more drinking. Understand?"

His faculties slowly returned as reality began to come into focus. Damon brought a hand to his head, and he wasn't sure if the wetness was booze or blood. Maybe both.

****

It was time to get shit handled. Caleb cocked his rifle, the muzzle right at the man's temple. "Drop the bottle and step back. Nice and slow, asshole."

He dropped the broken bottle neck and put his hands halfway up as he complied. "You must be Caleb."

"You know my name. That doesn't bode well for you. I like my privacy."

"Nothing personal. Just a job."

"You fuck with my brother, it's personal," said Caleb. "Stand there. Don't move."

He reached down and helped Damon to his feet. His brother was a brick house, so to see him swaying on his feet showed how hard he'd been hit on the head. "I'm sorry, Caleb. I won't drink again."

He frowned. "Damon, snap out of it." Caleb gave his brother a little slap on the cheek. "Where's Opal?"

Hearing her name seemed to bring some sense back to his brother. "Opal. She's in the house." Just then a shot rang off inside the cabin.

"Fuck." Caleb grabbed the arm of the trespasser and pulled him along as he raced to the front of the house with Damon. Once on the wraparound porch, he shoved the trespasser into his brother's arms. "Here, hold him."

Caleb got his rifle at the ready before kicking the front door in. He froze in place when he saw the fat bastard lying on the floor and Opal still holding a gun with her arms outstretched. It was an eerie scene, but he still felt the flood of relief seeing Opal alive and well.

He set his rifle down and took the handgun from her, prying her fingers apart one by one. "Opal, look at me." She was in shock, her body rigid and eyes glazed over. "Opal, it's okay now."

Caleb cupped her face in his hands and kissed her lips.

"I shot a man."

"I'm sure he deserved it." He kissed her again before leading her to the sofa to sit down. She was shaky and needed time to come to grips with the horror of what she'd been through.

Caleb used his boot to roll the body over. The pig had a bullet wound to the shoulder, but he'd live. At least Opal wouldn't have to live with any guilt that she was a murderer.

"How'd he get out of the chair, baby?" asked Damon.

"He had a pocket knife. When he stood up I just shot him without thinking. I didn't mean to. I'm sorry," she said.

"Are you kidding? I'm glad you did it." Damon shoved the other man to the floor beside his friend, but nearly toppled over himself. He was covered in blood, his face stained red.

"Damon, sit with Opal. You have a concussion and you've lost a lot of blood."

Another shot rang off, making Opal squeal. Caleb nodded, pleased with his handwork as the second man fell down and grabbed his knee. "That's my insurance policy. Neither of you move a fucking muscle until the cops get here."

He got on the phone and called the cops. It would take them at least a couple hours to get to their neck of the woods, but they had the time. There were only two trespassers, so now that they were debilitated, Caleb was in control again. That was the last time he made a town run on his own. He'd brought back enough supplies and batteries to get them through until spring.

"Who hired you?" he asked, aiming his gun at the skinny man's good knee.

"I don't know. It was just some guy at the dock. He was paid a pretty penny to get rid of you two. Said he'd give us a thousand dollars if we took care of it for him."

"Why us?"

"I don't know."

Caleb twisted the end of his rifle into the fresh wound. The man squealed like a pig. "You better know something."

"Something about trees! Fuck, we just wanted the easy money."

"If you were willing to kill two innocent men for cash, then you both deserve to rot in jail for the rest of your lives."

It was the damn loggers. They'd been trying to buy off their land since their parents were alive. Since they'd moved back home over a decade ago, they'd been harassed into selling off their land countless times. It only served to piss them off.

No price was good enough. This was their home, their land, and they wouldn't be bullied into giving up their legacy.

Caleb set his weapons aside and hogtied both men securely.

Opal left for the bathroom and came back with a damp washcloth. She wiped Damon's face, taking gentle care of him. He watched for a moment, realizing they all had the same agenda, and their mutual love for each other was growing stronger. Everything didn't have to fall on his shoulders because they were a family, a team.

He tossed a couple more logs into the fireplace and continually checked the windows to ensure there weren't more of them lurking around. Caleb thrived on the responsibility of caring for Opal and Damon. It gave him purpose. He'd always loved his younger brother, and now he had a woman in his life. That missing element they both desperately needed.

"I'm going to hook up the new battery, then I'm running you a bath," he said to Opal. "After what you've been through, you need to relax."

She shook her head. "I'm okay. Damon's the one we need to worry about." Opal continued to wipe the blood from his face and neck.

"No arguments, sweetheart. I'll take care of both of you."

Chapter Eleven

It had to be the most frightening night of her life, but the cops came and handled everything. They dealt with the men, taking them away in cuffs, and Caleb and Damon had a lawyer come up to the cabin. Opal didn't understand a word of what was being said, but figured it was important, seeing as her men seemed to understand.

A company had paid to have them killed so they could take the land and start cutting down the surrounding forest. There was a lot of money to be made, and seeing as the Whites hadn't sold, the logging company wanted them out of the way. She'd never seen a lawyer look so excited at the thought of going head to head with a large company before, but he told Caleb and Damon not to worry about a thing. There was a lot of evidence and the crazy trespassers were ready and willing to spill their guts to the cops.

She had given her statement, and from there, nothing else had happened, which she didn't mind. It was better to forget that nightmarish day and focus on the positive.

One good thing came out of the crazy night. One of the police officers found Bear on one of the trails miles away. He must have been spooked or disoriented. She knew the brothers were worried about him, so it was good the dog was home safe and sound.

The days seemed to pass, and with it, the brothers made a great deal of repairs around the house. She noticed they put more locks in, and also talked about sensors on their land, which they installed. The nights belonged to all three of them, and Opal lived on cloud nine. She never for a second thought her life could be like this.

One evening, nearly two weeks since the incident,

after making sure the stew was just right, she made her way toward the bedroom. She'd already picked out the dress that she hoped would totally blow away her men. The straps were thin, and didn't leave room for her to wear a bra.

She wanted to set the mood, and one thing she loved about both Caleb and Damon, they loved her curves. Whenever she was near with minimum clothing on, they couldn't resist her, and she was more than ready.

With the dress on, she stared at her reflection. Opal had always thought her breasts were too big and sloppy, but seeing herself through the brothers' eyes made her fall in love with herself.

The dress clung to every single curve, and with it, the outline of her panties, which she didn't want. Wriggling out of her panties, she felt sexy, and maybe a little naughty. She'd never done anything like this in her life before, and it felt … good.

Tying her hair up, she stared at her reflection one more time, and didn't even bother with makeup. Out here, makeup didn't have a place, and her men loved her exactly the way she was—all natural.

She had no doubt of their love. Not only did they tell her every single night, but their actions spoke a hell of a lot louder than any words. The way they looked at her, touched her, and it wasn't just about sex either. It was about the little things. Like the way Caleb couldn't seem to resist touching her hand as he passed.

He'd take hold of her, and give it a gentle squeeze, or Damon would touch her neck. There was nothing sexual in the act. It was comforting. At nighttime she snuggled between the two of her men, and they held her close.

Those moments when she woke up and was able to turn her head either left or right, and watch them sleep, were the best of her life. Their love and warmth surrounded her, and there wasn't anything she wouldn't do for them. Her loneliness was finally gone.

Staring at her reflection, she smiled, feeling confident in herself. The tour she went on didn't help her at all. Being surrounded by men and women of wealth had only made her realize what little she had in the world.

The time spent with Caleb and Damon White had shown her who she was as a person, as a woman, and she liked what she saw. She no longer saw the useless fat woman she'd believed was there.

No.

She was a woman of worth who not only loved with her entire being, but also deserved love as well.

"You're happy now. You're good, and you're going to live an amazing life." She took a deep breath, and made her way to the living room.

The scent of the food made her mouth water, and her excitement at the night she had planned filled her up.

The main door opened, and she turned to see Caleb and Damon talking as they entered. They hung up their heavy coats and stomped off their boots.

The moment they saw her, they both went silent.

"Hey, guys," she said, running her hands down the front of her dress.

"Now that is the best way to come home, baby," Damon said, moving toward her. He wrapped his arms around her, and she didn't care about the chill from his body from being outside.

"What is all this?" Caleb asked.

"Well, I thought we should celebrate."

Damon cupped the back of her head, bringing his lips down on hers. She wrapped her arms around his neck, moaning as he traced his tongue across her lips, and she opened up, needing him. "You taste good," he said, pulling away.

She didn't have long to wait before Caleb pulled her into his embrace, and took his kiss. Their differences were slight but she'd be able to name each one with her eyes closed.

Her pussy was already slick, ready, and desperate for the both of them. "Did you do all of your chores?"

"Yes."

"Good." She pulled away from them. "I thought we could have some food."

"That's not all that's on your mind though, is it, Opal?" Caleb asked. He stole a bread stick, taking a bite out of it.

Heat filled her cheeks, and she offered them both a smile, shaking her head. "No, it's not all I want."

Damon stood beside Caleb, and she watched the two of them. "Then why don't you tell us what you want?"

****

Caleb had never seen such a sexy sight in all of his forty years. The way the dress molded to her curves, he was ready to take her to the floor and fuck her long and hard for hours. The heat in her cheeks was also a turn on. He loved that air of innocence that came with her. No matter how many times he was deep inside her, he wouldn't ever forget that look.

Opal wanted to be fucked, and hard. She was sweet and naughty mixed together in an irresistible package.

Not only that, he'd seen the change inside her. In the past few days, her happiness grew and spread, surrounding every single part of her, and he loved it. He wanted her more than anything else in his life.

The only thing that would make her look any

better was her heavily pregnant with their baby. Fuck. Just the thought of it and he was ready to blow his load.

Damon tapped his arm.

He didn't need to look at his brother to know what he wanted.

Reaching into his pocket, he held the ring that had once belonged to their mother. He'd been wanting to give this to Opal for some time now.

"Actually, Opal, there's something we've been wanting to ask you, and we need to do it before you try and have your wicked way with us."

"Oh, what is it?" she asked.

He saw her nerves, and he hated that.

Grabbing Damon's arm, he pulled him down onto the floor, one knee bent, and together they held up the ring. She gasped.

"We know it's sudden, and we know that this life is not for everyone, and I could probably list a million different ways that you shouldn't agree."

Damon slapped him around the back of the head.

"You're meant to name a million ways why this is a great idea," Damon said.

"I'm giving her all the facts," Caleb said.

This brought a laugh to Opal. "Yes."

"We've not asked yet," Caleb said. "Now, I can think of a million reasons you should go back to the city. Hot water all the time. No worries about backup generators. Not having to cook everything from scratch, and of course, not having to garden." This brought another smile. "But the city doesn't have us, and I know for a fact you'd miss us. The one reason I think you should stay is that we love you. Both of us love you more than anything in the world, and we'll protect you always."

Tears filled her eyes, and he hated making her

cry.

"That has to be the best proposal in the world," she said.

"Is that a yes?" Damon asked.

"Yes, of course, yes. A million times yes."

She stepped toward them as they stood. Damon held her hand as he slid the finger in place. "We'll make sure you'll never regret this."

"I know I never will. I love you both. This is the greatest day of my life." She cupped his face, and kissed him hard.

Reaching behind her, Caleb grabbed her ass, pulling her forward. His cock pressed against her stomach, and they both moaned. Damon moved to stand behind her, trailing kisses down her neck.

"I want both of you together. At the same time," she said.

"Are you ready for that?"

"I'm more than ready."

"You want one of us inside your pussy, and the other to take that ass?" Caleb asked.

"Yes."

"I think we should give the lady what she wants. We don't want her to think for a second that we're not up to her standards," Damon said.

She chuckled. "Neither of you could ever disappoint me." She tilted her head back, and he watched as Damon claimed a kiss.

Caleb ran his hands over her body, touching her heavy tits, moving down to between her thighs, and cupping her pussy. He groaned when he discovered she wasn't wearing any panties. "You're a naughty girl."

"And you love me like that," she said.

He certainly wasn't going to complain. Stroking between her slit, he felt how wet she was. Pulling his finger out of her pussy, he licked her cream off, and moaned. She tasted exquisite as always.

Taking the straps of her dress, he lowered them down, tugging the dress as he did. Damon gripped the edge of the fabric, and her tits sprang free.

Damon cupped them, offering them up to him.

Taking one nipple into his mouth, he sucked on the hard bud. With the other, he pinched, enjoying her gasps of pleasure as he teased her body. She was on fire already.

She wriggled out of the dress, and he broke from her nipples to push it to the floor. With only a pair of heels on her feet, she looked so fucking inviting, and it made him ache for her.

"I'd be so happy if we came home and found you like this every day. Naked, desperate, waiting for us," Damon said. His hand was on her stomach. Caleb stood, gripping her chin, and forcing her to look at him. He wanted to breed her, to fill her with his seed.

"You want me to fuck you?"

"Yes."

"You want me to lick your pussy first?"

"Yes."

He nodded at Damon, and got his brother to move her toward the couch. Damon sat down, and placed Opal on his lap, spreading her legs open wide, so not a single part of her was hiding.

One of the things he was sure to buy when he was in town was lots and lots of lube. They planned to share their women often. He had tube in the drawer of the coffee table, in close reach.

Kneeling down on the floor, he stared at her pretty pussy, which was already wet and ready. He wanted to taste her. Sliding a finger between her slit, he teased across her clit, then moved down, to push inside her. She gasped, arching up, and her cunt tightened around his finger. He added a second finger, watching as she wriggled on his brother's lap.

He smiled, seeing the pain on Damon's face. All in good time.

The best things in life came to those who waited, and he was ready to torment and tease Opal until she was an aching ball of pleasure.

The night was young after all, and he had the patience of a saint.

****

Damon didn't know how much more he could take. Caleb was really driving Opal wild, and the feel of her ass rubbing against his dick, was nearly too much. He watched his brother lick her pussy, opening her swollen lips before sucking on her clit.

She cried out, and he supported her gorgeous tits, teasing her big nipples.

On and on, his brother pushed her toward her orgasm only to deny her, driving her need higher and higher.

Caleb pulled away. "She's so wet for us. Have a feel, Damon."

He couldn't resist, and so he placed his hand between her thighs, and teased around her nub, sliding down to fill her drenched pussy. She was indeed soaking.

Suddenly, Opal moved. "You're both overdressed."

Going to her knees before him, she attacked his belt, pulling it from the loops, and tossing it to one side. She didn't stop there.

In a matter of minutes they were all completely naked, and Opal had kicked off her heels. She pressed her body against his, kissing him hard. She turned to Caleb, doing exactly the same, and keeping a hand placed on his chest.

Her hand moved down, wrapping her fingers around the length of Damon's cock. She did the same with Caleb, working his length simultaneously. It was the sexiest thing he'd ever seen.

"Suck him," Caleb said.

They were on the carpet, and Damon went to his knees before her. Caleb moved Opal so that she was on her knees, and he watched as his brother filled her in one forceful thrust. At the same time, she took his cock into her mouth, and started to suck on him. Wrapping her hair around his hand, he guided her, pushing into her mouth. Each thrust that Caleb did inside her pussy had her moaning, and the vibration in her throat had him so close to wanting to come.

He held off, loving the feel of her taking him, her lively tongue making his eyes loll back in his head. When he hit the back of her throat, she didn't pull away, and kept him, taking him even more.

It wasn't enough though.

"I want her pussy," Damon said, pulling out of her mouth.

Changing places, he ran his hands over her back. Sliding down, he pressed two fingers inside her, and she gasped.

Replacing his fingers with his cock, he thrust all the way inside her and groaned as her heat gripped him tightly. She was pure heaven.

He closed his eyes, staying still within her, just enjoying the feel of their connection.

Slowly, he began to fuck her, watching his cock appear, her cream coating his dick. Spreading the cheeks of her ass, he stared at her puckered hole. It made him harder yet. With how wet she was, he used her arousal to coat his fingers, and placed them at her ass.

Coating her anus, he teased her, taking his sweet time.

The moment he touched her, her pussy tightened around him, and he felt her get wetter.

"You like that, baby?" he asked.

She pulled off Caleb's cock, and nodded. "Yes."

"Good girl."

Pumping inside her, he stroked over her anus, getting her used to feel of him. After a few minutes, he pushed his finger inside her. At first, the tight ring of muscles held him back, and he didn't stop. Pressing against her ass, she relented, and he filled her to the knuckle.

Taking his time, he got her used to his finger before adding a second, and when she could take them both, he spread her open, scissoring his fingers.

"I'm taking her ass," he said.

Pulling out of her pussy, he gripped his length and coated it with the lube Caleb bought, and the pressed the tip at her ass. He made sure to go slow, waiting for her to open up to him.

"Relax for me, sweetheart. Don't tense up."

She released a little gasp, and he paused, waiting for her ass to open up to him.

When she started to press back against his cock, he gripped her hips, and inch by inch, he filled her virgin asshole until he was balls deep.

"How are you feeling?" Caleb asked.

"It feels ... weird," she said.

Caleb pushed some of her hair off her face, and Damon closed his eyes, feeling her ass tighten around him. Fuck, it was even tighter than her pussy.

"Are you ready for me inside you?" Caleb asked.

"Yes!" She was panting now, wanton and eager.

Damon moved so that he was on the floor. His

cock still deep within her ass, and she was spread open, ready to take Caleb. She held onto his hands, and when his brother pressed inside her pussy, he groaned.

With every added inch, her ass squeezed him even more.

"I knew this was going to be good but I didn't realize it was going to be this fucking good," Caleb said.

"I feel so full, so out of control," said Opal.

"Let go, baby. Enjoy yourself."

Caleb worked his cock inside her pussy until fully seated, and they both stayed still, giving her time. Only when she was ready did they both move, creating a rhythm that took the pleasure to the next level.

The instant he saw Opal, he knew she was the one but right now, deep inside her, loving her with his brother, there was no doubt.

He loved her more than anything else in the world, and would give her whatever her heart desired. She held his hand, kissed his brother, and thrust against both of them, taking and giving with equal measure, and he fucking loved it, more than anything.

She was incredible.

"You feel so good," Caleb said.

"The best," Damon agreed with him.

"Please, I need it, please," she said, begging.

Reaching between her thighs, he teased her clit. With a few strokes, she came apart, screaming their names. Her release set off his orgasm as her ass squeezed him like a vise. He saw stars dance before his eyes as he filled her with wave upon wave of release.

Seconds later, he heard Caleb groan. All three of them finding their pleasure with each other. He couldn't help but wonder when she'd become ripe with their child. He could hardly wait.

They collapsed on the floor before the fire. The

comforting scent of burning wood and cedar mixed with the dinner waiting for them.

"Do you think we'll ever make it to the bedroom?" Opal asked.

"I don't know. I'm getting quite attached to the floor," Caleb said.

Damon laughed. "I think we're going to need to buy a fluffier rug. My ass has carpet burn."

They all burst out laughing.

"I love you guys so much," said Opal.

Damon cupped her cheek, and pressed a kiss to her lips. "You're our entire world."

Chapter Twelve

Four months later

Opal wore her rubber boots as she navigated the thawing trails. With each step, her boots suctioned into the muck. She didn't care because it meant spring was on the way in and winter on the way out. The birds sang in the trees above, dozens of different melodies. She'd fallen in love with the land, and couldn't imagine life in the city ever again.

The men were busy making outdoor pens for the animals they'd purchased. They were arriving next week, so they had to get things finished in time. They bought two milking goats, a dairy cow, and half a dozen hens. The fresh eggs, milk, cheese, and butter would make life even better for them. It was empowering to live independently without having to travel to town too often.

She'd hiked farther than she had before, but she felt the need to be alone for a while with her own thoughts. In the distance, she saw a structure, and discovered a small wooden shack. It was still on the brothers' land because they owned thousands of acres, way too far for her to wander beyond. Her curiosity soared.

Opal lifted the wooden lever holding the door closed and then gave it a push. The hinges whined loudly as the door swung open. Dust motes danced in the beams of light coming from the small windows. There wasn't much inside, just an old stone fireplace, a square dinette table and chairs, and a wooden cupboard. She ventured inside, opening up the cabinet to find some old preserves in glass jars. Opal wondered who put them there and how long they'd been stored. The glass windows had a thick layer of dust, making them nearly opaque.

She sat down on one of the chairs, imagining fairy tales like *Goldilocks and the Three Bears.* Opal giggled to herself. She'd never felt so at peace with herself and her life.

There were some marks on the wood in one corner, so she got up to investigate. They were growth marks for different years when Caleb and Damon had been kids. She smiled, trying to imagine the brothers as children. Even at twelve they'd been taller than her.

A shadow passed by the small window, making her gasp. She hadn't heard any footsteps and, in the light of day, she didn't expect any animal encounters. Her carefree mood shifted to caution.

The door was still ajar, so she waited to see what would appear in the doorway after rounding the corner. She held her breath, biting her lower lip in anticipation. *Please don't be a bear or another crazy man.* When nothing showed up, she wondered if she'd really seen anything.

She closed the cupboard and walked tentatively to the door. There were only the soothing sounds of nature waiting for her, so she pulled the door shut.

"What are you doing way out here?"

Opal gasped and twirled around into Damon's arms. She looked up into his eyes, her heart still racing.

"You scared me."

"Good. You were naughty wandering so far." He opened the door and forced her to walk backwards into the cabin.

"What is this place?" She had no fear of Damon. His words only inspired desire inside her.

"Before our parents built the cabin, this was home for over a year. Then it was our playhouse." The shack was tiny. She couldn't imagine the four of them living comfortably.

"You had it rough."

He shook his head. "It was an adventure." Damon hoisted her up to sit on the wooden table.

"Now, tell me why you're here, Opal."

She snuck her hands under his padded jacket, running them up against his warm, bare skin. "I needed time to think, to reflect."

"If you want to talk, you can always talk to either of us."

"I know." She brought her hands back down, dragging her nails against his firm flesh. He growled, staring at her like a wild man, a bushman.

"We just took a break from work, and I needed you, but you were nowhere to be found." He leaned over and kissed behind her ear. "I had to track you."

"You've found me now," she whispered.

"I have." He tugged her pants over the curve of her ass, then down her legs. Her pants and boots dropped heavily to the wooden floor. She braced her hands against the edges of the table to avoid falling off. "I need you. Open those legs for me, baby."

She still felt a bit shy being so exposed, even if the brothers had explored every inch of her body, over and over again. Opal positioned her heels on the ends of the table and let her knees drop open, leaving her slick pussy exposed to him. She still had on her coat and toque, the cool air giving her legs goosebumps.

He unbuttoned his jacket and she watched as each button opened. She loved his body, every hard-earned muscle. He turned her on so effortlessly.

The sound of a zipper lowering caught her attention. Damon released his thick, hard cock. God, he was impressive, and all she could think about was him filling her. But he toyed with her, rubbing the mushroom head up and down her moist slit, teasing her until she was panting.

"Give it to me," she demanded.

"Hush now, little one. You're lucky you're getting anything after worrying me like you did." He pressed in an inch as he licked his lower lip. His lips were thick and this stubble coarse—all man. When he pulled back out, she was dizzy with need.

"Please!"

Then the door opened and Caleb stepped in.

****

"Getting started without me?" Caleb asked.

What a sight he walked in on. Opal was braced on her elbows on the table, her legs spread wide. The entire shack smelled like sex and his cock was already hard.

"Don't worry. We were waiting," said Damon.

"You found our fort," he said. "We used to play here for hours. Not like this, though." He ran his finger along her inner thigh, making her shiver.

"Please, Caleb. I'm horny."

He smirked, giving Damon a sideways glance. His brother was punishing her, getting her hotter than hell before they shared her. She deserved a bit of sweet torture for hiking so far from home. He liked her close by so he could protect her from anything. At this distance, he wouldn't have been able to hear her scream.

"Damon's here," he said.

She shook her head. "He won't give me his cock. Give me yours."

He smirked. Fuck, he wanted to give it to her. It took all his resolve not to plunge inside of her heat to take away her ache.

"Patience, sweet thing." Caleb braced both arms on the table at either side of her waist and kissed her hard on the mouth. She was completely wanton, her tongue tracing the inside of his mouth as they kissed. "Go on, touch yourself."

She reached down to rub circles over her clit, but quickly pulled her hand away. "No, I want the real thing."

"What do you want?" asked Damon.

"I told you I wanted your cock." She scowled. "You're being mean."

Damon leaned down and lapped his tongue along her folds, just one. She cried out, trying to grab his head. "Say please."

"Please."

"Okay, baby, you've been punished long enough," said Damon. He positioned himself between her legs before sinking in deep. She sighed, tossing her head back. Damon growled and began to fuck her, holding her hips as he pistoned in and out. The small table creaked and groaned, the sounds of sex growing louder by the second.

"I want more. I want both of you," she said, writhing on the table. Her body arched up, needed more, needing to be double-fucked. Of course, Caleb was ready for anything. He'd hoped that after following Damon he'd find just this scenario. After working with his hands all day, he wanted to drown in Opal's curves. He felt for the lube in his pocket, his hard cock ready to blow off his zipper.

"Pick her up," said Caleb. There wasn't much room in the small shack. The bunk beds were burned long ago after the mattresses went moldy. It had been hard when they'd had to live and sleep there when their parents were building their homestead. But it had been full of love, and they were mostly outside working or playing, regardless. He couldn't wait to make those same sweet memories with Damon, Opal, and their children.

Damon hoisted her up, his cock still deep in her

pussy. She wrapped her legs snuggly around him and held his neck.

"You'll drop me," she said with a squeal.

"Oh no, I've got you, baby," said Damon. Compared to their massive size, Opal was a lightweight.

Caleb lubed his cock and pressed a finger full of the sticky substance slowly into her asshole. She tensed, then sighed, knowing what was to come. "Caleb, oh God."

He aimed his cock at her cute little rosette and pushed in with a slow, firm motion. She panted, holding Damon tighter as he forced his dick in to the hilt. "Fuck, you're tighter than a fist with Damon inside you."

"I feel so full," she said.

"You are, Opal. Full of our cocks," said Damon. "Soon you'll be full of my seed."

It had been almost six months since her arrival, and Caleb wondered if their constant breeding would ever pay off. He knew he'd love his woman the same, but his desire for a family was strong.

Once she'd adjusted to their combined size, they worked her body, taking turns to fuck and pull out. They moved like a well-oiled, synchronized machine. In their current position, both of them standing and supporting her weight, he was able to sink in even deeper. It was pure heaven.

"I love your little cunt," said Damon before growling. It was a herculean effort to hold back, but they always waited for Opal to orgasm first. Her pleasure was their number one concern.

"It feels so good. I'm going to come," she said between gasps. "Yes. Yes. Yes!"

When she came, she screamed, but no one would hear. Her ass clamped down impossibly tight on his dick, bringing him to his own release in seconds. After the minutes faded away, only the sounds of their heavy breathing could be heard in the small room.

Caleb slipped out of her ass, and Damon set her gently back on the table, his cum leaking out of her pussy. He used one of his clean work rags from his back pocket to clean her up, then he helped her back into her pants.

"You're amazing," Caleb said.

"I'm so tired, I don't know how I'll make it home," she said with a smile.

"We can wait it out for a while. I haven't been back to the shack in ages," said Damon.

"I saw your growth charts carved into the wall," she said. "You were big boys."

"Still are." Damon winked.

"Yes, very big boys." Opal kissed his brother before he sat in one of the chairs, pulling her down onto his lap.

Caleb walked to the window, tracing his finger along the jagged marks in the wood. So many memories. Their parents were taken too soon.

"I like to imagine I'd be a good dad like my father," said Caleb, reflectively. "He taught us a lot, but what I remember most was his patience and how much he loved his family."

"You'll both make excellent fathers," said Opal.

Damon kissed her temple. "And you'd make the sweetest little mother."

She smiled and her eyes filled with tears.

Caleb got down to one knee in front of her. "Don't cry, sweetheart."

"They're not sad tears."

****

Damon cupped her cheek, using his thumb to whisk away a tear. "What's going on?"

He'd already been suspicious when she went wandering off by herself, hiking miles farther than she usually did. For the past few days, she'd been off, something just not right. Damon wasn't sure what it was exactly, but she'd been more quiet and reflective lately. He hoped to God she wasn't reconsidering her decision to stay in the wilderness with them.

"I have something to tell both of you. I feel bad for not saying anything sooner, but I wanted to be sure."

Caleb's eyes darkened, and Damon could only imagine how broken his older brother would be if she left them now. There would be no replacing her. She was perfect.

Damon held her hand, fiddling with the ring they'd given her, their mother's ring.

"Go on," he said.

She took his hand and brought it round to her stomach, making him cup the rounded bulge.

"Are you sick?" asked Caleb.

"Not exactly. I'm pregnant."

Opal always had a little tummy. Her entire body was curvy, so he hadn't noticed anything different. Now, he circled her stomach with his hand, imagining there was actually a little White baby growing and developing inside her. It was surreal.

"Are you sure?" asked Caleb.

"I wanted to be sure before I told either of you because I know how much you want this. I'm only a couple months along, but so far so good."

"I just, I can't believe it. We're going to have a little family out here," said Caleb.

"We'll be daddies," said Damon.

The reality was starting to trickle in. They had a million things to do in preparation. Having the responsibility for a new life was not to be taken lightly.

They had to finish their pens, work on the barn, and build a crib. Damon loved working with wood and the plans were already taking shape in his head.

"I'm a bit scared though," she whispered.

Damon cupped her cheek and kissed her lips. "Why? We'll take care of everything."

"That's not what I mean. I'm worried I won't be a good mother. My own family was so cruel, and I've been on my own for a long time. What if I screw up?"

Damon smiled. "You're not like them. If anything, you're the opposite. You're kind, sweet, caring, and you'll be perfect. I know it."

"It's a chance for us all to make things right. We'll have a family of our own," said Caleb. "And I'll do everything in my power to take care of every one of you."

Money would never be an issue. They received a massive private settlement from the logging company, thanks to their eager lawyer. Now that the company was on the radar, they wouldn't be bothering or threatening them again. But money was only an insurance policy. They preferred to live simple, to be close to nature without relying heavily on modern conveniences. It gave them the ability to appreciate the little things, to love harder, and live healthier.

"I wonder if it'll be a boy or a girl," said Damon.

"Doesn't matter," said Caleb. "That's in God's hands."

"If it's a girl, I want her to look just like her mother." Damon held her close, a new level of protectiveness filling him to the marrow.

"If it's a boy, we can teach him to track and fish and build," said Caleb.

"Hey, I know you never had sisters, but you can teach all those things to a girl, too," said Opal.

"Then we win either way." Caleb dropped to both knees and hugged her around the waist, resting his head on her lap. "Thank you," he said. "Thank you for rescuing us, giving us hope, a baby, a family. I can never thank you enough."

Damon felt his own emotions bubbling to the surface, but he fought to stay strong. It was difficult to see his stoic brother break down, but he was finally happy and at peace.

"Is that why you've been quiet lately?" asked Damon.

She nodded. "It's a lot to think about, but I know this is the perfect place to raise our children. Fresh air, simplicity, and lots of love."

Children. Maybe they'd have another in the future. He'd love to have a big family, but right now he'd focus on baby number one.

They began to button up for the trek back to their home. It wasn't bone chilling outside, but the wind still carried a sharp bite in the shadows of the trees.

"Are you okay to walk?" asked Caleb as they walked hand in hand, Opal in the middle.

"I won't break. Promise," she said. "But I am glad we have hot water for my baths."

"Don't be surprised if we're a bit protective of you now," said Caleb.

"More than you already are?"

"Hell yes," said Damon. "You've got precious cargo, so we'll be doing lots of pampering."

Opal giggled, the sweet sound mingling perfectly with the song of the wild birds. He wished his parents could meet her and their grandchild, but at least they were keeping the family traditions alive and well.

The house came into view after their long hike along the muddy path. A slow plume of smoke coming from the stone chimney.

"There it is," said Caleb.

"Yep," Damon agreed.

Opal stopped, looking fondly at their little cabin in the woods. "Home."

The End

www.samcrescent.com

www.staceyespino.com

EVERNIGHT PUBLISHING ®

www.evernightpublishing.com